Praise for **ANNE GEORGE**'s Southern Sisters Mysteries

"A sassy series."
Chicago Tribune

"It's always a pleasure to keep company
with Mouse and Sister . . . George's sunny
Southern sisters are like comfort food, as good as
grits and almost better than biscuits."
Virginian Pilot and Ledger-Star

"George's low-key humor and engaging characters
keep you flipping pages."
Orlando Sentinel

"Great fun . . . George portrays a Southern family
and all the connections that go
along with it perfectly."
Greensboro News & Record

"The characters are so opinionated you half expect
them to fire your babysitter, and the action so real
you think it's happening next door."
Los Angeles Times

"It's never too late to meet
this zany pair of slueths."
Florida Times-Union

ANNE GEORGE

Murder on a Girls' Night Out

A SOUTHERN SISTERS MYSTERY

AVON BOOKS
An Imprint of HarperCollinsPublishers

This is a work of fiction. Names, characters, places, and incidents are products of the author's imagination or are used fictitiously and are not to be construed as real. Any resemblance to actual events, locales, organizations, or persons, living or dead, is entirely coincidental.

AVON BOOKS
An Imprint of HarperCollins*Publishers*
10 East 53rd Street
New York, New York 10022-5299

Copyright © 1996 by Anne George
ISBN: 0-380-78086-0
www.avonbooks.com

First Avon Books paperback printing: February 1996

Avon Trademark Reg. U.S. Pat. Off. and in Other Countries, Marca Registrada, Hecho en U.S.A.
HarperCollins® is a trademark of HarperCollins Publishers Inc.

Printed in the U.S.A.

30 29 28 27 26 25

For Mary Elizabeth, who makes life fun

Acknowledgments

My thanks to Bill Maddox for the necessary encouragement; to Malu Graham and Fran Boudolf for their reliable and kind critiques; to Maxine Singleton, who was generous with both her computer skills and laughter; and to the "Center Point Girls"—Jean Burnett, Elsie McKibben, and Virginia Martin—for their patience and help.

One

Mary Alice flung her purse on my kitchen table, where it landed with a crash, pulled a stool over to the counter and perched on it. "Perched" may not be the right word, since Mary Alice weighs two hundred and fifty pounds. The stool groaned and splayed, but it held. I began to breath again.

"I have decided," she announced, "that I am not going gentle into that good night."

"Thank God," I said. "We were all worried about you. Last year when you dyed your hair Hot Tart—"

"Cinnamon Red."

"Well, whatever. We all said, 'There she goes gentle.'"

Mary Alice giggled. She's sixty-five years old, but she still giggles like a young girl. And men still love it.

"That was a little much." She patted her hair. "This

is just plain old Light Golden Blond. It's what you ought to use, Patricia Anne.''

"Too much trouble.'' The timer went off on the stove and I took out a batch of oatmeal cookies.

"It would charge Fred's batteries.''

"There's nothing wrong with Fred's batteries.'' I went around her to get a spatula and opened the drawer too hard, banging it against my leg. How long had it taken her to get to me this time? One minute? No record. In the sixty years we have been sisters, I figure the record is somewhere below zero, into the negative integers of time. Absolute proof of the theory of relativity.

"Well, your hair sure could use some help.''

I scooped up a hot cookie and handed it to her. Burn, baby, burn.

Mary Alice blew on the cookie. A couple of crumbs fell on her turquoise T-shirt, which declared "Tough Old Bird'' and which had a pelican with a yellow beak peeking around the words. Given the expanse and jiggle of Mary Alice's chest, that bird was having a rough flight. "Hand me a paper towel,'' she said. I tore one off and gave it to her. She sank her small teeth into the cookie. "Ummm,'' she said. "Ummm.''

"Good?''

"Ummm.''

I put the plate by her. "You want some tea?''

"Ummm.'' She reached for a second cookie. "Mouse,'' she said, "these are great.''

I banged the ice into the glasses. Mouse. The old childhood nickname.

Mary Alice looked up. "I'm sorry. It just slipped out.''

I sighed. "It doesn't matter.''

"And mice are little and cute.''

"And can bite."

"Yeah. I'd forgotten about that." Mary Alice has a crescent scar on her leg where I bit her when I was three and she wouldn't let me play with her Shirley Temple doll. Daddy had liked to tell the story and said he thought they were going to have to wait until it thundered to get me to turn loose, a reference to snapping turtles. He and Mother had called me Mouse, too, though. And say what you please, if Mary Alice and I hadn't been born at home, I know they would have been at the hospital having the records checked to make sure we hadn't been mixed up. Whereas Mary Alice had been born a brunette with olive skin, I had been a wispy blonde and pale. She had been healthy and boisterous; I, sickly and quiet. My big teeth should have been hers. You name it; if it could be different, it was.

"I know a woman named Jean Poole," Mary Alice said. I smiled. We had been thinking the same thing. "What I came to tell you, though, is I've bought a country-western bar named the Skoot 'n' Boot. Up Highway 78."

I laughed and reached for a cookie.

"When Bill and I were in Branson, Missouri, last spring, we learned how to line dance, and we've been going out to the Skoot 'n' Boot every Thursday night. It's a lot of fun. You and Fred ought to try it."

"Are you serious?"

"Of course I'm serious. Y'all don't do enough. Fred's only sixty-three. Bill's seventy-two and he just loves it. He's hardly out of breath when it's over." Bill Adams is Mary Alice's current "boyfriend." I swear that's what she calls him. He showed up trying to sell her a supplement to her Medicare and he never really left.

"No, I mean about buying this place."

"Sure I'm serious. I told you I wasn't going gentle into that good night."

"Nobody thought you were, Sister."

"And country-western bars are hot right now. Everybody's going to them, getting dressed up in their fringy clothes and boots."

"Fringy clothes?"

"Stuff with fringe on it. You know." Mary Alice stretched her fingers out from her chest as if she were pulling bubble gum from the pelican's beak. "Fringe. Tassles."

"Where is it, this bar?"

"The Skoot 'n' Boot. I told you. It's about twenty miles out Highway 78. Bill and I were in there the other night and got to talking to the man who owns it, and he said he was trying to sell it, that he needed to go back to Atlanta because both his parents are sick and he needs to be near them. He says he hates to leave because the club's doing so well. There was a crowd out on the floor line dancing and I thought, Well, why not? Roger would have liked his money invested this way. So we met at the bank this morning and I bought it."

Roger had been Mary Alice's third husband. They had all died rich and, thanks to Sister, happy. She had given each of them a child, which, considering their advanced ages, was more than they had expected. And I think she really loved them—the husbands. She has them buried together at Elmwood Cemetery for convenience. She got a deal on a whole plot when the first one departed and swears they wouldn't object. Their children, my nieces and nephew, are wonderful. And I'm sure Mary Alice is right. Roger would probably be delighted to have his money invested in the Skoot 'n' Boot if that was what she wanted.

Mary Alice reached for another cookie. "I want you to come with me to see it."

"Now?"

"Sure."

"I need to get supper started. You know Fred likes to eat soon as he gets in so the food will get by his hiatal hernia before he goes to bed."

"Give him an Ultra Slim Fast. They go down quick."

So I wrote Fred a note that I had gone to Sister's new country-western bar, the Skoot 'n' Boot, and left, wishing I could see the expression on his face.

"What is line dancing, anyway?" I asked as we went out the door.

"Fun."

October is the second most beautiful month in Alabama, the first being April, when the dogwood and redbud are blooming. Most people are surprised when they come here for the first time and see the mountains. Granted, we're at the end of the Appalachian chain, but we have some pretty respectable mountains and beautiful color in the fall. The day Mary Alice and I set out to see the Skoot 'n' Boot was the kind you think of when you think October. Seventy-five degrees, a cloudless sky and everything golden as buttered biscuits.

"Oh, my," I said, leaning back and looking through the sunroof of Sister's car at the cobalt-blue sky. I pushed my glasses up on my head and relaxed. "This is nice."

"Absolutely." She leaned over and got another cookie out of the plastic bag I had brought. "You know what I've been thinking?"

"What?"

"We can have your fortieth anniversary at the Skoot 'n' Boot. Wouldn't that be fun? All the kids would

come. That'll be great. We'll make a family reunion out
of it."

I got this mental picture of all of us dancing in some
kind of conga line, with Fred leading the line.

"You know, I think Fred looks like Ross Perot when
he has a short haircut." Her mouth was full of cookie.

Again we were thinking the same thing. "Better-
looking," I said.

"We could have champagne and music, all the things
you didn't have at your wedding because of the Hollo-
wells. I always thought that was real tacky. It was your
wedding, after all, not theirs."

"It was best to start off on the right foot with my in-
laws."

"What could they do? Not come visit you? Tough
titty. Every time that old woman showed up, you acted
like you kept a kosher kitchen." Mary Alice blasted the
horn and whirled around a pickup truck. "God, that was
hard to do."

"Pass that truck?" I looked back.

"Keep a kosher kitchen. Have you forgotten my darling Philip?"

I hadn't. Philip Nachman, her second husband.

"Well, he insisted on a kosher kitchen."

"You never kept a kosher kitchen."

"I know it, but it was so hard keeping him from finding out."

Mary Alice blew the horn again and waved at a
woman at a farm stand. "I want to get some pumpkins
there on the way home. You want some pumpkins for
Halloween decorations?"

"Sure."

"We could even have a renewal of your vows. A lot
of people are doing that now. The minister could stand
where the Swamp Creatures play and y'all could stand

on the glass boot. How does that sound, Mouse? I'll bet you could still wear your wedding dress. How much do you weigh, anyway?''

"A hundred five." I was beginning to feel out of breath like I always do when I'm around Mary Alice for a while. Swamp creatures? Glass boot?

"You were always anorexic."

"I've never been anorexic!" I reached into the bag and put a whole cookie in my mouth. I was still chewing on it when Mary Alice pulled into the parking lot of the Skoot 'n' Boot. It was not at all what I had expected. It looked like it had at one time been several small shops in an L-shaped building.

"They knocked the walls out," Sister explained.

"But where's the front door?"

"Don't talk with your mouth full. Over there. See the sign?"

She pointed upward. On the roof, a huge boot, with "Skoot 'n' Boot" emblazoned on the side with what looked like rhinestones, pointed its toe downward toward an arrow that said, "Enter."

"The sun was in my eyes," I lied. Sister is always accusing me of not seeing the obvious, and this time she was right.

She leaned back and looked at the sign with admiration. "At night it lights up. You know how the lights used to run around the front of the Alabama Theater? That's the way these do. It really stands out at night. You can see it way down the highway. A few of the bulbs are out, though. I meant to stop by Kmart and get some. Bill said he would put them in."

Bill? Seventy-two-year-old Bill, climbing up on the roof and then up the sign? "Mary Alice," I said, but she was already getting out of the car.

Once out, she held up her arms like the Indian in a

picture Grandma used to have, invoking the Great Spirit or something. "Beautiful!" she said.

I am a sixty-year-old woman. I am five feet one, one hundred and five pounds, gray hair, married to the same man for forty years, mother of three, grandmother of two, sister of two-hundred-fifty-pound, five-foot-ten, golden-haired Mary Alice Tate Sullivan Nachman Crane, a sixty-five-year-old bar owner and line-dancing loony. Lord!

I climbed out of the car. "Sister," I said, "don't you let Bill get up on that sign."

"He'll be okay." Mary Alice reached over, grabbed my shoulder and crunched me to her. "Don't you just love it?"

"Wuump," I said against her ample bosom.

"I just knew you would. Come on, let me show you the inside." She let me go and I staggered a few steps while she hauled her purse up from where it hung around her knees and started looking for her keys. Sister's purses are never ordinary purses. They are huge and have straps so long that on most women they would drag the ground. She orders them custom-made from somewhere. She can never find anything, though. I have a little hook on the inside of my purse for my keys, and I gave Sister several until I saw she wasn't going to use them. I knew if I opened my purse right then, my keys would be on their hook, neat as anything.

She was about to empty her whole purse out on the car seat when the Skoot 'n' Boot door opened and a man called out, "Mrs. Crane!"

Sister beamed. "Hi, Ed," she called back. "I didn't think you'd be here yet." She put her purse strap back over her shoulder and grabbed me by the arm, pulling me toward the now open door. "He's the one I bought it from," she explained.

"Quit pulling me!" I hissed to no avail.

"Ed, this is my sister, Mrs. Hollowell. She was dying to see the place, so I brought her out."

"How do you do, Mrs. Hollowell." Ed greeted me with a damp, limp handshake, which surprised me, since he looked like he could be the club's bouncer. He was in his thirties but was already beginning to bald. The white T-shirt he was wearing showed off not only his muscles but also a tattoo of a hula girl with the message "Hail Maui, full of grass" on his forearm.

He rubbed the hula girl against his sweating forehead and said we should come on in. "I've just been cleaning up some."

"Well, aren't you the sweet one." Mary Alice swept by him. I followed her. Once inside, she did the Indian-upraised-arms thing again. "Mouse, I ask you. Is this not the most darling place you have ever set eyes on?"

I couldn't see a thing. I stood there waiting for my eyes to adjust from the bright October sunshine. From the left came the sound of trickling water. "Is there a water leak?" I asked.

Mary Alice laughed. "That's the wishing well. It makes you want to pee, and the more you pee, the more beer you drink. Right, Ed?"

"Right, Mrs. Crane."

"Mary Alice!" I fussed.

"Pee happens, Patricia Anne."

The running water and the recent iced tea were making me all too aware of that fact of nature.

"Where's the rest room?" I asked.

Mary Alice and Ed both laughed as if I had said the funniest thing they had heard in a month of Sundays.

"I'll show you." Mary Alice took my hand and started leading me through the semidarkness.

"How can you see in here?" I bumped into a chair.

"I don't have trouble with my rods and cones like you do."

"There's nothing wrong with my rods and cones."

"Sure there is. You never have been able to see in the dark. Didn't eat enough carrots. Didn't eat enough anything." Mary Alice opened a door and turned on the light. "Here you are. I'll be out talking to Ed. I'll turn the lights on over the bar so you can see when you come out."

"You don't have to go?"

"My bladder's better than yours."

Larger, anyway, I thought as she closed the door, leaving me in a room decorated with wallpaper with boots on it. Someone must have looked a long time to find that paper. Even the mirror had a small boot etched in the corner. I half expected the toilet to be boot-shaped, but only the toilet-paper holder was. Where would a decorator find *that* item?

I came out feeling better and able to see Mary Alice and Ed sitting at the bar. The light was provided by a large neon boot—what else?—above the rows of glasses.

"You want a beer, Mrs. Hollowell?" Ed gestured to the bottles in front of him and Sister.

"She'll take a Coke," Mary Alice said. "I'll get it. I've got to start learning my way around this place." She got down from the stool and went around the counter. "Where are they, Ed?"

He reached over the counter and pointed. The hula girl tattoo stretched a little.

"I can make her dance," he said, noticing my glance. "See? I'm double-jointed and I turn my elbow just like this and tighten my fist like this. And there she goes."

"Nice," I said, feeling a slight slip in my personal reality cog. An hour before, I had been baking oatmeal cookies in a suburb of Birmingham and worrying about what to give my husband for supper, and now I was sitting at a country-western bar watching a man with shifty eyes make his tattoo dance. I wondered if Sister had noticed those eyes. They were way too close together. I hoped she had studied the papers good before she signed them and that Debbie had done the legal work. Debbie Nachman is Sister's second daughter, a lawyer and the single parent of the most precious twin girls God ever put on earth.

"Here you go," Sister said, handing me a cold, wet can.

"Are there any napkins?"

"I don't see any."

Ed pointed again and she came up with a handful. "Patricia Anne doesn't drink," she explained to him. "She won't even eat stuff with alcohol in it. We had an uncle used to send Patricia Anne and I chocolates from England with rum centers. Lord, they were good! And I got to eat every one of them."

"Me," I said.

"What?"

"He sent Pat and *me* candies."

"Picky, picky." She came back around the counter. "She taught school for thirty years," she told Ed, shaking her head in a pitying gesture.

"I'm allergic to alcohol," I explained to Ed, though I don't know why I felt the need to justify myself, but Mary Alice does that to me. "My throat closes up, my eyes swell up, my nose turns bright red—"

"She also upchucks," Mary Alice said. "Mouse, I'm sure he gets the picture." Ed had, indeed, backed away a little. "Come on, let me show you some more of the place."

Tables and chairs were packed in so tightly it looked like an army could be crammed into the place. Mary Alice had to twist and turn to get through without rearranging the furniture.

"Here's the dance floor," she said. "Wait a minute and I'll turn on the lights so you can see." She wandered off into the gloom. "Ed," she called after a moment, "where is the switch for the dance-floor lights?"

"When did you say he was leaving?" I asked.

"By the window. Left side," Ed said.

"Okay," Mary Alice called back, ignoring my remark.

In a moment lights recessed around the dance floor were glowing on shiny hardwood. A series of spotlights hanging from the ceiling alternately flashed red, green, and yellow against the small stage and the black curtain that declared SWAMP CREATURES with what looked like real tendrils of Spanish moss hanging from the letters. The same black curtain continued around and covered the window, on the side wall, where Sister stood flicking light switches.

Green, red, yellow. The spot was affecting me like alcohol.

"Ed!"

He came over and fiddled with some switches. All three lights stayed on at the same time. "I'll give you a walk-through before I leave," he promised Mary Alice.

"Thanks. Can you turn on some music?" Sister looked at me. "Listen to this," she said.

"Rockytop" came blaring out with enough decibels to deafen a robot.

"Isn't this great?" Mary Alice hollered over the music. "Come on, let's dance."

I put my Coke down and we moved onto the dance

floor in a jitterbug she had taught me when I was eight and which we had eventually turned into a pretty complicated routine. Surprisingly, it fit the music beautifully. It had been so long since we had danced, I'd forgotten the sheer fun of it. The Tate sisters dancing again.

"Don't sling me up too high," I screamed.

"You've got to be kidding!" Mary Alice led us into the quick walk that would end with each of us whirling around and coming together again to quick-step the other way. "Look at the boot! It's inlaid tempered glass! Cost a fortune!"

I glanced down as we glided over it. A colored glass boot centered the dance floor with a glow of light. "I'll look at it later," I yelled.

"Rockytop Tennneeessseeee-e-e-e." The song came to an end and we staggered to chairs as Ed clapped.

"Great, ladies." He came over and handed me my Coke and Sister her beer. "Y'all are professionals. Maybe we could get you on *Star Search* or something."

"Or something." Mary Alice rubbed the beer bottle against her forehead. "Do this, Mouse. It feels great." She was right. In a few minutes we were breathing normally again.

"God, that was fun. You okay?" she asked. I nodded. "Then come on, let me show you the kitchen. You're going to love this."

"Maybe Ed better go with us."

"There are knives in there, little sister. Lots of knives."

I laughed and followed Mary Alice into a large white kitchen. "Oh, my," I said. Any doubts I might have had about the Skoot 'n' Boot being a first-class establishment did not carry over into the kitchen. "This is wonderful."

Mary Alice beamed. "I thought you'd like it."

I walked around admiring the chrome mixers, the pots

and pans that gleamed from an overhead rack, the huge freezer. "Oh, my." I ran my hand over the Corian counter, the butcher block; checked out the utensils that any gourmet cook would kill for. Not that I am a gourmet cook, but I appreciate a beautiful kitchen. "This is wonderful, Sister. What are your specialties?"

"Buffalo wings, pizza, hamburgers. You know." Her voice trailed off at the look of pain on my face. "French fries, crab claws. What's the matter?"

"It's sinful."

"We have a chef's salad that's good."

"Bottled dressing?"

"Fat-free. Henry runs a tight ship."

"Let me guess. The cook?"

"The chef. And don't go getting on your high horse, Patricia Anne. Your kids used to beg to come to my house so they could have pizza."

It was true, the ungrateful brats, when they could have been having vegetables at home.

"But this kitchen! I can see all sorts of fancy things being cooked here."

"Who would eat them? Look, you can hold a piece of pizza and line dance at the same time. Simple."

"I guess so."

"The truth is that this was a caterer's shop. All Ed had to do was knock out the wall and there was his kitchen. Voilà."

"I wonder how much business the caterer did out here in the country."

"Not enough, I guess. And next door was a gift-and-craft shop. I think I'll open that up again. Ladies who come in for lunch could browse around."

I was too nice to point out that the gift shop had also been closed and that I could not see ladies swarming in at lunchtime for Henry's pizza.

"I can go to the merchandise market in Atlanta to stock it. Lord, I love that place. Remember the fun we had that time we went with Sally?"

Sally Delmar is a friend of ours who owns a Christmas shop. Sister and I went with her one year on a buying trip. Mary Alice bought everything Sally didn't, and I ended up back in the hotel so exhausted I thought I would die.

"I remember it well."

"We'll do it just like we did last time, only we'll stay an extra day. I saw all sorts of stuff I wish I'd gotten."

"You called back from home and had it all delivered."

"That's true." Mary Alice swept her hand across the gleaming countertop. "Don't you just love this, Patricia Anne?"

I answered truthfully that I did. "We ought to have Thanksgiving dinner here."

"That would be great. We could cook five or six turkeys and have all the kids and their in-laws and any friends they wanted to bring. And pans and pans of dressing." It didn't take much to get her started. Mary Alice was rattling on about cranberry salad or cranberry sauce or orange-cranberry relish or tons of each when I left the kitchen. I will never learn to keep my mouth shut.

The trickle of the wishing well and the Coke made one more trip to the rest room a necessity before we left. When I came out, Mary Alice was on the phone and Ed was leaning on the counter watching CNN on the TV built into the wall like a football the neon boot was about to kick. I looked around. The place really did have potential. There was a feeling of . . . I tried to put my finger on it, and came up with "hominess." You could relax here and have a good time. The lunch ladies I had my doubts about, but the beer-drinking, line-dancing crowd, yes. Sister just might have herself a winner here.

I told her that on our way home. The sun had dipped just below the horizon but was still shining golden at the tops of the tallest trees on the mountains. We glided through a valley of purples and blues as lights were being turned on in houses like sudden stars. A beautiful house that looked like something from *Gone With the Wind* was silhouetted against the sky. White fences crisscrossed pastures. Such a sight can make you feel kindly toward the whole world. So I said I really liked the Skoot 'n' Boot and thought it had a lot of potential.

"Yes," Mary Alice said. I guess she was feeling mellow, too, because she didn't say another word until we were almost in Gardendale, where she said she was going to stop at a Kentucky Fried Chicken, since she was starving.

"One of the great regrets of my life," she said, wheeling into a parking place, "was that Will Alec didn't live to eat any of the extra crispy. He would have loved it. Remember how he loved crunchy fried chicken skin?"

Will Alec had been her first husband, the one without a chin. He had lived just long enough to sire their daughter, Marilyn—who has a beautiful chin, thank God—before he succumbed to a heart attack. No doubt all that crunchy chicken skin.

"Come *on*, Patricia Anne. I know you won't eat anything, but at least keep me company."

I ate a drumstick, a thigh, slaw, mashed potatoes and gravy.

"You want some dessert?" Sister asked.

I shook my head no.

"God, you just pick at your food."

TWO

After I retired from teaching, I thought that I would sleep late every morning. Not so. The truth is that first light, my eyes pop open just like they did all those years of getting Fred and the kids and myself off to work and school. Force of habit, I guess. It's nice, though, knowing I don't have to get up. I'll snuggle over close to Fred, who could sleep through Big Ben and just drift for a while. I'll hear the furnace click on or the air conditioner and I'll smell the nice Fred smells of Gain and Bounce, soap, warmth, sleep, Prince Albert tobacco. Sometimes Fred turns over and we greet the morning in a rousing fashion that I'm sure would startle our children and grandchildren, who think passion is the province of the young. Somehow that makes it more fun. Familiarity doesn't necessarily breed just contempt.

But the morning after Mary Alice and I had gone to

the Skoot 'n' Boot, Fred was snoring lightly and I was
thinking about nothing more important than what to get
our daughter, Haley, for her birthday when the phone
rang. It's on Fred's side of the bed. It rang a couple of
times before he woke up enough to answer it. In fact, I
was reaching across him to get it when he woke up.

Phones ringing that early in the morning are seldom
good news, so my heart was beating a little faster.

"What?" Fred said. "What?"

"What is it?" I poked his side anxiously.

He handed me the phone. "It's your sister. She says
I'm dead," he said sleepily.

"What?" I grabbed the phone. "Mary Alice?"

"Oh, Mouse, Fred's dead!"

"No, he's not. He's right here. You're having a bad
dream."

"Not Fred. Ed. It's Ed who's dead. Oh, Mouse! I
meant to say Ed. Did I scare you? I know I scared you.
It's Ed. He's dead in the wishing well."

I put my hand over the phone. "It's Ed who's dead,
Fred. Not you."

"Thank God," he said. He got up and ambled to the
bathroom.

When I put the phone back to my ear, Mary Alice
was wailing, "Ed's dead. Dead in the well." She was
crying so hard I was having trouble understanding her.

"Died in the wool? What are you talking about?"

"Dead in the well, Mouse. Hanging in the wishing
well."

"Ed hanged himself in the well? My God!"

"His throat was cut and he was tied up on the pulley
thing!"

"How awful! He must have been desperate."

"Mouse!" Mary Alice wailed again. "Wake up. I'll

call you again in a little while. I've got to get some aspirin.'' The phone went dead.

''What was that about?'' Fred asked.

''It seems that Ed, the man Sister bought the Skoot 'n' Boot from, committed suicide last night by hanging himself in the wishing well after he cut his throat and tied himself to the pulley thing.''

''He did what?''

''Committed suicide.'' I thought about it for a minute. ''He couldn't do all that, could he?''

''I don't think so.''

''Somebody killed him, didn't they?'' I began to feel very cold. Fred came and sat down by me on the bed.

''What did Mary Alice say?''

''That he was dead. And that stuff about the well. She was pretty upset.''

''I'll bet she was. I wonder who called her.''

''I don't know. I don't know anything. I just assumed he killed himself. Oh, Fred.'' I held him as hard as I could. ''He could make his tattoo dance.'' I started shaking.

''I'll get you a robe and some coffee.'' Fred disengaged himself just as the phone rang again. I grabbed it.

''Somebody murdered him, didn't they?''

''Oh, Mouse, it must be awful. The police called me just a few minutes ago. Some men who had been at the lake fishing saw the door standing open and thought maybe they could get some coffee, and there he was.''

By this time I had the big-time shakes. ''Do they know anything?''

''I don't think so. They want me to come out there this morning. I don't know why.'' Mary Alice started the wailing again. ''Oh, Mouse, I don't want to see his body in a wishing well with its throat cut.''

"It's not the wishing well's throat that's cut. It's Ed's."

"What? What are you talking about?"

"Just correcting your grammar."

The phone went dead again. I got up and put on the robe Fred had handed me. It was the pink quilted one, the elegant one I'm saving for when I have to go to the hospital. Well, what the hell.

I went into the bathroom, brushed my teeth and splashed some water on my face. The phone rang again.

"Do not say a word," Mary Alice said.

"All right."

"Not a word. A man is dead. Murdered. A man we saw yesterday who clapped when we danced. Someone has wrenched the life away from this beautiful young man, maybe someone who was lurking around even while we were there. I think that's what the policemen want to ask us. If we saw anything."

Fred came in and handed me a cup of coffee.

"Well?"

I didn't answer, just sipped my coffee. What was this "we" business? I didn't want to see a dead body in a wishing well, either.

"Well? Patricia Anne?"

"You said not to say anything."

"Damn."

"Well, you did. Besides, he wasn't beautiful, anyway. His eyes—"

"One hour, Patricia Anne." The phone went dead again. It was closer to two hours before I heard the horn blowing in the driveway. When I went out, I saw that Mary Alice was wearing the largest, darkest pair of sunglasses I had ever seen.

"Can you see out of those things?" I asked. "You want me to drive?"

"Yes, I can see, and no, I'll drive. You aim at mail-boxes."

"I haven't hit a mailbox in forty-five years."

"Not from lack of trying." Mary Alice backed out of the drive and we headed toward the same highway we had taken the day before. How quickly things change. The sun was just as warm, the sky just as blue, but somehow our world had seemed more innocent yester-day.

"Well, tell me about it," I said.

"I told you all I know. He was going to close up right after we left, since the place isn't open on Monday. We said good-bye and that was that. We signed all the pa-pers yesterday morning and I gave him a check, but he said he would stay around and help for a couple of weeks. I didn't know anything about him, except the place is in pretty good financial shape and he said he needed to get back to Atlanta. I don't even know if he had a girlfriend or what. Bill and I only saw him when we went there to dance."

"It was robbery. He cashed the check and someone knew it."

"We signed the papers at Ed's bank and he deposited the check. I saw him. Besides"—Mary Alice shivered just as I had done earlier—"look at the way he died. The police said it was like an execution."

"My God!"

"I just hope they have everything cleaned up before we get there."

They did and they didn't. As we pulled into the park-ing lot, we saw the yellow canvas body bag being lifted into an ambulance. Mary Alice slammed on the brakes. "Eeee," she squeaked.

"Wuuuf," I wheezed as I catapulted forward against the seat-belt straps, which knocked the air out of me.

"It's Ed." Mary Alice covered her mouth with her hands.

I tried to loosen the seat belt, which was slicing me in thirds.

"Look, Mouse, they're putting Ed's body in the ambulance right now."

"I can't see," I said. "I think the blood supply to my brain is cut off."

Mary Alice reached down and unfastened my seat belt. "Just be glad it wasn't an air bag."

I rubbed my chest and looked at the scene in front of us. There were three police cars, a fire truck, a rescue squad (I didn't imagine there was much rescuing) and the ambulance, which was now being closed. While we watched, the attendants got back in the cab and drove out of the parking lot without the light flashing. Not that there was any hurry. It dawned on me for the first time that an ambulance without a siren and a light might be more sinister than one dashing through red lights.

Yellow plastic CRIME SCENE DO NOT ENTER tape was stretched across the front of the Skoot 'n' Boot as well as across part of the parking lot. Mary Alice parked in the far corner and we got out. The ambulance pulled into the highway in front of us and the driver waved as he passed. We both waved back, then looked at each other and put our hands down quickly, as if ashamed of the casual gesture.

"No blood," I announced. "I will not go inside. I mean it."

"I'm not going in, either, until it's cleaned up. Come on. We'll just talk to the policeman in one of the cars. We don't know anything to tell them anyway."

"Who are you supposed to see?"

"A man named Jed Reuse called me."

"You called Fred to tell him Jed said Ed was dead?"

Mary Alice stopped and glared at me. "Shut up," she said. "Just shut up, Patricia Anne. I can't take your mouth now."

She meant it. The truth is that I babble when I get nervous.

Babble and crack jokes, while inside I'm scared to death. I guess it comes from all those years of teaching.

"I'm sorry."

"Okay, but watch it." Mary Alice stomped over to the first police car and asked the young policeman in the driver's seat for Jed Reuse. He pointed vaguely in the direction of the front door of the Skoot 'n' Boot.

"Get him for me, please," Mary Alice said. "Tell him Mrs. Crane is here."

"Yes, ma'am." The young policeman hopped out and hurried toward the building. Mary Alice nodded at me. That the young man's mother had done a pretty good job of raising him went unsaid. I nodded back. She was probably right. On the other hand, my sister has no idea how formidable she can be. I would have been very surprised if the young man had not jumped when she said jump.

"Mrs. Crane?"

Jed Reuse was nobody's Columbo. About forty, he was tall and thin, with sharply ironed creases in his uniform and shoes polished so highly you could see yourself in them. Every reddish-blond hair on his head was in place. He held out his hand to Sister and then to me, offering both of us a firm handshake.

"My sister, Mrs. Hollowell," Mary Alice said. "She doesn't want to see any blood."

"I can't say that I blame her." Jed Reuse gave me a smile that was as warm as his appearance was crisp. I automatically looked down at his left hand, where a huge wedding ring shone as brightly as his shoes. Sister caught the glance and rolled her eyes. She says I ought to quit dragging men in for Haley, that Haley will find someone when she's gone through all the stages of grieving over her husband. Tom Buchanan was killed in an accident just about the time they started talking about having a family. Mary Alice says she is an expert on grieving over husbands. But every time she starts talking about the steps to take, I get an image of actual steps marked Denial and Anger, etc., and I wonder where Haley is on the staircase. In the meantime, her biological clock is ticking so loud, it must surely keep her awake at night.

"I'm going to have to ask you ladies to come in, though, to see if anything is out of place or missing since you were here last." Jed Reuse turned his smile on Sister.

"I'm not that familiar with it, Mr. Reuse." She frowned.

"Sheriff."

"Sheriff." Sister poured respect and dignity into the title. "I just bought the place yesterday, almost on impulse, and to tell you the truth, I haven't even looked at the inventory Ed got together for my lawyer. You know, when you come out to line dance, you don't pay any attention to what's around you." Mary Alice paused. "Long as it's clean."

The smile again. "What we're hoping, Mrs. Crane, is that there will be something that just strikes you as being wrong. You see, considering such a violent act, very little was disturbed.

"No chairs overturned, no sign of a struggle. There's even money left in the cash register."

"Maybe it was suicide," I said.

"Hardly." His eyes could turn steely, I saw.

"I don't want to go in there," Sister admitted. "It gives me the creeps."

"I'm sorry, Mrs. Crane." Sheriff Reuse turned and held up the yellow plastic tape for us to duck under. Sister had met her match.

The door of the Skoot 'n' Boot had been propped open. It looked dark inside, just as it had the day before, when we were coming in from another sunny October day. Once inside, though, we saw that the lights were blaring. Over the wishing well, which had ceased its trickling, was a spotlight. I averted my eyes and looked at the neon boot above the bar. I felt slightly nauseated as well as claustrophobic.

"I think I'm going to have a panic attack," Mary Alice said, echoing my thoughts exactly.

"No, you're not," the sheriff said gently. "You're going to look around very carefully and tell us what you see that might be even the slightest bit different. Please. It will help," he added.

I looked away from the neon boot, allowing my eyes to wander over the room. Every light was on, the spotlights, the recessed lights around the dance floor. I remembered the feeling I had had the day before of hominess. Forget that! Not now! Even the Spanish moss on the Swamp Creatures sign seemed threatening. I made myself turn and glance at the wishing well. It looked just as it had the day before. No blood, thank God.

"It looks the same," Mary Alice said, also looking at the wishing well.

"Take your time." The sheriff pulled out a chair. "Here, sit down." Mary Alice sat down and folded her hands on the table like a proper schoolgirl. Sheriff Reuse pulled a chair out for me. "Mrs. Hollowell."

We sat for a few minutes, not saying anything, just looking. I looked at the dance floor and the dark drapery across the side window; I looked at the bar and the shiny glasses.

"You see anything?" Sister asked.

"No. You?"

"No."

"I didn't even know his last name."

"Meadows. His name was Edward Meadows."

"Nice name."

"Yes." Sister drummed her fingers on the table. The sheriff drummed his fingers on the table. So did I. We sounded like the game where you have to guess what song a person is playing. I drummed the *William Tell* overture.

"Lone Ranger," the sheriff said. We all smiled at each other.

"I see something different," Sister suddenly said, looking over my shoulder. "The rope and bucket are gone from the well!"

"The rope went with Mr. Meadows and the bucket is already at the lab. We found it at the bottom of the well."

"Oh." Mary Alice sounded deflated.

"Why don't you just tell me all you can about Mr. Meadows and buying the Skoot?"

"Well, my friend Bill Adams and I learned to line dance in Branson, Missouri—"

"Excuse me," I said, "but is the rest room open?"

"Sure," the sheriff said. "We've already been over it."

They certainly had. Not only had they chipped a small piece out of the corner of the mirror with the etched boot on it, but they had also loosened the toilet-paper holder, so that it was just hanging on. I got my Swiss army knife (a gift to myself years ago) from my purse and tightened the screws. The holder needed a little more work, but it would be okay for a while. I came out feeling proud of my handiwork and saw that a man had joined Sister and the sheriff at the table.

"No way!" he was saying as I approached. "No way!" He looked up at me and the expression on his face changed to surprise. "Mrs. Hollowell?"

"Henry? Henry Lamont? It is you, isn't it?"

"Lord! Mrs. Hollowell." Henry jumped up and engulfed me in a bear hug. "Mrs. Hollowell. How about that!"

Henry Lamont had matured into a handsome young man. Like my son Alan, he had grown a couple more inches after graduation from high school and was at least six feet tall. His blond hair had darkened some, but in his late twenties, he still had the face that some men are blessed with that keeps bartenders asking for I.D. until they are forty.

"You two know each other," Mary Alice said.

"She taught me AP English for two years." Henry hugged me again. "Lord, Mrs. Hollowell, you remembered me."

"Of course I do, Henry. You were the best. Absolutely."

"No, *you* were the best. I still remember when you took us to see *Macbeth*. The way they brought his head out on the sword at the end and how they kept shaking a piece of metal for thunder.

"And Banquo's ghost. That was really something."

"Mutual admiration society meets at the Skoot 'n' Boot," Mary Alice said.

"Yeah. Speaking of murders, how about you people joining us for a few minutes?" The sheriff pointed at the chairs. Henry and I sat down, still beaming at each other.

"But what are you doing here, Henry? Last I heard, you were at the writers' workshop in Iowa."

"He's the cook," Mary Alice said.

"She was bragging about you yesterday," I said, patting Henry's hand. It was true he had been one of my most promising students, a gifted writer. I wondered what had brought him to become a short-order cook at the Skoot 'n' Boot.

"It's a long story," he said, reading my thoughts.

"You were saying 'No way'?" the sheriff said.

Henry turned to him. "That's right. Ed was straight as an arrow. I've been here six months and, take my word for it, he liked the ladies. All of them. But I never saw him coming on to one so much that it bothered their boyfriends."

"Regular customers?"

"Sure. Lots of them. I worked in back, so I wasn't out here much, but I would sometimes see faces I recognized." He smiled at Mary Alice. "Like Mrs. Crane here." Sister beamed back. "Bonnie could tell you more about that. Bonnie Blue Butler.

"Or Doris Chapman, except Doris quit a few weeks ago. I think she was moving somewhere. And then there's a new girl, Sadie somebody. She's only been here a few days, though."

"Anyone else in the kitchen?" Jed Reuse had his notebook out and was writing.

"We have two part-time people that help. Usually students from the junior college. Right now we've got Mark and Ted, and that's all I know about them. Mark helps me with the cooking and Ted cleans up. I don't even know where they live. Bonnie Blue probably does, though. She finds out about everybody."

The sheriff looked up from his notes. "We've already called her. She'll be in soon."

"Interesting name," I said.

"She swears she was conceived during the burning-of-Atlanta scene. Must have had a tremendous effect on her parents." Henry laughed. "May be true."

"*Casablanca* caused one of my kids," Mary Alice said. "You know, when she's getting on the plane and looking back at Humphrey Bogart. That just does me in. Late movie one night."

Jed Reuse cleared his throat loudly. We all looked at him. "Please. I'd like to continue."

"Go ahead," Sister said, having a hard time getting off the subject. "The other two were just vacations or carelessness or something."

A good disciplinarian, the sheriff used the old school-teacher trick of being totally quiet and still for just a moment too long. None of us moved.

"Mr. Lamont," he said, "do you know of anything unusual that has happened here in the last few weeks? An argument Mr. Meadows might have had with someone? Anything that comes to mind?"

A dead body in the well, I thought. That's pretty unusual.

But I kept my mouth shut.

"No." Henry took his time trying to remember. "He told me yesterday he had sold the place to Mrs. Crane and that he was going back to Atlanta in a week or two. He was always very nice to me, paid me on time, sometimes a little extra if we'd had an especially busy week."

"What were you doing here yesterday? The place was closed."

"He called me."

The notebook came out again. "Whatever he had to say, he could have told you today, couldn't he?"

"I suppose so. I guess he was just excited that he had sold the Skoot and wanted to tell somebody."

"What time was it?"

"About two, I guess."

"We saw him after that," I said. "We left here just before dark, and he appeared alive and well then."

The sheriff looked at me. "Mrs. Hollowell, I'm just trying to get some information. I'm not accusing your best student of murder."

Mary Alice kicked me under the table. I gave her a go-to-hell look.

"It's just that this was not a robbery or some random killing. This was murder, obviously, which means that someone, maybe one of you, is sitting on some information that you don't think has anything to do with the case but which might be just the key we need. Mr. Meadows didn't live in a vacuum, wasn't murdered in a vacuum. Someone wanted him dead. And from the way they did him in, I'd say someone really didn't like him." Sheriff Reuse spread his hands as if he were doing card tricks. "Now, Mr. Lamont, suppose you tell us why you left Iowa."

Henry cracked his knuckles, a habit of his I had forgotten. "Selling drugs," he mumbled.

There was a commotion at the door. "Woo-hoo, Henry!" It was as if a photographic negative of Mary Alice stood there. Six feet tall, two-fifty (at least), platinum hair and skin the color of dark chocolate.

Henry jumped up so quickly, his chair turned over. "Bonnie Blue!" He disappeared in the vastness of her embrace.

"The admiration society grows," Mary Alice murmured.

Three

Bonnie Blue Butler maneuvered through the crowded tables with an ease that belied her size. You could tell it was something she was used to doing. We caught glimpses of Henry following her as she made her way toward us..

His admission, just before Bonnie Blue's appearance, had startled me. Henry Lamont selling drugs! Any teacher will admit that occasionally a child touches her heart. He or she may not be the prettiest or the smartest or the neediest. But there is something that clicks, and both lives are enriched for it. Sometimes it is perilously close to the love you feel for your own children. During thirty years of teaching, there were perhaps four or five children I had totally lost my heart to. Henry was one of them. The thought of him not fulfilling his potential was painful enough. But selling drugs! He was right.

There was a long story here, and one I wanted to hear.

"Mrs. Butler." Sheriff Reuse got up and pulled out a chair for Bonnie Blue. "Please join us."

"I got a choice?" Bonnie Blue did not sit in the chair. Instead, she seemed to squat over it and fall. The chair creaked but held. The sheriff did not even attempt to push it back toward the table. He introduced himself and then us. Henry had eased warily back into his chair. He seemed uneasy. I glanced at him, but he avoided my eyes.

"I know Mrs. Crane," Bonnie Blue said, looking at Mary Alice. "You are one wicked line dancer, girl."

"Thank you." Mary Alice smiled, more a smirk.

"That Mr. Crane can move, too."

"Mr. Crane ceased all motion about twenty years ago," I said.

"Fifteen," Mary Alice corrected.

"I stand by what I said, Sister."

"You sisters? Lord, Lord! You don't look one thing alike. Henry, you know they're sisters? You think they look one thing alike?"

"Maybe around the eyes. And no, I didn't know they were sisters."

"And that man's your boyfriend."

The sheriff tapped his hand against the table. We all jumped. "Please," he said, sounding exasperated. "We've got a dead body down at the morgue. I'm sure this is all fascinating, but could we please get down to business?"

"Ready when you are," Bonnie Blue said. "Henry, honey, will you go get me a Coke? I swear I'm dry as a bone." Henry started to get up. "Diet, honey. And maybe everyone else would like something, too."

Mary Alice, Jed Reuse and I shook our heads. While

Henry was at the bar, Jed held the tips of his fingers pressed against his forehead.

"I think he has a headache," Mary Alice whispered. "You got any aspirin?"

I reached into my purse and found a bottle of extra-strength Tylenol. I handed it to Sister, who nodded and placed it quietly in front of the sheriff. Henry came back with Bonnie Blue's Coke.

"Get the sheriff one, too, Henry," she said. "He needs to take something for his headache. Acting just like a man, not wanting anybody to think he has feelings."

Henry put the second Coke in front of the sheriff, who promptly opened the Tylenol bottle and took several.

"Now," Bonnie Blue said, "you want to know what I know about Ed Meadows and who killed him, don't you?"

"Yes, it would be appreciated," Jed Reuse said as he got out his notebook again.

"Diddly."

"Who?"

"That's what I know about it. Diddly."

I swear I think the sheriff wrote "diddly" in the notebook. At least he wrote something. Then he got up, drank the rest of his Coke in one gulp and excused himself, saying he had to go check on his men but no one was to leave, he would be back in a minute.

"Nervy," Bonnie Blue said, watching him walk out the door. "You see his hands shaking?" She shook her head in sympathy. "That man's got one hard job." Bonnie Blue sighed. "Least he's got a job. What you gonna do here, Mrs. Crane?"

"Oh, I'm planning to open up soon as I can. I've got to get organized and see where we stand and where everything is. I'm not planning on anybody missing a payday, though.'' Sister folded and refolded a Kleenex she held in her hand. ''One thing that I've thought of is whether the murder will scare people away.''

''Lord, no. Bring them in by droves. Halloween we won't be able to move.''

''Bonnie Blue!''

''It's the God's truth, Henry, and you know it.'' She reached over and patted Sister's hand. ''Let that be the least of your worries.''

What Bonnie Blue had said was so terribly true that I started giggling. The others looked at me. ''Tickets to sit in the well,'' I said, and laughed harder.

''We'll get the bucket back.'' Sister was laughing now.

''Oh, God, this is awful!'' I put my head on the table and howled. ''Poor Ed.''

All of us were laughing so hard we were gasping for breath when Sheriff Reuse came back in. I think he thought something was wrong. He came hurrying over.

''Sheriff,'' Bonnie Blue said, ''I think I just peed my pants.''

That made us laugh even harder. Mary Alice always cries when she laughs, so she was holding the shredded Kleenex to her eyes. ''Me, too,'' she gasped.

''Mr. Lamont, when you get control of yourself, I would like to see you in the kitchen.'' The sheriff turned and walked stiffly away.

''He's got the piles,'' Bonnie Blue whispered. ''Look at that walk.''

Sister bumped her head against the table, she was laughing so hard.

Henry scraped back his chair. We looked up and saw that he was not laughing anymore. ''I'd better go,'' he said quietly, seriously.

"It'll be okay, Henry," Bonnie Blue called after him. He gave a backward wave of his hand.

"That was certainly an unseemly show of emotion, Patricia Anne," Sister said, wiping her eyes.

Normally, the way she said that would have started me laughing again, but it didn't. I was watching Henry's thin shoulders, the way he pushed against the kitchen door and disappeared.

Bonnie Blue wiped her eyes with the back of her hand. "Well," she said, "there's just no telling."

Sister and I nodded in agreement, assuming what she had said was connected to something. The laughter had drained out of us as quickly as it had exploded.

"That Ed was not a bad guy. I've seen worse." Bonnie Blue traced a finger around a wet circle her Coke had left on the table. "Full of it, but not the worst."

"Full of what?" Mary Alice asked.

Bonnie Blue looked at me.

"She's usually quicker," I said. "She's just a lot older than me and a whole lot older than you."

"She looks good."

"Plastic. Everywhere."

"Y'all cut that out," Sister said. "Tell us about Ed, Mrs. Butler."

"Bonnie Blue."

"Mary Alice," I said, pointing toward Sister, "and Patricia Anne."

"Okay." Bonnie Blue drank the last of her Coke, took the napkin that was wrapped around it and wiped the table. "Let me see. He bought the place from a man named Mullins, Sam Mullins. Used to have a filling station and bait shop here. Sold a lot of bait to people going to the lake. Called The County Line."

"I remember that!" Mary Alice exclaimed. "He had

an old tarpaper shack out in the back where he kept the crickets in cornmeal.''

"Sure did." Bonnie Blue looked pleased. "Anyway, Mr. Mullins made himself a bunch of money and decided The County Line wasn't uptown enough. So he tore it down and built this little shopping-center thing. He had the restaurant and his sister did catering and stuff. Lasted about two days. If there was anything on the menu had cornmeal in it or on it, people turned green."

"You worked for him?" Sister asked.

Bonnie Blue nodded her head. "But like I say, it didn't last long, and then he sold it to Ed. Went to Florida, I think. Grouchy old man. Should have stayed in the cricket business."

Sheriff Reuse came out of the kitchen and called for one of the deputies. Bonnie Blue turned and looked at the kitchen door, then continued.

"That was about two years ago, did I say that? Anyway, I came in one day and here was Ed and Mr. Mullins just beaming, and Ed said he was going to turn it into a country-western bar called the Skoot 'n' Boot; said he wanted me to keep on working. It took them about a month to get everything done, like the boots on everything and the dance floor. I went to see my sister in Detroit while they were working on the place and didn't have any idea Ed would pay me during that time. But he did. Amazed me."

Bonnie Blue glanced around. "All this stuff didn't come cheap, either. Took them days to build that well. Didn't seem to bother him, though. Even when business was slow at first, it didn't bother him. I asked him one day point-blank was he rich, and he just laughed. Must have been, though. Maybe this was like a hobby."

"You said Ed wasn't the worst, though, like something was wrong," Sister said.

"Honey, that man had PMS. I swear. You know Doris, the other girl worked here? I told her he had PMS, to watch and see if he didn't. And she said no way, he couldn't have any such thing. So I started marking it on a calendar and showed her. I made a believer out of Doris. We knew to start covering our butts beginning every twenty-six days. He'd get cranky and that would last for a couple of days and then he'd start drinking.

"Sometimes he'd get so drunk we would just lay him out in the storeroom and cover him up. And sometimes he would disappear and we'd know he was off somewhere, drunk. Mean drunk, too. What's today?"

"The date? October tenth."

"Well, that wasn't why somebody killed him, then. He wasn't due until next week."

"Anyway, what would you do when he was, well, indisposed?" Sister asked.

"Actually, he didn't do much of anything, anyway. Made his tattoo dance. Wasn't much good as a bartender. Most of the help comes from the college. They have this restaurant course and even a bartending one. Long as they're twenty-one, they can serve drinks. Most everybody just drinks beer, anyway. Henry would call asking for a bartender for a couple of nights. But they would know the call was coming. They have a calendar, too."

"That's the strangest thing," I said.

"PMS, honey. Remember?"

"I certainly do remember. It hasn't been *that* long."

"What about girlfriends? Wife? Family?" Mary Alice wanted to know.

"Boobs resting on the bar. Lots of them."

"What?" Sister said.

Bonnie Blue spoke slowly. "Women came to see him.

They were hanging over that bar all the time, like Ed
was a Moon Pie and they were craving sugar.''

"He looked perfectly resistible to me," I said.

"Me, too." Bonnie Blue motioned toward the kitchen
with her Coke. "I told Doris, I said, 'Listen, Doris, what
is this? Is there something I'm missing? 'Cause I don't
think I've missed much.' And she just laughed and said
I wasn't missing a thing if I meant what she thought I
meant, but had I ever just watched Ed? And I said,
'Watch him do what?' And she just grinned and said,
'Watch and you'll see.' So that afternoon, first woman
came, I watched just like Doris said, and sure enough, I
saw it right off." She paused.

"Saw what?" Sister asked.

"He touched her hand," Bonnie Blue said. "That's
all he did. A woman would come up and order a drink
or be sitting at the bar and he would reach over and
touch the back of her hand with his fingers. Just sort of
rub them across her hand. That's all. Those poor women
would just melt."

"From him just touching their hands?" Sister looked
incredulous.

"It was like he was telling each one of them that he
cared for them, that he understood," I explained. "Of
course, the booze didn't hurt."

Bonnie Blue frowned at me and then looked at Mary
Alice.

"What your sister said. Doris caught on before I did;
I was slow. Even Henry knew it. I asked him one day
if he knew about this trick Ed had and he said, 'Rubbing
his fingers across their hands?' Made me feel dense.
'Course, he never tried it on me. But I wasn't leaning
across the bar.''

"Maybe he didn't stop there and somebody's boyfriend or husband found out about it," Mary Alice said.

"Could be."

The three of us sat quietly for a few minutes. I didn't know about the others, but I was thinking about the lonely women who had been comforted by the brush of Ed's fingertips across their hands. It was a manipulative gesture. No doubt it had given him a sense of power. But I remembered his limp handshake and wondered how in the world the touch of that hand could be so appealing.

"There's no accounting," Bonnie Blue said.

"But so much loneliness," I said.

"And violence," Sister added. She pressed the tiny shreds of tissue against her eyes again.

Bonnie Blue eyed the kitchen. "I wonder what that sheriff's doing to Henry."

"Doing?" My breath caught. "You think he's doing something to him?" I started to get up.

Bonnie Blue reached over and caught my arm. "I mean I wonder if he's upsetting that child."

I sat back down. "He better not be."

Bonnie Blue looked at me, puzzled.

"Henry was Patricia Anne's favorite student," Mary Alice explained.

"That right? What did you teach that boy?"

"English. I was sure he was going to be the next Faulkner."

"Give him time. Henry is gonna be all right."

Mary Alice spoke up. "He told us about his little detour."

"An accident."

"He said he was selling drugs," I said.

"Accidentally."

I was wondering how a person could accidentally sell drugs when the kitchen door opened and the sheriff, deputy and Henry walked out.

"Uh-oh. What's wrong with this picture?" Sister said softly.

What was wrong was that the deputy's hand was around Henry's arm and he was leading him to the front door. Henry, his head down, didn't look our way.

"Henry!" Bonnie Blue cried, trying to get up. But she was too stuffed into the chair. By the time she was on her feet, Henry was out the door and the sheriff was standing by our table.

"Ladies," he said, "we're taking Mr. Lamont in for some questioning. I appreciate your coming out and know I can count on your cooperation. Mrs. Crane, I'll let you know when we are finished here so you can make plans about the Skoot 'n' Boot. In the meantime, if you could keep yourselves available."

"How come you're taking Henry?" Bonnie Blue hissed. The same height as the sheriff, she had her face so close to his that he backed up, bumping into a chair. She looked big enough to grab him by the shirtfront and lift him off the floor.

He straightened up. "There are some questions we need to ask him, Mrs. Butler. That's all."

"You listen. That Henry never did anything wrong in his life."

"Then he has nothing to worry about." The sheriff started to walk away. "Ladies, thank you again."

"Is he going to need a lawyer?" Mary Alice asked, but Sheriff Reuse either didn't hear or pretended he hadn't.

"Damn right," Bonnie Blue said. "You saw those handcuffs."

"Call Debbie," I told Sister. "Tell her something terrible has happened and we need her."

"Who's Debbie?" Bonnie Blue wanted to know.

"My daughter Debbie Nachman," Sister said. "She's a lawyer."

"Call her," Bonnie Blue said, reaching for the bottle of Tylenol that was still sitting on the table. "Lord, Lord."

Four

Debbie said she would be waiting for us at her office. It took both Mary Alice and me to tell her what had happened. She thought her uncle Fred was dead somehow in a well, what with Sister's babbling, and she was much relieved when I got on the phone and explained exactly what was wrong.

"You can tell me all the details when you get here, Aunt Pat," she said.

"But Henry was handcuffed. I would absolutely stake my life that he's innocent."

"When you get here, Aunt Pat. I have to get back to my client now."

I placed the phone back on the bar.

"She hung up on you, didn't she?" Mary Alice was moodily bending a straw into shapes. "Do you think this looks like a swan?"

"Don't be silly."

"I don't, either," she said, wrapping the straw around her finger.

"I mean she didn't hang up on me. That sweet child would never hang up on me."

"Of course she would. She just does it politely."

"She does not."

"Did you get her?" Bonnie Blue ambled from the rest room.

"She's meeting us."

"Good. You tell her that Henry's an angel."

"I already have."

"Too good for the ways of this world." Bonnie Blue hoisted her purse (the twin of Sister's) onto the bar. "By the way, somebody broke the mirror in the bathroom, Mary Alice."

"Probably the policemen." Sister's eyes narrowed. "I don't like that Sheriff Reuse."

Bonnie Blue's eyes narrowed. "Took that Henry out in chains!"

I listened to them bad-mouthing the sheriff and thought somehow we were missing the point here, mainly that a dead body had just been carted out with its throat cut. That didn't happen just every day in a person's life. I suddenly thought of a news story I had read the week before, about a woman finding her husband's body. The reporter had written, "When she saw that his head was missing, she became greatly alarmed." At the time I thought, *Alarmed*? What kind of a reporter would write something like that? Now I was beginning to understand how we can put horror in a little cubbyhole in our brains to deal with later.

"Let's go see Debbie," I told Sister.

It was good to get out of the Skoot 'n' Boot. The warm sunshine was a pleasant surprise. As we approached the interstate, we saw a woman with long blond hair riding a horse across the field toward the big house we had admired the evening before. It was a lovely picture.

Sister turned the car onto the interstate ramp. "I've been thinking," she said, slowing as a tractor-trailer rig thundered by, then pulling in behind it. "I think I may have jumped the gun buying that place like I did. I probably should have looked into it a little more."

I wanted to say, "No kidding," but decided the best thing to do was to keep my mouth shut. Which I did all the way to town.

Debbie's office is in an old, remodeled Victorian house on Birmingham's south side, where the wealthy lived a hundred years ago but which is now a neighborhood in transition. The huge old homes that were falling into disrepair are now being turned into smart apartments and offices. Debbie's house is both; her apartment is upstairs. She thinks it's wonderful, especially since it's right across from a park where Richardena can take Fay and May to play every day. She actually says that, having obviously inherited her mother's tendency toward rhyme. Mary Alice is suspicious of the neighborhood and the park, and if she sees two people talking together on the sidewalk, she is sure a drug deal is going down. Richardena, the nanny, is not beyond her suspicions, either, since she has had her own criminal tendencies.

"She shot him in self defense, Mama!" Debbie insists. "And she aimed for his foot!"

"Then how come she hit him about three feet higher?"

"An accident, Mama!"

At any rate, the judge believed Debbie, and Richardena escaped a prison tern just in time to get settled before the twins were born. She is a loving, gentle woman and May and Fay adore her. The fact that Richardena's ex-husband will never sire children bothers no one but Mary Alice. And probably the ex-husband.

Which brings up another matter that bothers Mary Alice: the sire of Fay and May. One day Debbie had announced to her mother that she was thirty-five years old, wanted a child and had taken matters into her own hands, so to speak, and been artificially inseminated at University Hospital.

"Do you believe that?" Sister had asked me. "I'll bet it was that Barney what's his name who has hair growing across his nose."

After the twins were born, Mary Alice was so enamored of them, I don't think she even looked for stray hairs across the bridges of those precious little noses. She even sent a large check to University's fertility clinic. She said it was in grateful appreciation. I figured she was planning on looking into their records someday.

The little girls were taking their naps when we arrived at Debbie's. Debbie was sitting on the front steps in blue jeans, eating a peanut-butter-and-banana sandwich and drinking a diet Shasta.

"My, aren't you casual," Sister said.

"I dress for court," Debbie said, unperturbed. "Y'all sit down. Want a Coke or something?"

"If I get down on those steps, I'll have to get up," Sister said. She pulled a wicker chair over. "Where are the babies?"

"Taking a nap."

"Richardena up there?"

"She's gone to the store." Debbie motioned to the monitor beside her. "I can hear them."

"I don't trust those things," Sister said.

Debbie turned to me. "Hi, Aunt Pat."

"Hi, darling."

"What's going on?"

Mary Alice and I both started talking at once. Debbie held up her hand. "Whoa."

"You first," I told Mary Alice. "It's your crime."

Sister started with line dancing and, almost without catching a breath, segued through buying the Skoot 'n' Boot (which Debbie knew about), to our pleasant visit the day before and Ed clapping to our dancing to "Rockytop" and ending up in the well, to Bonnie Blue having a purse almost like hers that she probably hadn't paid a fraction as much for, to Sheriff Reuse taking Henry away in chains.

She did a fine job of telling it all. Sister is a good one for details. When she finished, she looked at me. "Did I leave anything out?"

"The broken mirror in the bathroom."

"Oh, yes. That's another thing I want you to complain about, Debbie. Those policemen aren't being careful at all with my property. I want you to be sure and get that on the record."

Debbie looked at her mother and then at me. She took the last swig from the Shasta and crumpled the can up. (Her mother hates it when she does this!) "What?" she said.

"Those policemen are showing no respect for property."

"What?"

"What do you mean, 'what'?"

"The child's confused, Sister." I took Debbie's hand. "What do you want to know, honey?"

"What happened to Ed?"

"Dear God." Mary Alice came up out of the wicker chair with much groaning, though you couldn't tell who was protesting more, Sister or the wicker chair. "I'm

going to go fix me a sandwich and peek at those darlings. You tell her, Patricia Anne." She opened the
screen door. "I don't suppose you want a sandwich?"
I shook my head.

"Figures." She pulled the door to with a little pop-
ping sound.

"She's going to wake up the girls," Debbie said.

"Sure she is." We looked at each other and smiled.

"Okay, Aunt Pat. Tell me what happened, slowly, and
what Mama wants me to do."

I covered the same bases Sister had but stopped occasionally to breathe, allowing Debbie to ask questions.
The answers seemed to alarm her. When I finished, she
was actually gnawing at a cuticle, something I hadn't
seen her do in a long time.

"Good Lord. Execution style?"

I nodded. "My main worry right now, though, is
Henry. He's always seemed fragile to me, and no telling
what they're doing to him."

"What is this about him in chains?"

"Well, Bonnie Blue said she thought she saw handcuffs on him."

Debbie sighed. "I'll call and find out what's what.
Chances are they just took him in for some questioning,
just like the sheriff said, and he's already home. But I'll
see. They can't hold him for no reason, Aunt Pat."

"He writes poetry, Debbie."

"They can't hold him for that, either." Debbie
smiled. Then she frowned. "I wonder what Mama's got
herself into this time. This sounds scary."

The monitor beside us crackled suddenly. We both
jumped. Then Mary Alice's voice came in loud and
clear. "And are Grandmama's darlings awake already?
Are those tiny little eyes open?"

Ten minutes later, when she showed up with a twin

under each arm, she had the nerve to tell us they had been calling for someone to come get them.

"Mama!" each screamed and held out her arms to Debbie. They are fifteen months old and absolutely identical. Debbie and Richardena supposedly can tell them apart, but no one else can. They have dark, curly hair and the longest dark eyelashes I think I have ever seen on babies. Any sperm bank would be proud to claim them. Sister handed one of them to Debbie but held the other one. "Say Grandmama, darling. Grandmama."

"Dena," Fay or May said. They both began to cry.

"I'll get them some juice," Debbie said and handed her crying baby to me.

"They're sleepy," I accused Sister.

"Ponyboy, ponyboy," Mary Alice sang, jiggling her twin.

I suddenly realized that I had a splitting headache and was exhausted. Fay or May in my arms felt like a ton. I put my face against the dark curls and smelled the sweet smell of shampoo and baby sweat. I felt like crying, too. Too much had happened in one day.

Debbie came back with the juice and took Fay ("Come here, Fay, darling") from me. "You look green, Aunt Pat."

"She needs to eat something," Mary Alice said.

"I have a headache."

"There's some Stanback in the kitchen cabinet. Richardena swears by them."

"She lets these babies see her ingesting a white powder?"

"It is possible, Mama."

I got up. "I need some caffeine, I think."

"You want me to fix you some tea?"

"I'll fix it." I left Sister and Debbie exchanging slightly hostile remarks. The hall was dark and cool, furnished as the house might have been originally. The kitchen, however, could have been built yesterday. It was airy and light, and Debbie had added a glass sunroom onto the back. I found the Stanback, took one and heated water for tea in the microwave. I was startled to see that it was only two o'clock. How long could a day last?

Taking my tea into the sunroom, I sank down into a large leather chair. I would have to remember to tell Debbie how to get crayon off leather, I thought. Soon. I leaned back and looked up at the trees, and at the leaves that were just beginning to drift down. How golden everything was! I sipped my tea and closed my eyes. Ed was laughing and clapping to "Rockytop." I opened my eyes quickly. I didn't want my imagination to go any farther. But they wouldn't stay open. I put the tea on the table and made myself think about pleasant things as I sank into a delicious catnap . . .

"You were snoring," Sister said. "Drooling, too." She was sitting on the sofa across from me, looking at a *Glamour* magazine.

"Makes me feel sorry for old Fred."

"I don't snore." I wiped my still damp chin.

"Mash the button on that tape recorder by you."

"You didn't!"

"Sure I did. You didn't come back to the porch and I figured you had passed out or something in here, so I came to check on you and I couldn't resist. Go on. Mash the button."

I hadn't noticed the small recorder when I had set the tea down. Sure enough, the red recorder light was on.

"I'm going to kill you," I said. "In the most unpleasant way I can think of." I reached over and turned the machine off. "You act like a child."

"I know it. Isn't it fun?" Mary Alice put the maga-

zine down and leaned back in the comfortable leather
sofa. She propped her arms across her belly, for all the
world like a woman nine months pregnant. "Debbie's
gone to get Henry and talk to the police."

"They're not holding him?"

"No. They just wanted to ask him some questions."

"But what about the handcuffs?"

"You and Bonnie Blue watch too much TV. The way
you were snoring when I came in, it's understandable
that Fred keeps his distance."

I refused to rise to the bait. "Listen," I said, "is she
going to bring him back here?"

"I doubt it. You messed her whole afternoon up, you
know. She canceled all her clients."

"Where are the babies?"

"In the park with Richardena. I told Debbie we would
go on home. I think she just wants to talk to Henry. She
said she would call."

"Okay." I pushed up from the chair. "What time is
it?"

"Almost four. You had a long nap."

"Long enough to be stiff as a board." I stretched.
"You want to go by the market and get some boiled
shrimp? Call Bill and see if he wants to come for supper? That way we can tell the whole story at one time."

"Sounds good. I need to stop by the house and check
on Bubba, though." Bubba is the laziest cat who ever
lived. I could guarantee Mary Alice that he was right
where she had left him that morning. But she persists in
endowing him with all sorts of emotions, such as love
and loneliness. Her hands are constantly Band-Aided
from Bubba's "love bites."

"Okay," I agreed.

As we left, she blew the horn and waved at Richardena and the little girls, who were both bouncing up and

down on toy horses with springs under them. I felt
bleary-eyed, still not quite awake. I hate to take naps in
the daytime. They disorient so. I rubbed my eyes.

"You really do snore," Mary Alice said.

We picked up the makings for slaw and the shrimp.
Mary Alice decided we should make a recipe she loves
called Shrimp Destin, which is nothing but shrimp
heated in a butter-and-garlic sauce and served on toast.
Talk about cholesterol and indigestion! I told her Fred
and I would both be up at two o'clock looking for the
Maalox. She said wear a sexy nightgown.

"I'll just be a minute," she said when we got to her
house. "Come on in. It's too hot outside."

Mary Alice's house looks out over the whole city. I
love the view. You can see all the interstates and planes
landing and taking off at the airport. It is especially
beautiful at night. She has a whole wall of windows
where I love to stand.

The sun was getting low in the sky and rush-hour
traffic was beginning.

"I'm going to give this sweet Bubba a couple of
shrimp," Sister said. "He's starving, yes, he is." She
plucked the fat, starving animal from the counter where
he had been all day and headed for the kitchen, flipping
on her phone messages as she went by. "Maybe Debbie's home."

There were messages from the window washer and
someone named Jane about lunch, and a couple of hang-
ups. And then, loud, clear and unmistakable, my voice
came from the machine. "I'm going to kill you in the
most unpleasant way I can think of."

"My God!" Sister said, frozen in the kitchen door.
Her face turned white, as if she would faint. I knew how
she felt because I felt the same way.

Five

We both were so stunned we sat down in the nearest chairs. I put my head between my knees, which helped the dizziness but not the shaking.

"You did that, didn't you?" Sister's voice was still not normal.

"Did what?"

"Rigged it some way to get even with me for taping your snoring."

I raised my head. The room was standing still. "What?"

"That's it. You did it, didn't you?"

"How could I have done that? We turned off the tape recorder and left. We got right up and left. Remember?"

Mary Alice tried to smile. "Okay, you've won. You've got me scared. That was what you wanted to do, wasn't it?"

"I didn't *do* anything."

Sister turned the answering machine on. There was my voice again, saying I was going to kill her in the most unpleasant way I could think of.

"Turn it off!"

"You did it, didn't you?"

A thought even scarier than my voice threatening Sister lit up my brain. I jumped up. "Somebody's in Debbie's house, Sister! Call the police. Right now! Nine-one-one! Get them! Quick!"

"Oh, my God!" Sister suddenly believed me. She grabbed the phone and dialed with a shaking hand while I held my breath.

"Richardena? Is Debbie there?" She nodded. "Where are the babies? Right there with you in the kitchen? Okay. Listen, I'll explain this later, but right now I want you to take Kay and May and go next door to Mrs. Haddin's, and if she's not there, take them down to the drugstore. Somewhere where there are people. Please, Richardena, and don't go in the sunroom. Just leave. I'll be there in a little while and the police may be there, too." Mary Alice paused. "No, Richardena, you will not need a knife or a gun. Just take the children and leave." She hung up. "She wanted to know if she would need her knife or gun. The woman has a knife and a gun around my grandbabies!"

"Call nine-one-one," I said.

"I'm going to see if I can get Debbie on her car phone. I don't want her going into that house." She dialed again while I walked over to the window. The sun was touching the horizon now and some of the cars had their headlights on. Everything looked so normal, I began to think of some normal way my threat could have gotten on Sister's answering machine. Maybe Debbie had one of those phones where you just punched one button and one was for her mother's phone and one of the twins had been playing with it. But that reasoning didn't work out. The tape recorder would have had to be turned on, rewound. No toddler could do that. I started shaking again. I looked out at the cars going home. Fred was in one of them. Suddenly I wanted his arms around me so I could feel safe.

Sister was talking to Debbie. I could tell she was having a hard time explaining what had happened.

"Don't go in the house," she said. "Wait for us. The twins are either next door or down at the drugstore."

"She's not taking this very seriously," Sister told me, hanging up the receiver. "I'm going to get the tape out of the answering machine to take over there for the police to hear."

A noise from the kitchen made us both jump. Bubba appeared in the doorway with a shrimp in his mouth. A glance at the kitchen floor showed the whole package, ripped apart. Bubba hadn't been saving his strength all day for nothing. I grabbed him and put him out the back door. "Is Debbie calling the police?" I reached into the cabinet for a bowl and got down on my hands and knees to salvage what Bubba had left of our supper.

"She said she would." Mary Alice stood in the doorway biting her fingernails while I scooped the shrimp into the bowl.

"Good." I took the bowl to the sink, rinsed the shrimp—from which, hopefully, Shrimp Destin would kill Bubba's germs—put them in the refrigerator and got the mop from the broom closet.

"Come *on*, Mouse! We've got to go. You can do that floor when we get back."

"What?" I said. "What?"

She looked at me, puzzled. "I said we need to go."

"Mary Alice." I walked toward her with the mop.

"What?" she said, backing up slightly.

"Whose floor is this?"

"Mine."

I shoved the mop at her. "Get that shrimp juice up that your cat got on your kitchen floor."

She held the mop as if it were some kind of medieval torture tool. "And use Pine-Sol," I said and stalked out. I needed to talk to Fred. Maybe he was home by now. Sweet Fred. Sweet, soothing Fred.

"Where the hell are you!" he yelled into the phone when I said hi. "I've been worried sick about you."

Sweet, soothing Fred. "I'm at Sister's."

"I should have known. I called over there, though, and nobody answered. I saw the story about what happened at that hot spot she bought on the news. I want you to get home, Patricia Anne."

Hot spot? He had the Skoot 'n' Boot mixed up with our dog's skin rash. "She didn't buy the Skoot 'n' Boot on the news, Fred." Sometimes you know immediately that you have gone too far. There was a long silence. "Look," I said, "so much has happened today, you won't believe it."

"I'll believe it if Mary Alice was involved." His voice was cold. "Get home, Patricia Anne."

"I don't have a way."

"I'll be there in ten minutes." The next thing I heard was a dial tone. I put the receiver back in its cradle. The phone immediately rang, startling me. "Good-bye," Fred said when I answered it. I was smiling and once again thanking the marriage gods when Mary Alice came in reeking of Pine-sol and Victoria's Secret peach-hyacinth hand lotion.

"Was that Debbie?"

"Fred."

"Well, let's go." Mary Alice looked around for her

purse. "The police should be there by now."

"I'm going to wait for Fred. He's coming to get me. You don't need me over there, anyway."

"Okay. I'll call you later, Mouse, and let you know what the police say." Mary Alice slung her bag over her shoulder. "Let's see, I've got the tape. Do I need anything else?" She looked around. "Nope. Just set the alarm when you leave, okay?"

Trust my sister. I had been expecting all kinds of protests about not going with her, and wasn't even getting a small argument.

Not only that, she came over and hugged me.

"Thank you, Mouse, for all the help you've given me today."

She sailed out, leaving me with my mouth open just like she had been doing for sixty years, leaving me to face a disgruntled husband, who showed up a few minutes later and deposited an equally disgruntled Bubba in the foyer.

"Some fool," Fred said, "let the cat out."

One of the first lessons I learned after marriage was "Don't lie, but don't tell everything." It allows a certain amount of dignity to remain in the relationship. It is also a kindness. For instance, Fred had been perfectly happy for me to spend a quiet week in North Carolina with Mary Alice. He would have worried about the white-water rafting trip we took down the Nantahala. I saved him the worry. If he ever asks me if I went white-water rafting, I will, of course, say yes. I certainly don't believe in lying.

As soon as he came in with the cat, though, I forgot my "don't tell everything" rule and went from Ed in the well to the threatening phone message in about two minutes flat.

He listened, nodding at critical points when I stopped

to breathe. When I finished, I looked at him expectantly.

"What is that smell in here?" he asked.

"Shrimp, Pine-Sol, and peach-hyacinth lotion."

"Oh."

"It was our supper. The shrimp."

"We'll stop at Morrison's takeout."

I got my purse and set the alarm. When we went out, I noticed there was still a thin edge of light at the western horizon. This day had been a week long.

"Now," Fred said after we got in the car, "do you want to start from the beginning?"

I did. I started with Ed Meadows's body and how it had been found in the wishing well and how we had seen it lifted into the ambulance.

Fred said that was what he had seen on TV, the body being put into the ambulance.

I shuddered. "I wish that was the view I had."

Fred patted my hand. "I'm sorry."

"Me, too."

We were quiet for a moment, and then Fred asked, "What did the sheriff say?"

I thought I had told him all this already, but figured I had better not ruffle the waters. "He thinks it was a gangland thing, I think. Connected to drugs, maybe. I don't know. There was so much overkill."

"Overkill?"

"They beat him, cut his throat, drowned him, tied him up. Killed him about three times."

"Good God!"

"And then they arrested Henry Lamont. You remember me talking about my student Henry Lamont, Fred?"

Fred slowed to let a car enter our lane. "Faulkner, Welty and O'Connor rolled into one? I remember him. How did he get into this?"

"It's a mistake. He's the cook out at the Skoot 'n'

Boot and the sheriff found out he had been in trouble with drugs and took him in in chains. It was awful the way they treated him.''

"You saw chains?"

"No, I didn't, but Sister did. And Bonnie Blue."

"Figures. Who's Bonnie Blue?"

"She's a very nice lady who works at the Skoot 'n' Boot. She reminds me of Mary Alice, except she's African-American."

"Black?"

"I don't think that's politically correct anymore, Fred."

There was a silence while we stopped at a light. Fred drummed his fingers against the steering wheel. "What?" I said.

"What do you mean, what?"

"What are you thinking about?"

"An African-American Mary Alice. Two Mary Alices."

"When you meet her, you'll see what I mean. They even have purses alike."

Fred turned into the restaurant parking lot. "I don't want you to get involved in this, Patricia Anne. I really don't. Okay?"

"Okay," I agreed. "I'm sure the police are going to want to know why I threatened Sister, though."

"You threatened Mary Alice?"

"When she taped me snoring. Or at least she said I was snoring."

"Am I missing something here?"

I explained again about the message on the answering machine, though I had already told him once. While I was retelling it, I was reminded of the way Sister had gone rushing back to Debbie's without insisting that I go with her. She was over there now, talking to the police and in all sorts of danger, and here I was at Morrison's takeout parking lot. She could at least have argued with me a little.

"Probably some simple explanation," Fred said. He patted my leg. "What do you want for supper?"

This was what I needed to hear, wasn't it? Then why didn't it make me feel better? Because Fred was being patronizing? On the other hand, he wasn't the one who had been there, who had gone through the roller coaster of emotions that I had gone through today.

"Vegetables," I said. "It doesn't matter what kind. I'll wait in the car."

As soon as Fred left the car, I reached under the seat, got the phone and plugged it into the cigarette lighter. Sister had had plenty of time to get to Debbie's.

After the second ring, someone picked up and I could hear heavy breathing. Then there was a low moan, a gasped "Oh, oh!"

My heart nearly stopped. "Debbie! Is that you? Debbie?"

"Oh, hi, Aunt Pat. That was Fay saying hello. She's grabbing the phone away from me again. Say hello to her."

"Oh?" I could hear Debbie coaching her. "It's Aunt Pat, darling. Say hello to Aunt Pat."

"Oh?"

"Hello, sweetheart. Hello, my baby girl." My heart was assuming its normal rhythm.

"Oh. Oh. Oh. Oh."

I could just see that precious child with the phone. Sometimes I feel the lack of grandbabies living close by like a great void. Alan's two are teenagers and live in Atlanta, and Freddie says he doesn't want children. Besides, he's in Atlanta, too. My only hope is knowing Haley wants children so much. Sometimes I wish she would visit the University of Alabama at Birmingham sperm bank like Debbie did. But Haley wants a husband and a father for her children. She had known that kind of love once and knows it is possible.

"Aunt Pat?" Debbie's voice broke into my thoughts.

"What's going on over there, darling?"

"You mean about the message on the phone? Nothing. You know how Mama tends to exaggerate things. Richardena says she turned the tape recorder off when she went in and saw it was on, and the twins were with her, so anything could have happened."

"I thought we turned it off," I said. I didn't tell her I was the one who had fallen apart first when we heard the message.

"Did you call the police?"

"Of course not."

"You honestly think it was done accidentally?"

"Absolutely."

She sounded so positive and so unconcerned, I felt my fright begin to subside. Maybe I *had* overreacted. Maybe one of the babies *could* have hit the right sequence of buttons. It certainly wasn't impossible. I got to the second reason for my call.

"Did you see Henry?"

"He was already gone when I got there. What was this about handcuffs, Aunt Pat? Sheriff Reuse, who is a very nice man, incidentally, just asked him if he would come in so they could get some details straight about the people who worked at the Skoot 'n' Boot and the regular customers."

"The handcuffs were your mother's idea," I was proud to relay.

"Well, there weren't any. I'm sorry you and Mama got mixed up in this, though. Mama's sitting at the kitchen table right now having a 'toddy for the body' that looks like an eight-ounce glass of pure vodka.''

"Tell her I turned the alarm on at her house. You may want to drive her home.''

"She's fine, Aunt Pat. And don't worry about that phone call. That guy's murder has just spooked you. I'm sure there's a simple explanation.''

Fred's exact words. But somehow when Debbie said them, they didn't sound so patronizing. I told her I would talk to them later and hung up just as Fred got in the car and handed me a plastic bag.

"Macaroni and cheese, lima beans and mashed potatoes,'' he announced happily. "An orange, green and white vegetable. Just what the nutritionists recommend.''

I wondered if he was kidding and decided I didn't really want to know. "Did you get any dessert?''

"Egg custard pie.''

I reached into the bag, found the small Styrofoam container and took out the slice of pie. When I bit into it, I could taste nutmeg and cinnamon. It was the best thing I had ever eaten, sweet and comforting. I had finished it by the time we left the parking lot.

"Would you like my slice, too?'' Fred asked.

He was being sarcastic, but I reached back into the bag and found the other small container. By the time we got home, that slice was gone, too.

Six

I didn't sleep well that night. The pie that had seemed to go down so lightly lay in my stomach like a piece of lead; nightmares plagued me. I finally got up, went into the den and turned on the TV. That didn't help. The local channel I was watching had a replay of its ten o'clock news at 2 A.M. There was Ed's body being loaded into the ambulance, and I felt the same tightening in my stomach. I turned the TV off and tried to read. I finally fell into a fitful sleep on the sofa. Fred woke me with a cup of coffee.

"I started to let you sleep," he said, "but I wanted to know you were all right."

I took the coffee gratefully and assured him I was, though to tell the truth, I wasn't sure. I was stiff from sleeping on the sofa, which is really a love seat and too short for comfort, and I had a pounding headache. "I'm fine," I insisted, refusing to groan and moan like an old woman until Fred was out of the house.

Two aspirin and an hour later, however, I really was better. I decided to tackle the bushel of apples that we had bought over the weekend. My family says my applesauce is the best in the world. I use a recipe I found in *Southern Living* about twenty years ago, so there are no secret ingredients. In fact, I am suspicious that I am the only one who is willing to peel those apples and stand there stirring the pot. But that's okay. I really do enjoy the way it smells when it is cooking and the feeling of satisfaction I have when I put the packages into the freezer. It's one of my fall rituals.

I was standing at the stove stirring the first potful when the phone rang.

"Mrs. Hollowell? It's Henry." His voice sounded hesitant. "Is it all right if I call you at home?"

"Where else would you call me, Henry?"

"I guess so. I keep forgetting you aren't still teaching."

"I don't." I stirred the applesauce. It smelled like Thanksgiving and Christmas. "Are you all right today?"

"I'm fine." Henry cleared his throat. "Mrs. Hollowell?"

"What, Henry?"

"Do you think we could have lunch somewhere? I think I owe you some explanations."

"You don't owe me any explanations, Henry."

"I feel like I do."

I smiled. "My daughter has a T-shirt that says, 'My Mother Is a Travel Agent for Guilt Trips.' Maybe you should borrow it."

"I think I've become my own best agent." Henry sounded so despondent, it broke my heart. What had happened to the boy with all the promise?

"Where are you now?" I asked.

"At home."

"Well, I think talking is a good idea and I could use some help peeling apples. Why don't you come over?" I looked at the mountain of apples. "I think I've committed myself to a day in the kitchen."

"You're sure?"

"You'll have to peel apples."

"I can do that."

"Great. I'll see you after a while, then." I hung up the phone and stirred the applesauce. The morning sun came through the bay window I had had installed in the breakfast nook. We had talked about having that done for years, until finally I called a remodeling company. When Fred came home from work, the whole wall was torn out. "You can take your money with you," I said, "but you're not going to take mine, too." To his everlasting credit, he had laughed.

I set the first batch of applesauce on the back of the stove to cool and sat down with another cup of coffee. A squirrel was standing on his head on the bird feeder, trying to get some sunflower seeds; my climbing Peace rose was blooming along the fence. The violence of yesterday seemed as unreal as if it had happened in another world. I wondered how Mary Alice was today and glanced at my watch. Probably still asleep. I crossed my arms on the table and rested my head on them; the sun was warm on my back and the next thing I knew, I was dreaming the doorbell was ringing. When I sat up, both arms were tingling from the weight of my head and there was a small circle of drool on the table.

The doorbell rang again. "Coming!" I yelled, trying to get myself together. I grabbed a paper towel, wet it and swept up the drool. I ran my fingers through my hair. Damn! I must look like a wild woman.

Henry had my rolled-up newspaper in his hand, which again proved that I was not my usual self this morning. Usually the first thing I do after Fred has gone is take our dog, Woofer, for a walk. Then I come back, get the paper and settle down in the breakfast nook for a good read. It may be the best luxury of being retired. Today I had just thrown Woofer a couple of dog biscuits. Bless his heart, he never complains.

"Good morning. Here's your paper." Henry looked like he hadn't slept very well last night, either. I could smell aftershave lotion and his clothes were neatly ironed, but Henry's eyes were as bloodshot as mine, and there was the unfocused air about him that I had seen on thousands of tired children in my classroom.

"Come in."

He stepped into the foyer and smiled. "You know, you're so much smaller than I remembered you."

"I know. It happens to me all the time. I think maybe all adults seem large to children."

"I was in high school, though."

"Just my formidable presence."

"You really were pretty formidable."

"Was I? I never intended to be."

"Oh, formidable in a good way. You expected so much of us that we didn't want to disappoint you."

We smiled at each other, and for a moment we were once again teacher and brilliant student with the whole bright future ahead.

"Come on back to the kitchen and I'll get you some coffee. I wasn't kidding about those apples. I'm making applesauce."

Henry followed me down the hall. "It smells wonderful," he said. "This is the way every house should smell."

"I agree. I think that's one reason I enjoy it so much.

And it's like putting nuts up for the winter, too. I like to open the freezer and see all those packages. My parents had me right in the middle of the Depression, and Mary Alice was tiny and they had a terrible time. I think their attitude rubbed off on us. Well, on me, anyway." I pointed to the breakfast nook, where I noticed gratefully that the table was dry. "Have a seat and I'll get us some coffee. You want cream and sugar?"

"Both."

"How about some warm applesauce and toast?"

"Sounds great."

I busied myself fixing the food. If Henry was like my own two boys, Freddie and Alan, it would take several pieces of toast and a bowl of applesauce. Maybe two bowls. I sneaked a glance at him. He certainly looked peaked, as my mother used to say. Like he needed some good food.

"This is nice," he said when I set his plate before him, nodding his head to indicate he meant both the view and the food.

"Peaceful," I agreed. I poured the coffee and sat down. I watched him take his first bite of toast and applesauce, saw the pleased look. "I'll give you the recipe," I said.

Henry nodded and chowed down. He gave no sign that I had indirectly referred to his job as a cook. He seemed satisfied to eat and watch the squirrel still trying to get the bird seed. Which suited me. The applesauce was as good as ever.

"More?" I asked as he sopped up the last of the applesauce with the last of the toast.

Henry smiled. "No, thanks. That was wonderful, though."

"More coffee?"

Henry shook his head. "My wife died, Mrs. Hollowell, from a drug overdose. Or at least a reaction to drugs. Cocaine. The doctors said she had an underlying heart problem we didn't know about and she died. Atrial fibrillation. Maybe if I had gotten her to the emergency room quick enough. But who knows?'' Henry looked into his coffee cup as if he expected an answer.

"Oh, Henry, I'm so sorry." I was also startled at the suddenness of his confession.

"Her name was Barbara and she was twenty-three. She was a student, too, and we had been married only a few months. I was the one bought the coke and brought it home, even talked her into trying it." Henry twisted his coffee cup around and around.

"You were a user, then?"

"I wasn't an addict, if that's what you mean. Luckily. I was a recreational user. A stupid recreational user. In time things might have changed, though. I'd gotten to the point I enjoyed it more and more." Henry shook his head. "Stupid."

His coffee cup was in danger of sailing off the table. "Let me get you some more coffee," I said, rescuing it. Henry rubbed his hands together as if he hadn't noticed the cup was gone.

"They arrested me for manslaughter."

"But how could they do that? For not getting her to the hospital?"

"I didn't even know anything was wrong with her. I was in the bedroom, high as a kite, trying to write. Can you imagine?"

"Yes," I said, thinking of Faulkner and Fitzgerald.

"What they said was that I had furnished the lethal drug."

"But you didn't make her take it."

"Not physically. They couldn't make the manslaughter charge hold up. But the charge of buying and selling drugs did. A couple of times I'd let the guy next door have some coke. They found out.''

"Oh, Henry, I'm so sorry. What happened?''

"There's a mandatory one-year sentence.''

"You went to prison?'' I gasped.

"Well, I'd never been in any trouble before, so they put me into a program that's like a halfway house. You do community work and they even have some counseling for you. I ended up working in a homeless shelter. That's where I learned how to cook.''

I put the coffee cup in front of him.

"I've got a record, but I got off easy. I could even have gone back to school if I'd wanted to. But I didn't have the heart. I kept thinking Barbara was going to walk around every corner, or I'd see some girl with hair the color of hers and I'd forget for just a second what I'd done. That she was gone.''

Henry picked up his cup and looked me straight in the eye. "That was when I came back to Alabama. My father died when I was a child and my mother remarried and moved to Florida. She's dead, too, now. But Alabama's home, and I figured this was the place to get my life together again.'' He sipped the coffee. "Things like yesterday don't help, though.''

"No,'' I agreed, still trying to absorb all he had told me.

"I don't know anything about Ed's murder, Mrs. Hollowell.''

"I know you don't, Henry.''

We sat quietly for a few minutes.

"I was planning to call you when I got my act together, to say thank you.''

"To thank me? For what?''

"I was the only one at Iowa who always knew when

to use 'lie' and 'lay.' '' His ironic smile was sadder than it should have been.

"Oh, Henry." I smiled, but I felt tears burning my eyes. "Let's peel apples."

I spread newspaper on the table for the peelings and Henry pulled the bushel basket over so each of us could reach it.

"How did you end up at the Skoot 'n' Boot?" I asked, settling down with a paring knife and a big Rome apple.

"Through the junior college. They have a great food preparation and restaurant program, you know, and I knew I wasn't going to make a living writing. I hadn't even finished the course when Ed hired me. He needed a cook, not a chef. But I'm still in the class. I'll graduate this semester. And you know what?" Henry's face showed some real animation for the first time. "I really like it. I'm good at it, and I figure I can always get a job as a chef. In fact, one of the country clubs is already interested in me."

"That's great."

"I won't give up my writing, though."

"Good. How about a very literate cookbook?"

"Why not?" Henry pared his second apple expertly and held it up, gazing at it as if it were a crystal ball. "You know, I can't believe Ed was murdered like that. I keep thinking tonight's pizza night at the Skoot and I need to get there early to see if we need extra crust. I make it ahead and put it in the freezer, but if we've had a lot of pizza orders during the week, I'll need to make some more. But I guess it'll be a while before we have pizza night, or anything else out there. Somebody really hated that old boy, didn't they?"

"Did the sheriff seem to have any ideas?"

"If he did, he didn't share them with me. He ran a

background check on me and asked me who some of the regular customers were and if I had seen Ed arguing with anybody.''

"Bonnie Blue and my sister thought he had you hand-cuffed. 'In chains!' They convinced me, too. We were ready to come down and spring you.''

"That's what I heard. Bonnie Blue called me last night.'' Henry grinned. "She's wonderful, isn't she?''

"A hundred percent on your side, I'd say.'' I put my peeled apple in the pan. "The sheriff didn't give you any problems, did he?''

"No. I told him all I knew, which wasn't much. There are quite a few regulars there. Mrs. Crane and her boy-friend, for instance. And Ed had a lot of girlfriends, most of whose names I don't know. I never saw anybody sinister hanging around, though, and haven't even no-ticed any new faces in the last week or so. Like I told the sheriff, Ed just seemed like a pretty nice guy. You had to stay out of his way sometimes when he'd been drinking, but that wasn't too often. He didn't hassle the help, and if anybody got too loud or belligerent, he han-dled it easily. I was surprised he sold the Skoot, to tell you the truth. I think he had a real good thing going there.''

"I understand he was going to Atlanta, that his par-ents were in poor health and he needed to be near them.''

Henry shook his head. "That can't be right. I remem-ber telling Ed once that my father had died of lung can-cer and that it cured me of wanting to smoke, and he said both his mother and father had died of lung cancer within a week of each other while he was in the Navy and his wife had to stay in Charleston to settle every-thing.''

"Charleston?''

"Absolutely. I remember because he was talking about some beach property they had and how he was glad they sold it before Hurricane Hugo."

We looked at each other. "Did you tell this to the sheriff?" I asked.

Henry shook his head. "He didn't ask and I didn't think about it. You think I should?"

"Well, Ed was lying about his reason for wanting to leave town. I guess that could be important."

"Or maybe he was just trying to get away from one of his girlfriends. Didn't want her to follow him."

"Or one of the girlfriends' boyfriends."

"Maybe." Henry studied the peeled apple in his hand. "But I don't think his murder had anything to do with jealousy, do you?"

"You mean because it was so vicious and premeditated?" I shrugged. "Who knows, Henry? You've read your Shakespeare." I dropped an apple into the pan, where it landed with a metallic thud.

"That's true."

The phone's ring startled both of us. "Unless I miss my bet," I said, "that will be my sister, who probably suspects, God forbid, that my blood pressure is normal today." I was right.

"What are you doing?" she asked after I said hello.

"Making applesauce."

"Why? You can get Motts now with extra cinnamon or Lucky Leaf. They're both good as homemade."

I didn't argue. I just let my mind drift for the millionth time to the idea that one of us really was adopted. Probably Mary Alice. After all, I had my mother's short upper lip and blond hair.

"Mouse?"

"What?"

"You nearly scared me to death about that phone call last night."

Mary Alice definitely was the adopted one.

"There was a very reasonable explanation," she said.

"What was it?"

"Probably one of the babies. Children nowadays know a lot more about electronic stuff than we do." I didn't point out that the babies were fifteen months old. Sister would just get started on what geniuses they are. "Anyway," she continued, "I know you didn't mean to upset me, so I forgive you."

"Gee, thanks."

"And I need you to go to the Skoot 'n' Boot with me this afternoon."

"What for?"

"I'm going to meet with a contractor. To have some minor remodeling done."

"You're having the wishing well taken out."

"That and a few other things."

"You checked with Sheriff Reuse?"

"Not yet, but I will before we actually change anything."

"So you're definitely opening back up."

"Of course. What happened to Ed had nothing to do with me. I'm not going to be mixed up with the Mafia or doing drug trafficking or whatever he was involved in. All I'm going to do is have a nice, fun place for people to dance and have a good time."

"Shall I tell Henry his job is safe, then?"

"Sure. When you see him."

I glanced over at the table, where Henry was peeling an apple and seemed lost in thought. "He's here. Peeling apples."

"Well, tell him I'm glad he's not in jail. I'll pick you

up around two. And, Mouse? Bring me some of the applesauce.''

"What about Motts?" I yelled into the dial tone. Whatever had happened to saying good-bye before you hung up? I slammed the receiver down. "That was Mary Alice," I said to Henry, needlessly, as I sat down. He was grinning. "She's going to open the Skoot 'n' Boot back up."

"That's good."

"You really think so?" For a moment I saw Ed's tattoo dancing, saw his body being lifted into the ambulance. "You think it's safe?"

"Most probably."

It was not the answer I wanted to hear, and Henry knew it. We both reached for an apple at the same time.

Seven

In October, political advertisements bloom on all the signboards and at the interstate exits. If there is a space, there is a sign. They will stay there long after the elections, in fact until storms batter them down. Candidates are supposed to take them down the day after the election, but I have yet to see that happen. Half the candidates are too happy to bother; the others are too depressed.

On our way to the Skoot 'n' Boot, Mary Alice asked who I was voting for and then said, "Never mind. I know."

She was referring to the fact that I usually vote a straight Democratic ticket. She votes straight Republican. Always has, so she says. I happen to know she voted for Kennedy, though, and she knows I didn't vote for McGovern. He sounded exactly like Liberace when you listened to him on the radio. Not that I had anything against Liberace, but I couldn't take him seriously as President. I'm sure Mr. McGovern was a very nice man and I felt terrible about it, but there it was. Abraham Lincoln wouldn't be elected today and we all know it. Or at least he would have to have that mole taken off. I've always worried about it being a melanoma, anyway.

"What factor sunscreen do you use?" I asked Sister.

"Thirty." She looked over at me. "Worrying about Abraham Lincoln again?"

"That mole was very dark." Sometimes it's scary the way Sister can read my thoughts.

"Worry about something you can do something about."

Lord, she sounded like Mama.

"I know, I sounded like Mama, didn't I?"

I nodded. Sister flicked her right turn signal and we exited up the ramp, which was lined with political posters.

"Speaking of politics," she said, "you know who lives over there? Richard Hannah, Jr." She was gesturing toward the house across the fields that I had noticed the first time we had left the Skoot, the Tara house that had been silhouetted against the setting sun. "I'm invited to a party there next week for the Republican Women's Committee. You want to come with me?"

Dick Hannah was the Republican candidate for the U.S. Senate. He just might win, too. My candidate was, admittedly, old and ugly. His slow speech made him seem retarded at times. He was, though, as our father used to say, dumb like a fox. And he was a known quantity. Dick Hannah was young and handsome, and some advertising agency in Memphis had done a wonderful job of promoting him as the ideal family man with his beautiful wife and two little girls. Yes, he probably *would* win.

"You want to come, Patricia Anne?"

"No."

"Sure you do." Mary Alice stopped at the top of the ramp for an old pickup that was huffing and puffing down the county road. So much smoke was pouring from it, it reminded me of the little engine that *could*.

"I think I can. I think I can," it gasped.

I wasn't at all sure it could, but the driver seemed confident, waving to us. We followed him as closely as the exhaust fumes would allow. Two old hounds watched us mournfully from the truck bed. It was a relief when he turned into a dirt road.

"See?" I said. "That's why I vote Democratic. That old fellow has Social Security and Medicare at least, thanks to Franklin Roosevelt and Lyndon Johnson."

"Are you crazy?" Mary Alice looked at me and laughed. "That old fellow needs Social Security like he needs a hole in his head. That was Jackson Hannah, Richard's uncle. He and his brother—ex-governor Richard, Senior—own half of north Alabama. Coal, lumber, cattle, trucking. You name it, they own it. Jackson even ran for governor one time. Remember?"

How could I forget? The Hannah family has been involved in Alabama politics for years. Richard, Senior, had served one term as governor and probably would have been re-elected if he hadn't been injured in a small plane crash during his second campaign. And now his son, Richard, Junior, was campaigning for the Senate. But it was brother Jackson Hannah's one foray into the political arena that had left the most indelible image.

"He's the one who pulled off his shirt on TV to show how much hair he had on his chest?"

"Well, somebody had called him a wimp, questioned his manhood, he said."

"Good Lord, is that who that was?" I turned to look at the truck, which was disappearing in a cloud of red dust. "I remember his wife trying to get his shirt back on him and he fell backwards over a chair. One of Alabama politic's finest moments."

"Jackson has had a little problem with alcohol, I understand."

"I'm sure the host of that TV show would agree with that."

"Water over the dam," Mary Alice said, turning into the empty parking lot at the Skoot 'n' Boot. "We're dealing with a whole new generation of Hannahs now. Dick and Sara are very nice, and their house is supposed to be as gorgeous inside as it is outside. Don't you want to see it? It's going to be a fancy party, and I've got plenty of invites. I contributed to his campaign fund."

"I don't have any Republican clothes to wear," I said. "They dress elegantly at these parties."

"Don't be silly. Nobody'll notice you."

"Thanks," I said. Sister missed the sarcasm as usual.

"The guy's not here yet." She pulled into the handicapped parking space almost in front of the door. "Let's go on in."

"You're in a handicapped space!"

Mary Alice looked around the empty lot. "Oh, the shame! And all those handicapped people without a place to park."

"It's the principle!"

"There's nobody else in the whole place!"

"Move your car!"

Mary Alice sighed, backed the car up and moved two spaces down. Just as we were getting out, a pickup with a large butterfly painted on the door, with the words

"Monarch Remodeling" forming the antennae, pulled into the lot. This truck, I noticed, wasn't in much better shape than Mr. Jackson Hannah's. Blue exhaust fumes floated behind it like contrails. These truck owners, I thought, had every reason to pray we never had another oil embargo.

The truck stopped in the parking space on the other side of the handicapped place, and an old hippie got out. Well into his fifties, he wore his waist-length graying hair in a ponytail. His hairline was receding badly, as if the weight in the back were pulling it out of the front. The result was a look of permanent surprise.

"Mrs. Crane?" His rubber flip-flops made squishy sounds as he came toward us. "I'm Fly McCorkle." He was not as tall as Mary Alice, but he had broad shoulders and gave the impression of strength. His handshake was warm and firm when Sister introduced us.

I was glad to see him. I had been dreading going into the Skoot and seeing the wishing well. I knew it was silly, but I got a funny feeling in my stomach just thinking about what had happened there. Fly McCorkle's presence was obviously going to be a comforting one.

"I know the old Skoot well," he said while Sister found her keys. "And Ed." He shook his head. "Nobody deserves that. You know?" We agreed. "He was a pretty good old fellow. Went fishing with me a couple of times."

Sister handed him the key as if she were as reluctant to enter as I was. He fit it into the lock.

"Did my lady tell you I don't work on Fridays? I go fishing Fridays. Can't miss that. Friend of mine's got a son named Smith, 'cause we were fishing at Smith Lake when the baby was born and his wife didn't want him to forget it. He told her, he said, 'Woman, I promise you only one thing. When you're nine months pregnant, Fly and I won't fish at Weiss Lake.' '' He grinned and opened the door. "Got grandchildren now."

He held the door open for us. I was smiling at him and didn't realize Mary Alice had stopped dead still. I walked right into her with a *whump*, barely catching my glasses as they sailed off. "Lord, Sister!"

"Oh," she said. "Oh."

"For heaven's sake, I didn't hurt you. Move."

"Ohhh." It was almost like a long-indrawn breath.

"What's the matter? Turn on the lights."

"Here." Fly McCorkle reached around me and flipped a switch.

"Oh," Mary Alice said. "Ohhhhh."

"Good God!" Fly exclaimed.

I couldn't say anything. The Skoot 'n' Boot was a total wreck. Tables were turned over, chairs were slashed with padding spilling onto the floor, broken glass shimmered everywhere.

"I didn't know it was this bad," Fly said, looking around, stunned.

I found my voice. "It wasn't. Somebody did all this last night."

"I think I'm going to be sick." Mary Alice nearly knocked Fly and me down getting out the door.

I felt sick, too. I had never seen such devastation. They had spared nothing.

"We better call the sheriff. I got a phone in the truck."

We backed out carefully, our shoes crunching glass. Why hadn't I noticed that crunching sound when I took my first step inside?

"Fly's calling the sheriff," I told Sister, who had her head propped on the steering wheel and the air conditioner on full blast. "You want a Tums?"

She nodded, and I found one in the side compartment

of my purse for her. There was another one down in the corner with the old receipts and recipes. It was a little dusty, but I chewed it up. I had the feeling I was going to need all the help I could get.

In a few minutes there was a tap on the window. "She okay?" Fly asked me.

Sister answered for herself. "I need a Valium."

Fly looked around me. "You got a mantra?" he asked Mary Alice.

"Of course."

"We both do," I added.

"Then close your eyes and say it until the sheriff gets here. He said it would be a few minutes."

Mary Alice moaned.

"You say that mantra now," Fly cautioned. "You, too, Mrs. Hollowell." He went back to his truck, turning to wave. I waved back.

"Dear Lord, Patricia Anne," Sister said. "You've always had a thing for hippies, haven't you?"

"Feeling better, are we?"

She put her head back against the steering wheel. "Say your mantra."

Sister was right. The whole hippie movement was one that fascinated me. I had been too old to be one, my children too young. But there was something so innately romantic about handing out flowers in a park in San Francisco. The darker side of the movement I didn't like to think about. It was the innocence that touched me.

I closed my eyes, but what I saw was the terrible vandalism inside the Skoot 'n' Boot. My mantra went sliding by, refusing to stick in my brain. "I'm going to walk around," I said.

"Don't mess up any clues."

"Like what?"

"Footprints or something."

"Don't worry."

Fly McCorkle was talking on his phone when I passed his truck. I admired the butterfly on the side, and for the first time, it dawned on me that "Fly" must be a nickname for "Butterfly." Good for him, I thought. Moon, Sunshine, God. You don't hear those old hippie names much anymore. Like their owners, most of them have faded into corporate America. God Jones just doesn't get it for a stockbroker.

I walked to the end of the building and down the side. In the field behind was an old apple orchard, overgrown, neglected, but with a few of the trees still bearing. I wondered about the people who had owned this land, who had planted this orchard. Surely there had been many October days like this when they had come out to pick apples under a sky that looked freshly Windexed. Sister says I romanticize the past, and she's probably right, but there was the peaceful old orchard before me and the asphalt parking lot and Skoot 'n' Boot behind me. The comparison was enough. I went over and sat under a tree. A few apples had fallen and bees were going mad over them. I kept my distance, though the bees were too busy to notice me.

I leaned back against the tree, closed my eyes and let my thoughts wander. Why had someone torn up the Skoot 'n' Boot like that? For that matter, why had someone killed Ed? He had to have been deeply involved in something others felt passionate enough about to want him dead. Maybe partners with some people in a robbery and he had held part of the loot back from them? Money, jewelry?

The tattoo on Ed's arm danced against my closed eyelids. I saw him laughing as Sister and I danced; I saw his body being lifted into the ambulance. I shuddered and rubbed my fingers in a circular motion on my temples.

Drugs. It was all going to boil down to drugs and we all knew it. What else could it be in a little country-western night spot on a county road in Alabama? And my sister had bought right into the middle of the mess. Well, given the condition of the Skoot now, she was just going to have to accept her mistake and eat her losses. She needed to get as far away from this place as possible.

"Get up, Mouse, the sheriff's here." Mary Alice's voice seemed to be coming from a great distance. "You're drooling again."

I wiped my mouth and sat up straight. I couldn't believe, given the state of my nerves, that I had fallen asleep.

"You okay?" I asked. Mary Alice was white as a sheet; her eyes were bloodshot, and smeared eye makeup made them appear sunken.

"I am now. The mantra and the Tums both failed me. I lost my lunch in the dumpster."

"You want some gum?"

She held out her hand while I rummaged in my purse, finally coming up with part of a stick of Freedent. She picked the foil off while I groaned my way up from the ground.

"The sheriff's already gone in. He wants to go over the damage with us."

"Us? I don't know anything about that place." My voice sounded like Prissy in *Gone With the Wind*, squealing, "Lordy, Miss Scarlett!"

"I don't know anything about it, either. There's an inventory somewhere."

"You should have been more businesslike about this whole thing," I grumbled. "Leaping and then looking. Just like always."

I regretted it the minute I said it, but Sister seemed not to notice my harsh words.

"It's nice out here, isn't it?" she said. "Fly McCorkle says his wife's church group usually picks these apples for the Jimmy Hale Mission; wanted to know if it would be okay. I said sure."

"This orchard belongs to you?"

"I think so. Come on," she said, helping me brush my skirt off. "Let's go talk to the sheriff."

The inside of the Skoot 'n' Boot was as bad as I had thought when I first saw it. Sheriff Reuse and a deputy were walking around examining the devastation, the sheriff had his notebook out, of course, and Fly McCorkle sat at the bar with a bottle of beer. I couldn't imagine where he had found an unbroken stool to sit on and an unbroken bottle of beer. The place looked like a bulldozer had been in it. The sheriff saw us and picked his way through the mess.

"Ladies, would you like to sit down?" he asked.

We glanced around. Fly seemed to have found the only seat in the whole place.

"The kitchen isn't too bad."

We followed him into the kitchen I had admired so much just two days before. He was right. Drawers had been pulled open and utensils scattered around, but it was not the total wreck the rest of the place was. Maybe because kitchens are just sturdier. Or maybe the vandals had been tired when they got to it. At any rate, there were unbroken stools by the Corian counter. We sat down.

"Why on God's earth would anybody do this?" Sister said. She wasn't really asking the sheriff; she was thinking aloud.

He answered, though, with another question. "Maybe looking for something?"

"They could have looked without tearing everything up, couldn't they?"

"It depends."

"I mean, I'm always looking for things like my reading glasses or the mate to a shoe. And, Mouse, when I was over at your house looking for my Gucci scarf you borrowed and didn't return, did I tear up your house? No. Ask me, this was pure vandalism. All this destruction. And why?"

"You were looking through my house for your scarf?"

"Just in your dresser, and see? You couldn't even tell."

"But if something was hidden," the sheriff insisted.

"Nothing was hidden in the wineglasses and the bottles of liquor. They didn't have to break all those." Sister motioned around the kitchen. "And look at the pots and pans and the cuts in the counter. It doesn't make a grain of sense."

"Neither does setting forest fires, but we see it all the time. There are more sick people out there than we like to admit." Sheriff Reuse opened his notebook and scanned it. "I know there's an inordinate amount of damage, but I still think they were looking for something. From what I've seen, there was a fairly methodical pattern to their search. The stuffed chairs, for instance. They didn't miss a single one of them. If they had just been vandalizing, two or three would have sufficed. I think the glassware was an afterthought. Maybe they didn't find what they were looking for and were mad. Or maybe they wanted it to look like vandalism."

"You went through my dresser drawers?" I asked Mary Alice.

"Oh, for heaven's sake, Patricia Anne. You should have returned the scarf." She turned back to the sheriff. "You think they're looking for drugs?"

Her question was answered by the deputy standing in the door. "I just found this, Sheriff," he said. He held out a tiny plastic bag with some white powder in it. "It was in the toilet-paper holder in the ladies' room."

I wondered if it was the holder I had fixed the day before with my Swiss army knife. If so, my fingerprints would be all over it. "Oh, my," I said, putting my forehead down against the cool kitchen counter.

Eight

Haley came to supper that night. Usually I try to fix something special for her. Alan has his wife and children, and Freddie seems to find girlfriends who like to feed him, so I know there's nourishing food on their tables, but Haley is alone and stops by the pizza shop too often on her way home. She's an RN, working in open heart surgery, spending the day unclogging other people's arteries and the night clogging her own. She swears this is not true, but I know better. So on Haley's supper visits, it's veggies, every color. All beta carotenes and antioxidants.

But after Sheriff Reuse had got through questioning us and had us walk through the Skoot, just as he had done the day before, to see if we saw anything different (stuffing out of chairs didn't count), and Mary Alice had talked to Fly McCorkle about the repairs (yes, indeed, she had decided she was going to open back up!), and she had to stop at Hardee's for a peach milkshake to settle her stomach and wondered why I was mad at her since I left the key out there in that plastic rock, anyway, for anyone to come in my house, and she had seen an advertisement for a dog turd that you hid a key in that would be a lot better than that old rock, a fake dog turd, of course, and she would order me one, and why wouldn't I talk to her, that she hadn't done anything but look in my dresser and it hadn't been very long since we had had one dresser for the two of us, had I forgotten?

"Fifty years ago," I said.

"See?"

"You always had the top drawers."

"That's better, Mouse. Now we're communicating."

By the time she let me out at home, I barely had time to go to the store. I grabbed a slice of ham steak, a can of green beans and an angel food cake. With the applesauce I had made that morning, it would do.

Haley and Fred came in at the same time. I am always amazed at how Fred's features became so beautifully feminine on Haley. She looks just like him, but she is lovely. No one would ever call her Mouse. Like Mary Alice, she had received the gift of beautiful olive skin from some unknown progenitor. Combine this with reddish-blond hair and brown eyes and you have a knockout. The only way anyone would know I was in the delivery room is that she is small.

"Hey, you two," I said.

They both gave me a hug.

"Ham?" Haley looked over my shoulder. "You're giving me *meat* to eat?"

I popped the ham steak covered with a raisin sauce into the oven. "Don't get used to it."

"I'm just impressed. You want me to set the table?"

"Please. I've been out to the Skoot 'n' Boot with Sister. You wouldn't believe all that's happened out there."

"Something else happened today?" Fred stopped on his way out of the door.

"No more murders, thank goodness. Go get cleaned up. I'll tell you all about it at supper."

"I'm not happy about you being out there, Patricia Anne."

"I know, honey."

"Your sister is a dingbat."

"I think so, too, honey."

Fred nodded solemnly as if we had reached an important agreement. Then, clutching the evening paper under his arm, he headed toward the bathroom. Haley and I grinned at each other.

"Have you heard all that's happened?" I asked her.

She opened a cabinet door and took out the plates. "I stopped by Debbie's to see the babies. She told me. Good Lord, Mama, an execution-style murder! Does Aunt Sister know anything about this man? Debbie says she bought the place on a whim. What a thing to get mixed up in!"

"They found drugs there today."

"At the Skoot?"

"In the toilet-paper holder in the ladies' room. When we got there, someone had torn the place up, obviously looking for it."

Haley put the plates on the table and reached into the silverware drawer. When she turned around, her mouth was pursed exactly like Fred's. "I think Papa's right, Mama. This sounds like a place to stay clear of."

"It's a real neat place." I found myself defending the Skoot. "Or at least it could be. It's the kind of place

your Aunt Sister would have a wonderful time with. You
know how she likes to be the world's hostess and ply
everyone with food and drink. She would be in her element there.''

"It sounds like an element is already there that you
and Aunt Sister don't need to get mixed up with."

"You may be right. According to Bonnie Blue Butler,
though, and even Fly McCorkle, there's never been any
trouble. Sheriff Reuse admitted he hadn't had a call to
the Skoot in over two years, and that was somebody
backing into the Swamp Creatures' van and leaving." I
finished chopping up a small onion, dumped it into the
beans and put the pot on to simmer. "You want some
corn bread?"

"Bonnie Blue Butler?"

"She works out there. Wonderful person."

"Fly?"

"An old hippie who's going to fix the place up. Wonderful person."

"Sheriff Reuse?"

"Seems competent."

Haley reached for the glasses. "I'm almost afraid to
ask this. The Swamp Creatures?"

"The band. I haven't met them yet." I put the lid on
the green beans. "Hey, you want corn bread or not?"

Haley shook her head. "It's too much trouble." She
put the glasses down, came over and hugged me. "It's
just that I worry about you."

"Don't worry about me," I said, patting her shoulder.
But I knew she would. Tom's sudden death had taken
from Haley the sense of invulnerability that is the blessing of youth. Until his death, the patients in the operating
room were people she didn't know, sick people she
cared for professionally; their families were strangers.
Now she was one of them. Anything could happen to

anyone at any time, and did. The knowledge had come to her too soon.

"I'm going to make corn bread, anyway," I said. "You can feed Woofer for me. I'm sure he's feeling neglected."

Haley opened the pantry door to get the dogfood. "Debbie told me about Henry Lamont, too. I remember you talking about him."

"Debbie was just a font of information, wasn't she?"

Haley laughed. "I have an idea Debbie hasn't even scratched the surface."

I reached over her for the cornmeal. "You're right," I admitted.

At supper I told them everything I knew, including about Fly McCorkle's pickup with the monarch butterfly on it and the old apple orchard behind the Skoot. I told them about Ed's tattoo and the stuffing torn out of the chairs and the cocaine in the toilet-paper holder. They ate and listened. I opened a can of peaches and sliced the angel food cake and told them about the Swamp Creature sign and the lights that ran around the outside sign like the marquee at the Alabama Theater. They ate and listened. I told them about Henry, though I didn't tell them about his wife. Finally I poured coffee, sat down and said, "That's it."

Haley and Fred both put exactly a half teaspoon of sugar in their coffee and stirred. If the Olympics had a synchronized coffee-stirring event, these two would have been gold medalists, I thought. They looked from the coffee to me, coffee to me. Their expressions were so alike, it was eerie.

Fred finally raised his cup to his mouth. So did Haley.

"You're right," Fred said, his words blowing steam across the cup toward me. "That's it."

Haley nodded.

Fortunately, just then the phone rang. Haley reached behind her to answer it. "It's for you," she said, handing me the receiver.

"Who is it?"

"Some lady."

"I'll get it in the den." I picked up my coffee cup and left the kitchen. Fred and Haley watched me silently.

"Patricia Anne? It's Bonnie Blue."

"Hang the phone up," I yelled to Haley. I heard the click.

"Hey, Bonnie Blue, how are you?"

"I'm okay. Just wanted to know if you've heard from Henry."

"He came by here this morning."

"I mean since they found the dope at the Skoot."

"No. How'd you hear about that?"

"Fly McCorkle told his wife. AT&T ought to snap that woman up. She could teach them some shortcuts. Anyway, I've been trying to get Henry, and I can't find him."

"You worried about him?"

"Just wanted him to know. Thought the sheriff might be calling on that child again."

"Oh, my God." I couldn't believe I hadn't thought about such a logical course of events. "You're right."

"Henry tell you all that's happened to him?"

"Yes."

"Bless his heart." Bonnie Blue sighed mightily. "Patricia Anne, I think we need to do some talking. Can you have lunch tomorrow?"

"Sure." There was a tone in her voice I had not heard before, a tightness. It made me anxious. "You *are* worried about him, aren't you?"

"I guess so."

"Just tell me where to meet you," I said.

"Shoney's on Eighteenth at eleven-thirty suit you?"

"I'll be there. You going to call Mary Alice?"

"I want just you and me to talk."

"Fine. Bonnie Blue, if I should hear from Henry, you want me to have him call you?"

"Sure do. He knows my number."

"I don't, though."

"You got a pencil?"

I did, wrote the number down and put it in the side compartment of my purse before I went back to the kitchen.

"Who was that?" Haley asked.

"A lady from the church wanting me to make a cake for the Christmas bazaar." Lie detectors aren't necessary for people like me; my voice gives me away. Fred and Haley both looked at me disapprovingly. "You want some more coffee?" I asked.

During the night, I got mad at Fred. He was lying there snoring lightly, twitching occasionally just like Woofer does when he dreams he's chasing rabbits. I wondered who Fred was chasing, and the more I thought about how well he was sleeping and dreaming in the pajamas I had bought and washed for him, digesting the supper I had cooked for him, the madder I got.

I punched my pillow and tried to get comfortable, but I couldn't. What made him think he had the right to tell me what I could and couldn't do? Make me have to lie to him? Telling me I could do this and I couldn't do that and Mary Alice was a dingbat. Which she was, but he shouldn't have said that about my sister, and Lord knows what he would do if he knew she had come into our house and gone through my dresser drawers, which was another matter, but damn!

I got up and put on my robe and slippers.

"You okay?" Fred mumbled.

"You're not the boss of me," I said.

I went into the kitchen. It was three o'clock. I got a glass of milk and a cookie and took them into the den. It was cool, so I lit the gas logs. Haley, too, I thought. Even Haley bossed me around just like her father and aunt did. And the boys weren't much better. Alan trying to tell me how to invest my retirement money. I had enough sense to invest my own money, thank you. And a nice little income I was getting from it, too. I didn't have to listen to Fred or Sister or anybody. Or solve anybody else's problems. I was an independent woman. I might even move down to Gulf Shores, never cook another supper, just sit on the beach. With a lot of sunscreen, of course.

Woofer scratched on the back door. I got up and let him in. "You can go with me," I told him, rubbing his ears back. "You don't boss me around." When I let him go, he went straight to the coffee table, gobbled up my cookie, then pranced into the kitchen and looked expectantly at the box of cookies still on the counter.

"You just knocked yourself out of a life at the beach," I told him.

I woke up to the doorbell ringing. For a moment I was confused, and then I realized I was on the den sofa and that the slant of the sun against the wall was mid-morning bright. I could hear Woofer barking in the backyard. Fred must have let him out.

The doorbell rang again. I ran my fingers through my hair and went to see who it was. They were going to be in for a shock, I thought, when they saw me.

I looked through the peephole and saw a florist delivery man getting into his truck. I opened the door, and on the porch was a large gardenia bush full of blooms.

"Ohh," I said, bringing it inside, burying my face in the fragrance. "Ohhh." It was suddenly May. Graduations and proms and dances and kisses and weddings. I couldn't believe it.

I carried the plant to the kitchen table and circled around it, admiring it. This was October! Somebody had spent a fortune on this!

I opened the card, knowing what it would say. Something like, "Enjoy! Mary Alice." What I got instead was one of the dearest surprises of my life. The card said simply, "I love you. Fred." I sat there smiling. How about that? I guess I would have to take the old bastard to Gulf Shores with me.

Bonnie Blue was waiting for me when I got to Shoney's. We both ordered the Senior Soup and Salad Bar and went to get our soup. She was wearing a dark nylon wind suit and looked neither as large nor as formidable as she had seemed at the Skoot 'n' Boot. In fact, she seemed subdued today.

"Cream of broccoli," she said. "Hmm. My favorite."

"Mine, too." I filled my bowl and added some oyster crackers.

Bonnie Blue looked at me in surprise. "You going to eat all that?" she asked.

"Sister's been talking to you, hasn't she?"

Bonnie Blue grinned.

"Well, you can forget my anorexia. It exists in her fertile imagination."

We walked carefully to our table, balancing the soup. It was still a little early for the main lunch crowd, so we had a corner to ourselves.

"Did you find Henry?" I asked.

"No. And he's still not answering the phone."

"You don't suppose he left town, do you?" But the

minute I said it, I knew it wasn't so. "No. I know better than that," I told Bonnie Blue.

She was stirring ice from her water glass into her soup to cool it. "Maybe he did," she said, "if he's smart."

"What do you mean? You know Henry didn't have anything to do with Ed's murder or with the drugs, either. Why would he need to leave town?"

Bonnie Blue looked straight at me. "That sweet boy has things working against him. The sheriff'll find it out."

"What, Bonnie Blue? What do you mean?"

Bonnie Blue shrugged. "Things that happened between Henry and Ed."

"What kind of things? Henry said he and Ed got along fine."

"They did, usually. But you remember I told you Ed had these spells like PMS? Well, a couple of months ago, he had the worst one ever. I mean, there was no living with that man! And he got to drinking and got mean as a snake. Usually he would just sleep it off in the office, and that's where we thought he'd gone until we heard Doris screaming. Doris, the girl who used to work there?"

I nodded.

"Well, Doris is nobody's spring chicken and nobody's beauty, but I guess Ed was so drunk he couldn't see straight. Anyway, he decided he was going to get him some right in the walk-in cooler, of all places. Doris walked in and there Ed was, ready for action. Backed her up against the counter, and her just a-screaming. He slammed the door—locked it, the fool. If they'd been there by themselves, they'd have frozen, I reckon." Bonnie Blue grinned. "That brings an unusual picture to mind, I must say." She tasted her soup to see if it was cool enough. "Anyway, it was the middle of the day, and we all heard Doris yelling, but we didn't know why. Henry grabbed the key and opened the door and there they were, poor Doris with Ed all over her. Henry yelled for him to quit, but I think old Ed was too far gone by that time. Anyway, Henry had a frying pan in his hand and he hit Ed with it. Took Ed's mind off what he was doing, all right. Knocked him cold. The trouble was, when he fell, he cut his head on the corner of a metal shelf. Had to have fifteen stitches. I took him to the emergency room and told them he was drunk and fell and cut his head, which was true. But Doris couldn't keep her mouth shut. She told everybody about Henry hitting Ed with the iron skillet and saving her honor. Huh, he saved something, all right, but it wasn't Doris's honor." Bonnie Blue took a spoonful of soup. "I wish I knew where she is. She knows what happened, but she left the next Monday, soon as Ed came back to work. And you know? I swear Ed didn't remember any of it. He never said a word to Henry about him hitting him or about locking Doris up in the cooler. Just acted like nothing had happened."

"Good Lord! I thought he just touched women's hands. Could he have been on drugs?"

"I don't know. I just know he was crazy. That was the only time I ever saw him *that* drunk." Bonnie Blue munched thoughtfully on a cracker. "The fight plus the dope I'm sure someone planted are gonna put Henry in a tight spot."

I remembered when I had put the toilet-paper holder back in the wall. There had certainly been nothing under it then.

"You think someone's trying to set Henry up?" Soup dripped from my spoon, which was frozen halfway to my mouth, and landed solidly on my white shirt.

"Damn, damn," I said, grabbing a napkin. "Let me go see if I can get some of this off."

In the ladies' room, I wet a paper towel and worked on the spot. It takes more than a wet paper towel to get broccoli soup out of a white cotton blouse, but I got out enough to keep the spot from staining. The whole time I was working on it, I kept thinking about what Bonnie Blue had said. Why would someone want to set Henry up? Or was Bonnie Blue jumping to conclusions like Sister and I had done with the "I'm going to kill you" phone message, which, incidentally, still had not been explained to my satisfaction. But she was right about one thing: the cocaine, or whatever it was, had been put into the holder when the Skoot was vandalized. I could swear to this.

"I think you're right," I said, sitting back down at the table. "Whether someone is deliberately trying to set Henry up or not, he's in trouble. I'll tell the sheriff the dope wasn't in the bathroom the day Ed was murdered. I screwed the holder back in myself. I have this Swiss army knife." I reached into my bag and brought it out. "See? A little Phillips head. You think he'll believe me?"

"Probably. What we need is Doris, though. She's not at her apartment and nobody's seen her since she left the Skoot. I don't have any idea where she might be, and I've got a temporary job at the truck stop on 78, so I don't have much time for looking. I'll keep trying, but I was hoping you'd help me. Help Henry."

"Sure I will. Just give me the details." I pushed my cold soup away. "Hit him over the head with an iron skillet?"

Bonnie Blue grinned.

"I'll bet *that* made his tattoo dance," I said.

Nine

My house smelled wonderful when I came back from my lunch with Bonnie Blue. It smelled like my wedding day, I thought, the bouquet of gardenias I had carried. I went into the kitchen and admired the plant that I had put on the breakfast room table in the bay window. I would have to move it before we ate, it was so large. Where in the world had Fred found a huge gardenia blooming in October? He was going to be forgiven a lot for this.

I listened to my phone messages: Mary Alice, call her; Debbie, call her; Sheriff Reuse, please call; Becky Bates, about cupcakes for the church bake sale. The last one shook me up more than the sheriff's call; I'd been expecting that. Becky's call was proof positive that lies will catch up with you. How had she known?

I called the sheriff first. He wanted to know if I could

come in at my convenience to talk to him, that I should just call to make sure he was in. I said I would, the next day, and would he mind telling me what it was about. He assured me he was just trying to clear up a few little discrepancies and would appreciate my time. I wanted to ask him if he had Henry there, but decided I'd better not.

Debbie was next. She wanted to know everything I knew about Henry. I told her, including his wife's death and the fight he'd had with Ed, if you could call it a fight. More like a rescue. She thanked me but wouldn't tell me why she needed the information.

Then Sister. The black dress I had worn to Myrtle Teague's funeral would be fine to wear to the Hannahs' party if I hemmed it a couple of inches, maybe three, and wore an important necklace.

"Fine to wear where?"

"To the Hannahs' dinner party. You know. Richard Hannah, our next senator."

"Oh." I'd forgotten about Sister's invitation.

"Just above your knees. You've got great legs, Patricia Anne, and never show them. At least three inches, okay? And an important necklace."

"I don't think I have an important necklace, whatever that is."

"I do. I'll let you borrow one if you'll return it."

"Look, I just forgot that old scarf."

"It's a Gucci."

"Well, if I decide to go to the party, I'll come up with my own important necklace. Okay?"

"Fine." The line was quiet between us for a moment; then Mary Alice said, "Sheriff Reuse wants to talk to me tomorrow."

"Me, too."

"I don't know what on God's earth that man thinks *we* can tell him, do you?"

"Of course not."

"He won't even let Fly McCorkle get started fixing the place up. Won't even let *me* go in. Said he would let me know when they were through with their investigation."

"Hmmm," I said. I was admiring the way my gardenia looked in the afternoon sun.

"You want to go together?"

"Sure. You want me to drive?"

"God, no. Let's try for the morning, okay?"

"Sure."

"I'll bring some necklaces so you can choose one. And three inches at least."

"Three inches," I repeated. Sister hung up.

I got the piece of paper I had written the information about Doris on and studied it, trying to decide what to do. I wondered if Doris's version of what had happened would be necessary. Surely if the sheriff heard about it, he would know what Henry had done was what any decent man would have done. On the other hand, he might consider hitting Ed over the head with an iron skillet a little overkill, so to speak, and there would be only Bonnie Blue and Henry to say the cut had come from Ed's falling into a metal shelf. Besides, Ed wouldn't have fallen if Henry hadn't hit him. But he'd been trying to rape Doris. I sighed and reached for the phone and dialed the number Bonnie Blue had given me.

"Hi," the answering machine said. "You have reached the Chapman residence. I am unable to answer the phone at this moment, but if you will leave a message, I'll return your call as soon as possible. Thanks."

Doris's voice surprised me. It sounded very young, a Marilyn Monroe whispery quality to it. I hung up. No

use leaving a message. Bonnie Blue had been doing that
for three days. I looked again at my notes. Doris Chapman, fortysomething, single, no steady boyfriend as far
as Bonnie Blue knew, phone number, address in Fultondale, probably a size 12, fell into a peroxide bottle. Bonnie Blue's exact words. I don't know why I hadn't just
put "blond."

I got out a map of the Birmingham metropolitan area
and found Doris's street in Fultondale. It was just two
o'clock. I had time to go out there before I had to cook
supper. And the gardenia deserved a very special supper.
On the other hand, if she wasn't at home, what good
would the trip do? Ask the neighbors if they had seen
her? Or knew where she had gone? Maybe one of them
was feeding her cat.

It was worth the trip, I decided. And I would give
Fred stir-fry for supper. He loved that. I could get the
stuff already cut-up at the salad bar at the grocery. What
did it matter who cut up a carrot?

But first I tried Henry's number again. If he had answered, I don't know what excuse I would have used
for calling. You hate to tell a grown man that you were
just worried about him. He didn't answer, though. I gave
Woofer a couple of dog biscuits and apologized for ne-
glecting him, grabbed my keys and headed for Fultondale.

The address turned out to be a nice town house in a
new development. Each town house was painted a different pastel color, which was startling against the red
clay bank that rose, stark and bare, behind them. The
builder had come in with a bulldozer, cleared off every
tree, cut a hill in half and wedged the town houses in.
Doris's place was yellow. A small tree with no leaves
was planted in her postage-stamp yard and enclosed in
some kind of wire frame—for protection, I supposed.

By the front door was a round concrete planter filled with dead and dying geraniums. If Doris was home, she certainly wasn't taking care of her plants, I thought. Not that they stood much of a chance, anyway, with that mud slide in the back just waiting to happen. It couldn't have rained hard since these places had been built.

I rang the doorbell and heard "War Eagle," the Auburn fight song, instead of the usual "Avon calling." That was all I heard, though. I rang the bell again and picked a few dead leaves off a geranium. Finally I went to the blue town house on the left.

This time I heard footsteps, and the door was opened just as far as the security latch would allow. "Yes?" a woman asked.

"I'm looking for Doris Chapman," I said. "Do you happen to know if she's out of town?"

"Why?"

I thought quickly. "I'm the new owner of the Skoot 'n' Boot, where she worked. It's about her health insurance." God forgive me!

"She's in Florida," the woman said. "Gone to spend the winter down there."

"Do you know where?"

"Destin, I think. I hope she left some heat on. Like I told her, her pipes burst, my house floods."

"You don't have a phone number or anything?"

"No. But if you give me your name and I hear from her, I'll tell her you were looking for her. I probably won't, though."

I tore my name off a bank deposit slip and handed it through the crack in the door, thinking for the thousandth time that I needed to get some cards printed.

"Thanks," I said.

"You're welcome." The woman shut the door, but as I turned away, she opened it again. "Hey," she said, "I just thought of something. There's this guy keeping her dog. I'll bet he knows where she is. Fixed the kitchen floors here last time it rained. Got a real funny name. Some kind of bug. Wait a minute, I'll think of it.'' She drummed her fingers against the molding.

A light dawned. ''Fly?'' I asked. ''Was his name Fly McCorkle?''

''That sounds right. I knew it was some kind of bug.''

''Thank you,'' I said. ''Thank you very much.'' I fairly skipped back to the car. As I was backing out of Doris's driveway, it occurred to me that in spite of the mud-slide hazard and the lack of landscaping, these town houses had not come cheap. Minimum wage and tips at the Skoot didn't buy pastel town houses in nice neighborhoods. Nor did they allow for winters in Florida. I shook my head. Another puzzle to add to the pile.

I added a Mrs. Smith cherry pie to my supper shopping. Usually, by the time you get them home they are thawed enough to be put in your own pie plate to cook. Which is what I do. My daughter-in-law has never forgiven me for not giving her the recipes for my wonderful pies. It's the old Mom-apple-pie cliché and I'm caught right in the middle of it, hiding my Mrs. Smith boxes. There are certain lies you have to live with.

The pie, the stir-fry, and my obvious gratitude for the gardenia put Fred in an unusually good mood.

''Hear anything more about the Skoot 'n' Boot today?'' he asked cheerfully, settling back in his recliner.

''No,'' I said, taking out my needlepoint.

''Do anything special?''

''No. Just had lunch with one of the girls.''

''Good.''

''Promised to take a couple of dozen cupcakes to the church bazaar.''

''That's nice.''

The house smelled like gardenias and my husband was smiling at me. Like I say, there are certain lies that just make life easier.

"Do I look like I haven't slept a wink in three days?" Mary Alice asked, backing out of my driveway. This is one of her damned-if-you-do, damned-if-you-don't questions.

"Absolutely not," I said.

"You're lying." She waited for a pickup truck to go by and turned into the street. "I have bags under my eyes so puffy, it looks like I've been in a fight." She pulled her dark glasses down. "Look."

"Hmmm," I said, like I have been doing for sixty years when she puts me on the spot. She bought it again and pushed her glasses back up on her nose.

"And my earlobes are numb, particularly the left one. That always happens to me when I don't get enough sleep. Numb earlobes. You know how I've always told you about my numb earlobes."

This was the first I'd ever heard of numb earlobes. "Hmmm," I said.

"One night I couldn't sleep because of the murder and you screaming about somebody being in Debbie's house and scaring me to death, and last night I was worried about the break-in."

"That's just two nights."

"And three days." The tone of her voice left no room for arguing. I changed the subject.

"Fred sent me a beautiful gardenia bush yesterday," I said.

"Why?"

"Because he wanted to."

"Doesn't sound like Fred."

I changed the subject again. "What could the sheriff want with us today?"

"The man's a little martinet, Patricia Anne. It's as simple as that. He loves to see people jump when he says jump. God help the wife who has to put all that starch in his shirts and iron them to suit him."

"He doesn't have a wife," I said.

"What?" Mary Alice pulled her glasses down again and looked at me. "How do you know?"

"Watch where you're going," I said, pointing at the intersection ahead. "Henry told me."

Mary Alice didn't question how Henry might have known this. Actually, it was Bonnie Blue who had told me at lunch the day before, but I didn't want to go into all that.

"He has a ring. His wife quit him?"

"She's a neighbor of your husbands."

"At Elmwood?"

"Yep. He's a widower. Two years."

"Hmmm."

"Just the right age for Debbie."

"Shut up, Patricia Anne." She turned up the interstate ramp. "Besides, Haley irons better than Debbie."

It was my turn to say, "Shut up."

Sheriff Reuse's office was as Spartan as his appearance. There were three chairs, the usual file cabinets and bookcases, and a desk on which there was a computer and nothing else. Not a scrap of paper or a manila folder. Not an empty Coke can or a Styrofoam coffee cup.

He motioned us to the two chairs that faced his desk, sat down behind it and thanked us for coming.

"Laundry," Mary Alice said to me. I looked at his starched shirt and nodded in agreement.

"What?" the sheriff asked.

"I'm reminding my sister I need to pick up my laundry," Mary Alice said, not hesitating for a second. "Since everybody's gone back to cotton, it's a godsend for the laundries, isn't it? Of course, some people still wear polyester." She looked at me so pointedly that the sheriff turned my way.

"It's a blend," I said, holding out the sleeve of my blouse for his inspection. "Forty-sixty."

"It's very pretty," he said.

"Thank you. The way I figure it, if God had intended for us to iron, He wouldn't have invented polyester."

"That doesn't make a grain of sense," Mary Alice said.

The sheriff rubbed his temples in the way that was becoming familiar to me and asked Mary Alice if she had done any kind of background check on Ed Meadows when she bought the Skoot 'n' Boot.

"Just how the place was doing financially. How much money he owed on it. That kind of thing. Why?"

"We're having trouble finding his next of kin. We need to notify them so they can arrange for a funeral and clear up his financial obligations."

"He was going back to Atlanta to see about his sick parents," Sister said. "They shouldn't be too hard to find."

"I think he was from Charleston," I said, "and his parents are dead."

"Who told you that?" Mary Alice asked.

I couldn't think of a lie. "Henry."

The sheriff nodded. "Mrs. Hollowell is right. We have his service record, which lists compassionate leaves for his parents' deaths. Apparently they died fairly close together. And we know he had a wife for a while, because the Navy paid her dependent allotment for about a year. Then that stopped. Marriage didn't work out, I guess." The sheriff drummed his fingers on his desk.

"And he didn't have any brothers or sisters who we can find any record of. We've had the Charleston police helping us."

"Well, what can we do?" Mary Alice asked.

"I thought maybe he mentioned some friends. Maybe somebody helped him get started with the Skoot. If we could find someone who knew him well, they might know about aunts or cousins, somebody."

"I never heard him mention a soul," Sister said, "and he paid cash for the Skoot. He didn't owe a dime on it."

The drumming on the desk got louder. "Then why did he want to sell it?" the sheriff murmured thoughtfully, as if he were talking to himself. Sister and I looked at him. We certainly didn't know.

"Maybe," I surmised, "he was going to go into some other kind of business. Or even the same business somewhere else."

"But why would he lie about his parents?" Mary Alice asked.

The sheriff shrugged. There were obviously bigger questions to be answered. Like who had cut the guy's throat.

"And if you can't find any relatives, what will you do about a funeral?" Mary Alice pulled her purse up from the floor like Grandpa used to pull a bucket of water from his well. It probably weighed as much. She fished around for a package of mints and offered one to the sheriff and one to me. We declined.

"Those are terrible for your teeth," I said. "You need to get the sugarless kind."

Mary Alice popped one into her mouth. "Sugarless leaves that awful taste at the back of your tongue. You know, like you ate something bitter a half hour ago or chewed on a peach branch."

"Chewed on a peach branch?" I had this mental picture of my sister chomping down on a peach tree.

"Not a whole branch, for God's sake. A twig."

I tried to remember chewing on a peach twig and how it tasted, but the memory escaped me.

"The county has a cemetery," Sheriff Reuse said, rubbing his temples. "We'll make every effort to locate some relatives, though."

"He's in the morgue now?" Sister asked.

The sheriff nodded.

"Frozen?"

A slight nod.

"There's no hurry, then. Who was it they kept frozen for so long, Mouse? Some celebrity." She thought for a minute. "Was it Kate Smith? Wasn't there some reason why they didn't bury her? You'd think the United States government would have given her a patriotic funeral at Arlington, wouldn't you? With some big star singing 'God Bless America.' Maybe Jessye Norman or that religious lady who does the 'Star Spangled Banner' so good when they're having the Fourth of July fireworks. The one whose name sounds like a mud pie."

"Sandy Patti. And I don't remember Kate Smith not getting buried. I know Billy Rose stayed frozen for a long time, though."

"Maybe that's who I'm thinking about. But I don't know why I would get him mixed up with Kate Smith, do you?"

"Who's Billy Rose?" Sheriff Reuse asked.

Mary Alice and I shook our heads at his ignorance. "Just the greatest showman who ever lived," she declared. "He did the Aquacade at the 1939 World's Fair in New York, and Mama and Daddy took Patricia Anne and I—"

"Me," I corrected, "and I was only three so I don't remember anything about it.'

"And all these gorgeous women swam and made designs in the water like in the Esther Williams movies, and the star's name was Eleanor Holmes. I remember she'd get out of the pool and come back five minutes later and her hair would be dry. I still wonder how they did that. I think he married her."

"Billy Rose married Eleanor Holmes?" the sheriff asked.

"She was so beautiful, you wouldn't believe," Sister declared. "It was the dry hair got me, though. You don't think they'd swim in a wig, do you?"

"Probably not," Sheriff Reuse said. "It would have been real hair back in 1939 and expensive as hell."

"He married Fanny Brice, too. Didn't he? In *Funny Girl*?" I asked.

"Barbra Streisand," the sheriff said.

"But she was playing Fanny Brice."

"No, that was Omar Shariff," Sister said. "I think it was the next one she married Billy Rose in. Anyway, I saw my first television at the Fair, President Roosevelt talking." She sighed. "He looked so handsome. Nobody knew until years later they had him propped up. Poor man." She thrust the package of mints at the sheriff. "Here. You look like you need some sugar."

He took one and chewed it. Mary Alice and I cut our eyes around at each other. Which one of us was going to tell him he should never chew hard candy? Neither, we decided. We watched him rub his temples and break his teeth.

"Is there anything else we can do to help you?" Sister asked. " 'Cause we don't know a thing about Ed Meadows."

The sheriff smiled, actually a very sweet smile, and

stood up. We took this as a signal that our talk was over and we got up, too.

"I don't believe so. But thank you, ladies, for coming in."

"You'll let us know when Ed's funeral is, won't you?" Mary Alice asked.

"I certainly will," he said.

"There just might be a place for him at Elmwood," I offered.

"Mouse!" Mary Alice swung her purse at me, landing it squarely on my rear end and nearly catapulting me out of the sheriff's office. "Enough!"

"He could have asked us what we knew about Ed on the phone," Mary Alice complained on the way home. "In fact, I think he already *has* asked us about a dozen times." She pulled into the curb market we had noticed on our first trip to the Skoot 'n' Boot, the one with pumpkins of every size stacked around it. "You know, Patricia Anne, I've decided we make him nervous. Have you noticed how he starts rubbing his head?" I nodded. "The thing about it that drives me nuts is he isn't rubbing the same way. One hand is going clockwise and one counterclockwise. I think it signifies something about his brain function."

"What do you mean, it signifies something?" I was chagrined that I hadn't noticed this particular aspect of the sheriff's mannerism.

"I don't know, but you try to do it." Mary Alice got out of the car. "You want a pumpkin?"

"Sure."

We walked around the orange stacks trying to find one without a flat side. I tried to rub my fingers on my temples in different directions. Mary Alice saw me and grinned.

"One for each of the babies," she said, putting her selections in the car, "and one for me."

"This one is for Fred." I put my pumpkin into the corner of the backseat so it wouldn't roll.

"Hey, ladies." The voice came from above us. We looked up to see Fly McCorkle perched on the roof of the curb-market shed. He was leaning over, grinning, and looked for all the world as if he were going to live up to his nickname. "Wait there," he said. "I need to talk to you."

Ten

Fly McCorkle scampered agilely down a ladder propped against the side of the building. His flip-flops squished against the rungs.

"You ladies out here at the Skoot?" he asked, wiping his forehead on a bandana he pulled from his back pocket.

"The sheriff won't let us in," Mary Alice said. "He called us all the way out here to ask if we knew any of Ed's relatives. I told him I hardly knew Ed, let alone any of his relatives."

"He's trying to find somebody to claim the body," I added. "I don't think they can have a funeral until they make every effort."

"What about his folks in Atlanta?"

"Dead," Mary Alice said. "In Charleston."

"What?"

"A long story. It seems that Ed wasn't exactly wed-
ded to the truth."

"Well, that's not news." Fly put his bandana back
into his pocket. "You knew half the time he was lying.
Like that tattoo. He had at least ten stories about where
he got it. They were so good, though, you had to appreciate them." Fly brushed sawdust from his arm. "I
believed that story about Atlanta, though. A sick
mother?"

"Nope." Mary Alice shrugged.

"I'll be damned."

We nodded in agreement.

"The sheriff say when you could have the Skoot
back?"

Mary Alice shook her head. "It wasn't mentioned."

"I've got a couple of good-sized jobs coming up. I
was hoping I could get to the Skoot before I started on
them."

"Won't the Skoot take a long time?" I asked.

Fly shook his head. "Looks worse than it is." He
brushed his arm again. "Damned dust."

"What were you doing up there?" I asked, pointing
at the roof.

"Place leaks like a sieve. My old lady closes it up in
the wintertime, and I said let's just put plastic over it.
She wouldn't go for it. Wants a rainproof roof." Fly
shook his head as if this were the most ridiculous thing
he had ever heard of.

"This is your wife's curb market?" I asked.

He nodded. "People go right by the Birmingham Far-
mers' Market, where she buys the stuff, and come out
here and load up. Guess they think it comes out of the
fields back there. Who knows?" He remembered we had
stopped to buy something and grinned. "What do you
need? Pumpkins? Tomatoes?"

"Pumpkins," Mary Alice admitted.

"Well, we got plenty of them. Y'all find what you want and I'll put them in the car for you."

"Thanks, we've already picked them out. I see one over there I like, though." Mary Alice wandered over to one of the piles of pumpkins, but I stayed back.

"Fly," I said, "I need to know where Doris Chapman is staying in Florida."

"Who?" he asked.

"Doris Chapman, the waitress at the Skoot 'n' Boot."

"Oh. Doris. I don't have any idea."

"I thought you did."

Fly looked at me blankly, and I remembered that the lady who had told me about the dog hadn't remembered the exact name of the man who was keeping it. I was the one who had supplied "Fly."

"I guess I was mistaken," I said.

Fly shrugged. "Wish I could help you. Mrs. Crane thinking about trying to hire her back?"

"Yes," I lied.

A black BMW pulled into the parking lot. Fly looked up and waved. "That's Dick Hannah," he said. On his face was unmistakable relief.

My children have always sworn they couldn't get away with the slightest lie, that somehow I always knew when they weren't telling the truth. And they were right. It's a kind of radar; something blips onto the screen that shouldn't be there. Right now I felt like a traffic controller at a busy airport. I watched Fly walk over to the BMW. He had definitely been lying about Doris. The question was, Why?

Dick Hannah unfolded himself from the car. He was a big man, more handsome in person than he was on TV, which meant very handsome indeed. I guessed him to be about six foot two or three. At thirty-eight, he still had the build of the star football player he had been at the University of Alabama. If looks could do it for him, he was a shoo-in for the Senate. And if the polls were right, he was a shoo-in.

"Oh, my," Mary Alice said right into my ear. I jumped. I hadn't heard her come up beside me. "And he's just as smart and nice as he looks."

"He's already got my vote," I murmured.

"Mine, too," Sister agreed. "Have you ever noticed, Mouse, how much easier it is to suffer a fool if he's handsome?"

I cut my eyes around at her. "You just said he's smart."

"Oh, he is. I meant fools in general."

Sister seldom means things "in general." I wondered if Bill Adams, the line-dancing devil, was not about to be pushed from their love nest. He had already hung in there longer than most of her men. Except the husbands, of course. I didn't get a chance to ask her, though, because Fly and Dick Hannah were heading our way. Halfway across the parking lot, they stopped for what seemed to be the punchline of a joke Dick was telling. They both roared with laughter, Fly slapping his leg like an old man. He looked diminutive beside Dick Hannah, probably coming up to his chin. They were still laughing when they reached us.

"Sounds like we missed a good one," Sister said.

Dick Hannah gave us an "aw, shucks, ma'am, just a good-ol'-boy" grin and held out a hand to each of us. No limp cold fish there. His warm hand swallowed mine. "Just discussing foreign policy, ladies. How are you, Mrs. Crane?"

"I'm fine, Dick. Foreign policy, huh?"

"A laughable matter at times, Mrs. Crane." His teeth were so white they were startling. But there was no acrylic shine to them. A football star with beautiful teeth. Amazing.

"This is my sister, Patricia Anne Hollowell, Dick." Mary Alice introduced us.

I didn't say, "How do you do." I just blabbered, "I'm voting for you," which I hadn't been positive of until that moment.

Dick Hannah was used to flustered females. He simply said, "Thank you, Mrs. Hollowell. I appreciate that." He pointed toward the pumpkins. "I guess you ladies are here on the same serious business I'm on. I've got two kids can't wait another day for a jack-o'-lantern."

"I've already got some in the car," Mary Alice said.

"Well, well, well, Dickie boy. It's about time you got those babies their jack-o'-lanterns." A small woman who had to be Mrs. Fly had emerged from the shed into the parking lot. Short and plump, she was smiling widely.

"Cousin Katie." Of course, in Dick Hannah's Alabama accent, it came out "Cuddin Katie." He went over, lifted his cuddin' off the ground and gave her a big smack.

"Kissing cuddins," I murmured. Mary Alice gave me a black look.

"Quit that, Dickie Hannah." Cuddin Katie giggled.

"I'll protect you, Kate." Fly strutted over to the two, looking so much like a bantam rooster, it was unbelievable. "Unhand my woman, you lout." He doubled up his fists and danced around the laughing Dick Hannah, who held Kate away from him and lowered her to the ground as if she weighed mere ounces. Chances were, I realized, that we were not going to have just the handsomest senator in Washington, but also the strongest.

"Mind your own business, you old fool." Kate

smiled affectionately at Fly and, poking her shirt back into her jeans, came over toward us, calling over her shoulder, "Six dollars a pumpkin, Dick. No haggling."

Kate McCorkle, like Fly, was obviously an old hippie. Her light brown hair, liberally sprinkled with gray, was pulled back into a single plait that hung to her waist. Her jeans were bell-bottoms, which made her legs look even shorter than they were. She wore red rubber flip-flops, and her toenails (hopefully) were painted green, though they looked for all the world as if each had been slammed into a car door recently. Her brisk walk reassured me on that point. She wore no makeup and probably never had. Her skin was flawless, and like her husband, she had an aura of youth that made it impossible to guess her age. Fly came up behind her and introduced us.

"The Skoot?" she asked. She shook her head when Mary Alice said yes. "That poor Ed Meadows. You just don't think something like that'll happen to people you know and right in your own neighborhood. Fly worries about me being here by myself so much, but it's never bothered me. Maybe I trust people too much. I didn't even have a lock on the door for years, figured the only thing to steal was peanuts and turnip greens, and if they were that desperate, let them have them."

"Did you know Ed well?" Mary Alice asked. "The sheriff's trying to locate his family."

"He'd stop by sometimes. Liked boiled peanuts." Kate McCorkle sighed. "I liked him, you know? Never said anything about his background, though. Did he, Fly?" She turned to her husband, who was drawing patterns in the gravel with the toe of one flip-flop.

"That thing about his folks being sick in Atlanta."

"I didn't even hear that from him. You told me."

"Wasn't true, anyway. His folks were already dead.

That's what the sheriff told these ladies today. Seems Ed was from Charleston and his folks were dead.'' Fly shrugged.

"Why would he lie about it? That doesn't make a lick of sense." There was a look of chagrin on Kate Mc-Corkle's face, and I remembered what Bonnie Blue had said about her knowing and spreading all the news. Here was a tidbit that had obviously escaped her. It dawned on me that she might be the source of information about Doris Chapman.

Sister said that the world was going to hell in a hand bucket when people told such outrageous lies, that her daughter Debbie was a lawyer who said you couldn't believe half of what folks said in a courtroom under oath, wasn't that right, Patricia Anne?

The question was rhetorical, fortunately for me.

"God's truth," Katie McCorkle commiserated. Then she straightened her shoulders bravely and got back to business. "Well," she said, "you ladies finding what you want?"

"We've got four pumpkins in the car and I'm going to find one more," Sister said.

"I got a lady cans soup mix for me," Katie said. "Best stuff you ever put in your mouth. All you got to do is add a little stew meat, or just a bouillon cube if you're scared of the fat. She brought a new batch in yesterday and it's about gone already."

"Sounds great," I said. "I think I'll get some."

"Get me some, too," Sister said. "I'm going to pick out another pumpkin."

"I'll help you," Fly volunteered. "That stack over there where Dick is has some great ones in it."

I followed Katie McCorkle into the curb-market shed. The jeans, stretched over her ample behind, were alarmingly worn at the seams, in imminent danger of disintegrating. But they were bell-bottoms. Twenty years old? At least.

The shed had the smell of all old curb markets, the smell of overripe bananas and apples, the earthy smell of root vegetables. Open bins of corn, tomatoes and okra as well as other vegetables were lined up in two rows along the hard-packed dirt floor. Along the back wall of the shed, Fly, presumably, had built a small platform and counter on which were a cash register and a small TV. Shelves filled with jars of homemade jellies and relishes lined the wall behind the platform. *Jeopardy* was playing loudly on the TV.

"Up here," Katie said. I followed her up the one wooden step. The jars jiggled and clanked as we stepped onto the platform, which I hoped was not indicative of the quality of Fly's work.

"Huron!" Kate screamed suddenly, wheeling around.

I jumped backward so quickly, I nearly toppled down the step.

"Oh, God, I'm sorry." She reached out to steady me. "It's just that those idiots"—she pointed to the TV—"never know the answers to the Great Lakes. Much as they ask them."

I held my hand against my galloping heart. The past few days had shot my nerves to hell and back.

"You okay?" Kate asked.

I nodded. "You just surprised me."

"Sorry. It just ticks me off, though. They have to pass tests and everything." Katie scowled at Alec Trebek. "You think he's putting something on his hair? I don't think he's gray as he was last week."

I shrugged. Given Katie's emotional involvement with the program, I felt it best not to comment.

"Maybe not," she said, letting me off the hook. She walked to the shelves, motioning me to follow. "Soup

mix is here''—she pointed—''and here's new pear relish and chowchow. The pepper jelly's just come in, too.
Red and green both.'' She held two jars of the pepper
jelly up so the light shone through them. They reflected
against the wall, red, green, red, green. And for a second
I was back at the Skoot 'n' Boot and the music was
pounding and the lights were flashing on the dance floor,
red, green. There was something I should remember.
Something . . .

''Two and a quarter for the little jars,'' Katie Mc-
Corkle said. ''Three dollars for the soup mix.''

I must have had a strange expression on my face.
Katie read it as my being critical of the price. She
frowned. ''That's cheap.''

Some important fact was still gnawing at the edge of
my mind. But I was back at the curb market and Katie
McCorkle was holding the jelly and looking displeased.

''Even the jars cost a fortune nowadays,'' she said.

''I'm sorry,'' I said. ''My mind was a million miles
away for a minute.'' More like five miles, actually. I
could still feel the beat of the music. I took one of the
jars of jelly and admired it. ''How much did you say
this was?''

Mollified, Katie told me the prices again. When she
finished, she said, ''You remind me of Fly.''

''How's that?''

''Daydreaming like that. He's the worst, I swear. Yesterday, right in the middle of uncrating some canta-
loupes, he just stopped. Started staring into space. I went
over and tapped him on the forehead and said, 'Anybody
in there?' He jumped like he'd been shot. Gotten where
he does it a lot.'' Katie took two jars of soup mix off
the shelf. ''How many of these you want? I've got six
left.''

''I'll take them all. I'll help you.'' We carried the jars

to the counter. "And I want one of each color of pepper jelly and one chowchow."

Katie went back to the shelf. "Sometimes I think it's still all that acid he dropped years ago." She brought the jars to the counter and placed them beside the others. "You know that stuff can do permanent damage."

I nodded.

"Me, I was scared to death of it. Folks thinking they could fly and stuff. Seeing God. You know how it was." She began to put the jars into a sack.

Because I had been a teacher living in the suburbs with small children during the hippie heyday, my knowledge of LSD was from educational films, the precursors to the "Just Say No" movement. One puff of marijuana in those movies and the smoker went mad. The one on LSD had things flashing and turning different colors. A couple of kids threw up during that one, so we had to turn on the lights and get the janitor in with the cat litter. I think the film had the desired result by association.

"Fly thought he could fly?" I asked, then realized how dumb it sounded and grinned.

Katie grinned back. "How do you think he got his name?"

"I thought it was maybe from 'butterfly.' Like the one on the truck."

Kate shook her head. "He flew out of the third-floor window of a friend's apartment. You noticed him limping?" She folded the top of the sack neatly. "Weird thing is, he still swears he flew."

"Did he see God?" I was not being facetious. I really wondered if he thought he had.

"Not unless he was dressed like an intensive care doctor." Katie added up the bill and took my money.

"Sister's paying for the pumpkins," I said. I looked out and saw that Mary Alice had both Fly and Dick

Hannah loading the car with them. At the rate she was smiling, flirting and buying pumpkins, I might have to hitchhike back to Birmingham. The car would hold only so much.

Katie counted the change into my hand. "You know all the folks at the Skoot 'n' Boot?" I asked.

"Sure. Henry Lamont comes up here sometimes for salad stuff. That's about all the vegetables they serve there. And Bonnie Blue. She's a character." Kate looked outside at the pumpkin frenzy. "I swear, that Dick Hannah is a pretty man."

While I agreed with her thoroughly, I didn't want to stray from the subject. "What about Doris Chapman?" I asked.

"Had a falling-out with Ed a few weeks ago. Said he got her in the freezer and tried to rape her. Hnnn. Took off for Florida. Mrs. Crane want to hire her back?"

"Probably. You don't think he was trying to rape her?"

Katie slammed the cash register closed with her hip. "I'd say it was highly unlikely, since Ed cut a plug out of his weenie that day. Fly took him to the doc-in-the-box to get it sewed up and didn't sleep a wink that night. Just sweating. It's amazing, isn't it, how much men empathize with each other about things like that."

"Ed cut a plug out of his weenie?" Somehow Kate McCorkle had not struck me as the type to call that part of the male anatomy a "weenie." But Fly had mentioned grandchildren, hadn't he? It goes with the territory.

Katie gestured with a downward motion of her hand, thinking I hadn't understood. "His you-know."

"How did he do that?"

"He was unloading some crates that were on a metal shelf and the shelf came loose and fell and cut him. It's a wonder to me, the way they hang there like they do, they don't get hurt more. You know?''

The thought had occurred to me the first time I played doctor with Lewis Goodwyn and he showed me his funny looking little appendage. ''And you're sure this was the same day Doris said he tried to rape her? Maybe it was before the accident.''

''Fly was already home looking for aspirin and sweating, like I said, and here comes Doris saying she needs something with sugar in it 'cause she's about to faint, and I gave her a Nutty Bar and a Coke and she started this story about Ed being crazy and trying to rape her. I figured he might be zonked on pain pills, but I knew good and damn well he wasn't trying to rape her.''

''Did you tell her?''

''Sure. But she just took her Nutty Bar and Coke and stomped out. Called Fly the next day and asked if he'd keep her dog. Wouldn't even talk to me. Like I'd insulted her or something. Good thing I like that dog.''

''You know where she is?''

Katie looked at me with the beginning of suspicion in her eyes. ''You need her now?''

I backed away from the questioning. ''Of course not. Mary Alice is going to need some good help out at the Skoot, though, and she's heard Doris is terrific.''

''I wonder who told her that,'' Katie said.

Mary Alice and Dick Hannah came in just then to pay Cuddin Katie for their pumpkins. I tried to remember just one thing that was on the platform he was running on. Something about crime? Health care? Education? He smiled at me with those perfect teeth; there was a Kirk Douglas cleft in his chin. Oh, my. Politics are so complicated, so political.

I rode home straddling a huge pumpkin on the floor in the front seat. The drive was becoming a familiar one, but the fall colors seemed more vivid every day. This far south, it is usually November before the leaves peak. In the late afternoon, even with a pumpkin between your knees, you have to be grateful for the goldenness of it all.

Mary Alice was quiet, not even suggesting that we stop at a fast-food place for a snack. I took advantage of the quiet and tried to put things in perspective. Things such as why I was being so secretive. There was no reason for me not to tell Mary Alice about my lunch with Bonnie Blue and her request to find Doris Chapman. There was no reason not to tell her about Doris and Ed having the argument which Doris said was attempted rape but which couldn't have been, unless stitches and pain affected Ed very strangely. And Henry and the frying pan. More stitches. That had been a busy day at the doc-in-the-box for Ed! And all about Henry and his wife and the drugs and her death.

Was I just trying to protect Henry? I thought about this for a minute and decided that was part of it. But there was more.

I sneaked a look at Sister. She was concentrating on the road, reaching up occasionally to push her huge dark glasses back on her nose. She looked competent, like she had never hit a mailbox in her life or suffered the thousand slings and arrows of a younger sister. I stretched my legs around the pumpkin and smiled. For once, little sister knew a whole lot more about what was going on. It was something to savor.

Eleven

Indian summer held on. On Saturday, Fred pushed his riding lawn mower from the basement and gave the grass what he hoped would be the last cut before frost. It was wishful thinking since frost sometimes doesn't arrive in Birmingham until after Thanksgiving. But the yard looked nice and would for several days.

Saturday night, we had Haley and a friend of hers from the hospital, Amy Russell, over for supper. While I was fixing it, I realized you could trace American economics and cuisine through the meals we have shared with company: spaghetti to steaks to low fat turkey cutlets.

"Anything new at the Skoot 'n' Boot?" Haley asked.

"Your mother's not involved in that at all," Fred said.

"Oh, okay." Haley concentrated on her salad with fat free dressing.

"This turkey's great, Mr. Hollowell," Amy said. "What did you marinate it with?" Smart girl.

"What's Mary Alice doing this weekend?" Fred asked later as we were getting ready for bed.

"I don't know."

"She hasn't called."

"You want me to see if she wants to go to Tannehill with us tomorrow?"

One weekend a month, they have Trade Day at Tannehill State Park. It's one of our favorite things to attend. Fred heads for all the old tools and I migrate to the quilts, dolls and old dishes. We've never found a real treasure there, but it's fun. Mainly, we see a lot of things that are already in our basement that we thought was junk. That makes us feel good.

"Are you kidding?" Fred said. "The last time she went with us she bought all those weird birdhouses. Had the whole car full of them."

I slid into bed. "I expect she and Bill are staying busy."

"One of those birdhouses looked like an outhouse, little quarter moon and all. Remember that one, honey?"

"And one was shaped lik a mailbox with the name 'Jenny Wren' on it."

We both laughed. That's got to be the best way in the world to go to bed.

Henry Lamont, who seemed to have dropped off the face of the earth the past few days, had resurfaced when we got home from Tannehill, and was even, according to the message Debbie left on my machine, at this moment preparing a gourmet meal at her house that Uncle Fred and I were invited to come and partake of.

I called her and got Richardena, who said Debbie had gone to the store to get some unsalted crackers for the patty Henry was making out of ground up green peppers, onions and carrots. Pretty, like a pinwheel.

"What?"

"A pinwheel patty. Little circles you spread on crackers. They're great!"

I think this was the most emotion I had ever heard Richardena show, though, given her history, I certainly knew she was capable of plenty. I wasn't about to tell her I thought Henry was making a pâté.

"He's a fancy cook, isn't he?"

"He's a chef," Richardena corrected me. "He's going to sprinkle a little fresh basil over the lemon chicken just at the last minute, and he's stuffing cherry tomatoes to go on the side."

"What's he stuffing them with?"

"I don't know what it is, but it's not the stuff you stick up a turkey."

"No, I wouldn't think so." Though actually, that might taste pretty good. I'd have to try it sometime.

"And roulage for dessert. He even whipped the cream."

"What time does Debbie want us?" I asked. Usually I check these things out with Fred for politeness' sake, but when Richardena mentioned roulage, I knew Fred would be happy.

"Seven o'clock. The twins will be in bed by then."

"Sounds great. How are those angels today?"

"Fine. Mrs. Hollowell?" Richardena's tone had the slight impatience of a woman who didn't have time to waste on small talk. "I got to go chop basil."

"Okay, Richardena, you go right ahead. We'll see you at seven."

I hung up the phone, smiling. It sounded like Henry

had added a couple more converts to his admiration society. And getting invited out to dinner gave me time to
take my poor, neglected Woofer for a walk.

He was waiting for his food. When he saw the leash,
he turned away in disgust.

"You don't want to walk?" I asked, shaking the
leash. "We'll go down the block and speak to Miranda."

Don't tell me animals can't reason. Woofer leaned his
head one way: if he refused to go, I'd feed him now.
Then the other way: if he went, he would see that gorgeous collie. Maybe even get a few sniffs through the
chain link fence.

Lust won out as usual. We had a nice walk, and
Woofer and Miranda exchanged a few happy yelps. I
stopped for a chat with Mitzi Phizer, who lives three
doors down and who came rushing out with pictures of
her new grandson. Most of us have lived in the neighborhood since our children were little, before we had
central air-conditioning and cable TV. We sat on our
porches at night, walked down the sidewalk, drank iced
tea or beer together and visited while the children played
or fell asleep in our laps. Now we have planned cook-
outs and Christmas get-togethers, but it's not the same.
A lot of our old neighbors have retired and moved away.
Young couples are moving in, which is great. They are
inside, though, in the long Alabama twilights, watching
TV or, God forbid, doing housework, since they have
just gotten home from work. Or they jog by the house
and wave.

I was delighted to see Mitzi's grandbaby. His mother,
Bridget, is Haley's age and had been one of her best
friends when they were growing up.

"Isn't he something?" Mitzi said, beaming. "I
thought Bridget never would decide to have a family.

Now she says she wants a dozen.'' She took the picture back and made kissing noises toward it. ''Andrew Cade. Can you believe that?''

''He's wonderful,'' I agreed. ''Maybe you can get her to settle on a half dozen, though.''

Mitzi laughed. ''She'll change her mind soon enough.''

''You tell Bridget how happy I am for her,'' I said.

''I will.'' Mitzi stepped over Woofer's leash, which he had encircled us with. ''It's going to be Haley's turn next.''

''Keep your fingers crossed.''

Fred was pulling into our driveway as I walked home. He smiled when he saw me coming and waited for me. And at that moment I loved him. I mean, I *knew* I loved him, which is something entirely different. One of the things you learn in a long marriage is that these moments happen. You'll see him standing in line at the movie waiting to buy tickets, or walking toward you at the Winn-Dixie with a gallon of milk, squinting at it to see if the date is okay, and you think, Hey, I love this man. You also learn not to take these moments for granted. So we didn't. Woofer was furious when we finally got around to feeding him. And Fred had agreed, without any complaints, to go to the Hannahs' party on Thursday night.

Debbie was the second surprise of the night. She met us at the door dressed in a peach silk dress and bone-colored high heels. Her mother would have had a fit about those shoes because it was after Labor Day, and Mary Alice tends to be very rigid about shoes. No matter what kind of god-awful outfit she has on, her shoes will be darker than the outfit, never white before Memorial Day or after Labor Day, and never patent leather after five o'clock. I have three pairs of dress shoes—taupe, navy and black—and I wear them all year, so I miss her lectures. But I swear I've seen her look askance at nurses' white shoes in doctors' offices after Labor Day.

Nevertheless, Debbie looked lovely. The peach of the dress gave her skin a glow and made her dark eyes seem enormous. When she hugged me, I recognized L'Air du Temps perfume. When she turned to kiss Fred, I realized it wasn't just the dress that was so flattering. Debbie had makeup on! She was wearing mascara, eye liner, blush, lipstick. The works!

"Y'all come on in," she said.

"You look mighty fetching tonight," Fred said.

Debbie blushed. I mean a good old-fashioned blush like I hadn't seen in years. I didn't even know Debbie was capable of it. What in the world?

The answer came into the hall: Henry, wearing gray pants, a white dress shirt with a small gray stripe in it, and a red tie. Debbie turned and beamed at him; he beamed back. I did some quick calculations about their ages, which made me mad at myself. So she was seven or eight years older. So what? Would I have given it a thought if their ages had been reversed? I knew the answer to that. Debbie's father had been twenty-eight years older than Mary Alice, and had we batted an eye? Maybe one or two. Slightly.

"Kick me," I whispered to Fred.

"What?"

"Uncle Fred, this is Henry Lamont."

There was a flurry of handshaking and hugs. Then we went into the living room, on whose coffee table were the "pinwheel patties" Richardena had been so excited about, and flat wafers I had seen in the gourmet department at the grocery but had never tasted. Fred is not much for fancy imported foods.

"Something to drink?" Debbie asked. "Aunt Pat, how about club soda with a twist?"

"Sure," I said.

"And Scotch, Uncle Fred?"

Fred nodded, his eyes on the hors d'oeuvres. "Mmm, these are those Norwegian crackers, aren't they? I've always wanted to try them."

"You never told me," I said, watching him put a whole pinwheel on one and devour it in two bites.

"Oh, my." He reached for another. "These are wonderful." He fixed another one and handed it to me. "Here, hon. You'll love this." I had to agree it was delicious.

"Henry made them," Debbie said, bringing us our drinks.

"My compliments, Henry." Fred fixed himself another one. I tried to remember how much Maalox we had at home.

Fred and I sat on the sofa and Debbie and Henry sat on the love seat. Fred stuffed his face and Debbie and Henry smiled at each other. I could tell the evening's conversation was going to pretty much depend on me.

"The babies asleep?" I asked.

Debbie pointed to the monitor on the sofa table. "Like angels."

"Where's Richardena?"

A crash from the kitchen answered that question. "Shit! Shit!" we heard Richardena screech.

Debbie and Henry smiled at each other. "She doesn't talk that way in front of the children," Debbie assured us.

"Maybe I'd better go see what's happened." Henry got up and ambled toward the kitchen.

"People have been looking for him for two days, you know," I informed Debbie. "Bonnie Blue, me, the sheriff.'' For some reason, I was beginning to get irritated at Henry.

"Really? Why?"

"Bonnie Blue and I were just worried about him. I expect the sheriff has some questions about the cocaine they found and also about what he knows about Ed Meadows. It seems they can't find any next of kin.''

"Henry's been here," Debbie said.

"So I gather.''

Richardena came to the door, wiping her hands on an apron. "Everything's okay," she announced. "I just dropped a pan of angel biscuits. They'll be okay when they're cooked, though. Hey, Mr. Hollowell, Mrs. Hollowell.'' She disappeared.

"Did she have on an apron?'' I asked. "Richardena in an apron?''

"She's decided she's going to be a chef. I don't know where she found the apron.''

"For God's sake, Fred.'' He was scarfing down what had to be his tenth pinwheel.

"You want one?'' he asked, his mouth full of carrot, green pepper and wafer.

"No, thank you.'' I tried to remember that I had loved him a couple of hours ago.

"Your mother and I were out talking to the sheriff Friday afternoon," I told Debbie. "We stopped by the curb market and got some pumpkins for the children. She brought them yet?''

"Haven't seen her.'' Debbie sat there sipping her drink and smiling like a Stepford wife.

Henry came back. "The angel biscuits may not be quite as angelic as I had hoped for.''

"They'll be delicious,'' Debbie assured him.

Fred reached for another wafer, but I was quicker. I grabbed the plate and passed it to Debbie and Henry.

"We saw Dick Hannah at the curb market. He was buy-ing pumpkins, too."

"Kate McCorkle's curb market?" Henry asked.

I nodded.

"She's a character."

"That's what she said about Bonnie Blue."

"It's truc. They're both characters."

"I've got to meet some of these people Patricia Anne keeps talking about," Fred said. "I can't believe all that's happened up at the Skoot 'n' Boot this week. I wish she wouldn't go back there."

"Give it up, Uncle Fred. You know she and Mama are going to do exactly what they want to do." Debbie put the plate back on the coffee table.

"They mainly do what Mary Alice wants," he com-plained.

I hate it when they start talking about me like I'm not even there. "I'm voting for Dick Hannah," I said, hope-fully changing the subject.

"Why?" Fred asked.

"He's the best candidate."

"Best-looking, too," Debbie added.

"Doesn't hurt," I said.

"I'm not sure I can," Fred said. "Richard, Senior, was always under some kind of investigation when he was governor. And remember Jackson Hannah running for governor? I'm just glad they didn't have CNN back then."

"Dick's different," I said. "A gentleman."

"Jackson and Fly McCorkle are good friends," Henry said. "I see them at the Skoot sometimes, having a beer together."

"They're related some way," I said.

"Well, old Richard, Senior, is pouring a fortune into his son's campaign. It'll probably pay off." Fred reached for another wafer. Fortunately, Richardena came to the door just then and announced that dinner was served. I swear she did it with a British accent.

The food was as fantastic as Richardena had promised. Fred, who usually scrapes off anything sprinkled on food with an expression that lets you know what he thinks of it, dived into the basiled lemon chicken as if he were starving. The stuffed tomatoes and the tiny peas with mushrooms disappeared from his plate with a speed I hadn't known he possessed. I actually looked to see if he was chewing.

Debbie had brought out her best china and silver for the occasion. In the center of the table were three exotic pink lilies arranged in one of those stark Japanese styles where the lines are supposed to represent heaven and earth or some such thing. On my list of things to do since my retirement was to join a garden club. So far I hadn't gotten around to it, but I could appreciate the elegance of the centerpiece. I reached over and touched one of the flowers.

"Henry did it," Debbie said. Why was I not surprised?

Richardena glided in to pour more wine. She is a tiny woman and the voluminous white apron should have overwhelmed her. Instead, it gave her a dignity I had never seen before. We were her guests, her job was to make us comfortable, and by the look of concentration on her face, come hell or high water, she was going to do it. She topped each glass, but when she got to me and remembered I couldn't drink alcohol, she leaned down and whispered, "I got some Diet Pepsi in the refrigerator, you want it."

"No, thank you," I whispered back. "Maybe later."

"Later's coffee," she said.

"I'm fine with my water."

She nodded and disappeared back into the kitchen.

"Are you sure that's Richardena?" I asked. The sound of glass breaking and "Shit!" from the kitchen answered that it was.

"Excuse me," Henry said, and went to see what had happened.

"Tonight's a practice," Debbie explained. "Someday Henry wants to have a very special catering service for small dinner parties. Very elegant. All the hostess will have to do is invite the guests. And Richardena wants to help him, so y'all are sort of guinea pigs. I hope you don't mind."

"Suits me." Fred was mopping up chicken gravy with an angel biscuit. The best that could be said about this was that he was using his fork, not his fingers.

"Aren't there a few problems to be addressed first?" God, sometimes I sound exactly like an old aunt. A bitchy old aunt with pins to stick in balloons. But things were moving too fast here.

"I said someday, Aunt Pat. Not tomorrow. We know there are problems." Debbie sipped her wine. "This is good, isn't it, Uncle Fred?"

Henry reappeared, smiling. "Just an empty bottle."

I looked at this handsome young man and realized that I knew very little about him. He was extremely smart and talented. I knew that. He certainly had an extraordinary ability to charm women. In a few days he seemed to have captivated both Debbie and Richardena, and if Fay and May were up, they would probably be drooling over him. But who was he, really? A short-order cook with a police record who was a good talker? Or a decent man who had made some mistakes and who, with a little help, would overcome them and have a rich, productive life? At this point I really didn't know, but since it was my niece who seemed determined to do the helping, I decided I'd better find out some more about Mr. Henry Lamont. And I knew right where to start.

Richardena removed our empty plates and returned with the dessert. "Roulage!" she announced happily. "With real whipped cream."

"I've died and gone to heaven," Fred said. Quite unconcerned that he was a guest at a fairly formal dinner party, he reached down, undid his belt and unbuttoned the waistband of his pants. "Ahhh." He sighed happily.

Twelve

Fred slept like a baby that night. I think his esophageal reflux didn't bother him, because there has to be some space at the top for the food to reflux into. And Fred was, as our aunt Ida used to say, stuffed to the gills. He didn't even snore, probably for the same reason. I kept waking up, though, to see if he was breathing. When the alarm went off at 6:45, I was tired, headachy, and my eyes were scratchy. I tried to go back to sleep, but it was a lost cause. While Fred was in the shower, I got up, put the coffee on and downed a couple of aspirin.

The sun was reddish orange and the sky was hazy. Red sky at morning, sailor take warning? Red sky at night, sailor's delight? I thought that was right. Mary Alice laughs at me for still remembering things that way. But I know how many days there are in each month and when *i* goes before *e*. She's always having to ask me.

"Gonna storm later today," Fred said, coming into the breakfast room and looking out the window.

"Red sky at morning," I said, pleased.

"On the weather channel, they said it's our first cold front this year. It does look funny, though."

I poured coffee and cut up a banana into two bowls of low-fat granola. Last night's chocolate roulage with the real whipped cream's sludge was busily clogging our arteries, but there was no use giving it additional help. I reached into the refrigerator for the skim milk and saw a can of Dairy Whip. You would have thought Henry had hung the moon by whipping cream. Probably neither Richardena nor Debbie had ever seen it done before.

"You want me to fix you a lunch?" I asked.

"I'm eating out."

"Get vegetables," I said. "Steamed ones."

"Are you going to the Skoot 'n' Boot today?"

"God forbid."

As soon as Fred left, I pulled on some jeans and walked Woofer. The air was heavy with the moisture the approaching storm was pulling up from the Gulf, and my head still ached, so I cut the walk short. A couple of dog biscuits placated Woofer, bless his sweet heart.

I took a long, hot shower, and when I got out, my phone-message light was blinking. It was a little early for Mary Alice, but that's who it was. Why had I not told her Henry Lamont was staying at Debbie's and that we were having supper there? She and Bill had taken the pumpkins by and there they were, Debbie and Henry, snug as squirrels in a nest, and fortunately, there was some roulage left but that was all, and she really didn't appreciate it, Patricia Anne . . . The time had run out on the tape.

I went into the kitchen, took another aspirin and sat down with the paper and another cup of coffee. During the next hour, Mary Alice called twice more. I ignored her.

Robert Alexander High School was built in the early seventies when, for some reason, architects all over the United States decided kids spent too much time daydreaming out of class windows, so they did away with them. They also did away with the inside walls to encourage team teaching and self-discipline. Movable bookshelves defined classrooms, and students were encouraged to have a lot of group activities. The floors were carpeted in bright colors and there was no intercom blaring, no bells ringing to tell you when to change class. Soft music was piped into the library, from which each "pod" was entered. The result was a strange madness among the inmates. Many students as well as teachers couldn't take the closed-in feeling of no windows and had to be transferred. Others were frustrated by the loose organization and did nothing, or took their frustration out on the other students or teachers.

In most of the schools constructed in this style, walls were soon built to divide classrooms again, and windows appeared for students to dream out of. But not at Robert Alexander. Any money the school board had on hand had to go to maintain old schools. Alexander was a new one, a state-of-the-art one. What were we complaining about?

And some of us weren't complaining. After a year or two of getting used to being without windows and bells, we began to love it. Kids couldn't roam the halls because there were no halls. The group activities and team teaching became a reality. The biggest problem was that after lunch, we all tended to go to sleep. Given what I've seen in most schools, teachers pray for such a problem.

I pulled into the visitors' parking lot, a strange feeling. It was the first time I had been back since school started, and I had mixed emotions. There was so much about teaching I had loved, and this school was one of them. A creek, fed by a spring, ran by the side of the practice field. What appeared to be a biology class with dip nets was down there wading around. I waved and they waved back. It was nice to have so much land dedicated to a city school. On the other hand, from inside you couldn't see the creek and the trees because there were no windows. Go figure.

A sign on the door said that all visitors should report to the office, that no firearms were allowed on school grounds and that anyone selling drugs within a half mile of the school was breaking a state law and would be subject to immediate and terrible punishment. They wished. At least at this school there was no need for armed guards or metal detectors at the door. I walked in, and it was like I had never left. The turquoise carpeting, the buff walls, the bright posters, but most of all the smell. Every school smells exactly alike, a combination of chalk, books, sweat, lunch cooking and Lysol. It doesn't matter if the school has carpeting and central heat or wooden floors and a potbellied stove. The smell is the same.

The office is to the left of the entrance. Here, there was a wall, the top half glass. You could see what was going on in there, but you couldn't hear. Mavis Redfield and Lois Aderholt, the registrar and the secretary, respectively, were both hard at work. A student was signing the checkout list and another was waiting. I didn't know either of them. A glance into the principal's office told me Will Burnham was either roaming the building or at a meeting. Or selling real estate. His second job was a not-so-well-kept secret. Will was a potbellied man in his late fifties, gregarious and fair in his dealings with both teachers and students. He had been the perfect choice for Alexander High, rolling with the punches, his main weapon in the battle for discipline simply the fact that he liked everyone. It went a long way. No one wanted to disappoint him.

Mavis, who would never see sixty again, looked up, saw me and squealed, "Patricia Anne!" I had talked to her since my retirement and we had discussed getting together for lunch, but we hadn't. Mavis is one of my favorite people, one of the few I know who changes the color of her hair as much as Mary Alice does. Today it was so black it had a navy sheen to it. She and Lois both came over and hugged me and we caught up on children and grandchildren. Both of them particularly wanted to know about Haley. They had gone through Tom's death and Haley's depression with me. The staff at a school becomes an extended family. I felt guilty because I had not seen them since my retirement party.

"I hope you're here for lunch," Mavis said. "Chicken day."

After the dinner at Debbie's, I thought I wouldn't want to eat for days, but I could smell the chicken frying and I actually felt some hunger pangs.

"Sure," I said. "How long?"

The phone rang and Lois went to answer it.

"In a half hour?" Mavis asked. "I'm trying to get this damn computer to total the attendance right. It says ninety-nine thousand, nine-ninety-nine children are here today. Can you believe that?"

"Telephone, Mavis," Lois said.

Mavis rolled her eyes. "God, let it not be something about a computer."

"It's Will."

"Tell him I said hey," I said.

Mavis nodded and went to the phone. I already had my story planned out; I told Lois I had been asked to write a couple of recommendations for students for college and needed to look at their permanent records. Just as I had hoped, it didn't occur to her that October is not the usual time for recs.

"Sure," she said. "You know where they are."

I sailed through the door to the file room for all the world as if I had legitimate business there. The students' scholastic records and test scores have been computerized, but the old files are still kept in old-fashioned manila envelopes in old-fashioned cabinets and filed under the date of graduation. What year would Henry be under? 1984? 1985?

The 1985 file was the top one in a cabinet, one I couldn't reach. This was familiar territory, though. I knew where the little foldout ladder was kept under the counter that still held an old mimeograph machine, the kind that turned out tests printed in pale purple ink that the kids complained they couldn't read. I pulled the ladder out, climbed up and looked through the class of 1985's lives.

It's scary when you see how much personal information is in old school files, information that hasn't made it to the computer. Each year in our school system, until some group questioned the procedure and threatened to take the system to court if it wasn't stopped, teachers were required to jot down their personal assessment of a student. Actually write it into his permanent record. Most teachers, like me, covered their asses with remarks like "Very capable" or "Could work harder." But some actually wrote paragraphs complaining that Mary couldn't keep her hands off the boys or Johnny probably stole money. It was amazing, some of the things they wrote.

I don't know what I thought I was going to find in Henry's files. I had always made it a habit not to read personal remarks about a student, preferring to make up my own mind. The night before, though, I realized I was basing my opinion of Henry on the fact that he was a pleasant boy and a talented writer. Given all that had happened and the fact that he seemed to be moving in on my family, I needed to know more.

I found his manila folder in the 1985 drawer and took it out. It was a thick one, going all the way back to kindergarten. I spread it out on the mimeograph machine and began to read.

Henry Alistair Lamont (I'll bet not many people knew about the "Alistair") could read when he got to kindergarten, his teacher noted. His mother attended conferences; his father did not. His father was an insurance executive, his mother a housewife. No siblings. His I.Q. was 145. Recommended for enrichment program.

Lois came in, got a package of Xerox paper from under the counter and wanted to know if I was finding what I wanted.

I nodded, and she left. Henry Alistair Lamont had brought a snake into the classroom in the second grade. Much commotion, though he had tried to show the teacher the snake's eyes because they indicated it wasn't poisonous. In fifth grade he won the school spelling bee and came in second in the county. Below that notation, his teacher, a Mrs. Cochran, had written "Father passed," a good Southern euphemism. The next year he was removed from the enrichment program because of poor grades, and the next year he was listed at a new address with a guardian, an aunt, Miss Elaine Denny. No mention was made of his mother.

Apparently Miss Denny did something right. Henry's grades improved dramatically, as did his achievement test scores. In high school he was on the debate team, was a National Merit Finalist, and blew the top off the SAT. All this and "Most Popular" in the yearbook. Here was the Henry I knew.

I closed the file, relieved and ashamed that I had had any doubts. Henry was one of those people blessed with charisma and the luck to have a relative as caring as his aunt must have been. I was surprised I had never heard him mention her. I opened the folder and looked at the aunt's address: 7192 Highland Avenue. Why did that sound familiar?

I went into the office and got the phone book off Mavis's desk. Surely not. But there it was, in bold: Nachman, Deborah T., Attorney, 7192 Highland Avenue. Henry had come home.

I closed the book, put the file back into the cabinet and wondered what it meant. I've never been much of a believer in coincidences, probably because I've seen my sister arrange so many. Granted, they happened, but this one was a humdinger.

"You ready to eat, Pat?" Mavis stuck her head around the door. I put the notes I had jotted on the back of my telephone bill in my purse and headed for the lunchroom and chicken fried in so much oil that when you bit into it, little bubbles of one hundred percent polyunsaturated grease exploded against your chin. God, it was good.

It was good to see everybody at the teachers' table, too. Will Burnham came in and said he had been to a meeting down at the Board of Education. He probably hadn't, or he wouldn't have felt the need to explain, but nobody minded. Except maybe Chesley Maddox, the vice principal, who was patrolling the lunchroom and pointing accusing fingers at misbehaving students. And even he seemed to be enjoying himself. Would I rather be here or at home with a sandwich watching *One Life to Live*? It was not the first time I had asked myself that question, and I still wasn't sure of the answer. I left with Will's hug and the assurance that all it would take would be a nod of my head and he would leave Rhoda and the family high and dry for a life of unbridled passion with me.

"Someday," Mavis said, "he's going to say that to the wrong woman and have a sexual harassment suit slapped on him."

Will grinned. "I should live so long."

I really did miss seeing them every day.

The sun had become totally obscured by high clouds while I was in the school. I turned on the car radio and heard the forecast for thunderstorms that night, some possibly severe. Stay tuned for possible warnings. The next night there would be a light frost. Time to take in the plants and pets, folks. I made a mental note to get Woofer a bag of cedar chips for his igloo. No ordinary doghouse for Woofer. I had found exactly what he needed at the dog show, a plastic igloo with thermal walls. Fred would have had a fit if he knew how much I paid for that thing, but I slept better knowing Woofer was comfortable. Probably more comfortable than we were.

There was something I wanted to do first. I cut across Springdale Road and headed up 78 to Delaney's, the truck stop where Bonnie Blue worked. If she was still worried about Henry's whereabouts, I could set her mind at ease. Shacked up with my niece at his old house. And Doris Chapman was in Destin, Florida. Fly McCorkle knew exactly where but was reluctant to say for some reason. It's been nice meeting you, Bonnie Blue, but Henry obviously doesn't need any help, and the whole thing, including the murder, is tacky, tacky, tacky.

I had never been in a truck stop before, but they all look alike, unusually busy restaurants with a lot of big trucks parked to one side. Certainly nothing intimidating. I pulled into a parking space near the front door which had just been vacated by a plump blonde in a blue Mustang convertible. She gave me a casual wave and floored the accelerator. The parking lot was full of huge potholes, which she ignored. I expected her to be catapulted out each time she hit one. But she hung on. She wheeled onto 78 and was out of sight before I got out of my car.

That should have given me a clue that this was not your usual family restaurant, or maybe the cigarette smoke pouring out of the door should have. But no. I stepped in casually, dressed in my red suit and white silk blouse as if I were having lunch at the Blue Moon Tea Room. Take my word for it, I was the only person there in a skirt.

I spotted a table in the back and started toward it. I'm sixty years old with gray hair, and the only estrogen in my body comes from the pill I swallow every morning with breakfast. But it didn't seem to matter.

"Yo," said a burly, whiskered man who had turned to look at me. He was sitting at the counter eating a hamburger, and he held up a French fry in salute.

"Yo, Red Suit," said his twin next to him, also looking at me admiringly.

I gave a little wave similar to the woman's in the parking lot. And so on down the line. By the time I reached the table, I was, as Mary Alice would have been happy to point out, "switching my butt." What is that saying about older women being appreciative?

I took out the plastic menu that was stuck between the sugar and the salt shakers and which felt slightly greasy. I had been planning on some dessert, but maybe I would just have coffee.

I wasn't the only woman in the restaurant, but I was the only one in a red suit. The others seemed to be lady truckers. Truckettes? One had a baby propped on her hip. Lord, hadn't she heard of secondhand smoke? She needed to get that child out of here. I gave her the old schoolteacher stare and she turned abruptly and walked out. Ha! I still had it.

The truck stop was a male bastion, though. The women were outsiders, even sitting together away from their male counterparts. I wondered if any sociologist had ever done any studies of truck-stop social mores.

"Patricia Anne, what you doing?"

"Just watching their facial hair grow," I said, pointing toward the men at the counter.

Bonnie Blue pulled out the chair next to mine and sat down. "I'm not supposed to do this, but my feet are killing me."

"I found Henry," I said. "He's at my niece Debbie's house."

"Is that precious child all right?"

"That precious child is fine. And Doris Chapman is in Florida."

"I figured that."

"But, Bonnie Blue, I found out something else. You know when Ed tried to rape Doris?"

"Sure. I was there."

"Well, he probably wasn't trying to rape her. He had a cut weenie."

"A what?"

"His penis! He cut his penis that morning and had to have it sewed up!"

I had spoken louder than I realized. Suddenly, except for the corner where the truckettes were eating, there was silence. The words "penis" and "cut" had been amplified in the testosterone-laden air.

"Oh, Lord, Patricia Anne." Bonnie Blue looked upset. Some of the men were pushing their plates back, preparing to leave.

"But they sewed it up!"

There was a general rush for the door. Bonnie Blue groaned and stood up. "I'll call you tonight."

"No. Don't. That's what I came to tell you, that I'm not going to have anything else to do with this whole mess. Henry is okay and somebody will bury Ed and it's none of my business, anyway. I'm sorry, Bonnie Blue."

I got up and stomped out. Several of the truckettes waved at me and smiled.

Thirteen

I knew when I got home there would be a dozen messages from Mary Alice. Mama always taught us that we should exercise tenacity, but Sister didn't know the difference between exercising it and beating it to death. I might as well go by her house and tell her all I knew about Henry and Doris and even Ed. Tell her I couldn't believe I'd let myself get dragged into this, and then go home and take the phone off the hook for several days. If Henry wasn't involved in what had happened out at the Skoot, which of course he wasn't, in spite of the fact that he had moved in on Debbie under peculiar circumstances, then let him work things out himself with the sheriff.

As I pulled into her driveway, I was rehearsing what I would say and for a moment didn't notice the grungy man leaning against a porch column smoking a cigarette, which he held between his thumb and index finger. He had on a torn undershirt, torn jeans and rubber flip-flops. His long, greasy hair might never have been shampooed. Or was greased with the same substance that curled his mustache around like a ram's horns. I slammed on the brakes with every intention of backing out as quickly as I could. But just as quickly, I knew I couldn't leave Mary Alice at the mercy of this Charles Manson look-alike. I tried to think what I had in my purse that could be used as a weapon. All I could think of was a ballpoint pen and some breath spray. Neither would do much good against this guy, who was now looking at me curiously. He flipped his cigarette into the azaleas and walked toward the car.

"Hi," he said, smiling. He looked to be in his mid-thirties and his teeth were perfect and white in their mustache frame. At least he was brushing and flossing.

I had the breath spray in one hand, the pen in the other. "Where's Mrs. Crane?"

"She's in the house with the others. They made me come outside to smoke. I'm Kenny Garrett." He held out his hand. I had to drop the breath spray to shake it. "One of the Swamp Creatures," he explained.

"I'm Mrs. Crane's sister, Mrs. Hollowell."

"Oh, sure. You're Patricia Anne. She's been looking for you."

"I'll bet she has." I let the ballpoint pen slide to the car floor. I wondered if Kenny could hear my heart still thumping.

"Why don't you pull on up and come in? I'll tell her you're here." He ambled off toward the front door and I could see that his clothes were just as ragged in the back. He had to be freezing. The wind was really beginning to pick up.

I had stopped about halfway down the driveway,

which if Kenny had thought strange, he hadn't shown. I pulled up and parked by a van that looked much like Kenny, the worse for wear. The name Swamp Creatures was written on the side in cursive boa constrictor. Pieces of metal seemed to have sloughed off as if the vehicle were molting.

"Mouse! Come in and meet the band!" Mary Alice had on a fiery red nylon wind suit and seemed to fill the front door. I couldn't believe how glad I was to see her. I put the pen and breath spray back into my purse.

"You met Kenny, and this is Ross, Sparky and Fussy." The three other band members stood up politely and shook hands. Kenny was the one who was dressed best. Fussy would have been thrown out of any bag ladies' group for not meeting the dress code. The men were no better.

"We were just having tea," Mary Alice said. "You want some?"

"The cookies are delicious," Fussy added. "Look at these chewy chocolate chips." She held one out to show me and I noticed perfectly manicured fingernails.

"Thanks," I said. I sat down and gave the Swamp Creatures a closer look.

"Aren't they cute?" Mary Alice beamed. "Don't you just love Kenny's mustache?"

He laughed. "She thought Pancho Villa had taken over the hacienda."

"We're on our way to play for an anniversary party at the Jewish Community Center," Fussy explained. "The couple's children are surprising them."

"Oh," I said, as if that made it perfectly clear why they were dressed in rags.

"We just came by to check on the Skoot 'n' Boot," Kenny said. "We need the regular night work. Mrs. Crane says the sheriff is still holding things up."

"We never had any trouble there," Fussy added. "If we had, my daddy would have jerked me out of that place in a second."

Her daddy? I realized that under the makeup and the black hat pulled over her forehead, Fussy probably wasn't more than eighteen. Ross and Sparky were also much younger than Kenny.

"I can't believe somebody did Ed in," Ross said.

"Nice guy." Sparky reached for another cookie.

"Somebody didn't think so," Kenny said, then glanced at his watch. "We've got to get going. We don't want to be late for the event."

They stood, gathering their tatters around them. There were going to be some surprised elderly Jews in Birmingham tonight, I thought. Probably some younger ones, too.

"Supper's included at the party," Sparky said. He wrapped what might very well have been the original Count Dracula's cape around his shoulders.

"Thank you, Mrs. Crane. Mrs. Hollowell, nice meeting you. Hope we see you again soon." They left saying all the polite things mothers teach children to say.

"What?" Mary Alice turned to me after she had shut the door.

"What do you mean, what?"

"You expected to see *Helter Skelter* written on the wall in blood? For shame, Patricia Anne. Always judging people by their appearance."

"I didn't know these people from Adam's house cat. Kenny was out on the porch smoking marijuana when I pulled into the drive. I thought he was a hobo or something."

"They don't have hoboes anymore, Patricia Anne, and he wasn't smoking marijuana. It was cinnamon."

"Well, whatever. Besides, I was very polite to them."

"Your eyes weren't."

"My eyes weren't polite?"

"No, they weren't, Patricia Anne. You have got to learn to be more tolerant."

That did it. Only a few minutes before, I had been willing to risk life and limb for this impossible bitch.

One big, chewy chocolate chip cookie was still on the plate on the coffee table. I grabbed it and whacked Mary Alice right between the eyes with it.

"I'll learn to be tolerant tomorrow," I said, stomping out the door. I was proud of that exit line when I thought of it later. Miss Scarlett herself couldn't have done better. The cookie, I realized quickly, was pretty childish.

Just as I thought, my answering machine was full of messages, mostly from Mary Alice. There was one from Debbie, and one from a neighbor who wanted me to join her bridge group. I had played with them several times, but I wasn't ready to become a regular. I had already realized I wasn't the club type. I ignored all the messages and got out the vacuum cleaner.

I hate housework with a passion. When I was teaching, I had two women who called themselves The Jolly Maids come in once a week and clean. They were two of the most unjolly-looking women I had ever seen in my life, understandably, given the work they were doing, but not understandably considering they charged an arm and a leg for it. While I was working, I was happy to pay for their services. And they were good at it, too. But when I retired, the jolly ladies and I parted ways. I explained that I would have all the time in the world to devote to dusting tables and cleaning the stove. That was one of the few times I ever saw them smile.

The adrenaline was still pouring, so I decided to use it in a constructive way, a penance, really. I would vacuum the whole house, dust, and clean the bathrooms. I didn't even bother to take off my red suit and navy heels, just turned on the vacuum and got to work.

I finished the bedrooms and was starting down the hall when I saw someone sitting on my den sofa. My adrenaline shot through the roof again before I realized it was Haley. I turned off the vacuum and she looked up.

"What is this?" She motioned toward my outfit. "I've heard of people vacuuming in the nude, but this is ridiculous. You need to get out more, Mama."

"Where did you come from?" I entered the den and sat down, my hand pressed against my pounding chest.

"Work. We had a light day today."

"At the rate I'm going, I'll be in your heart O.R. any day," I said.

"Nah." She held up the can of Diet Pepsi she was drinking. "Want one?"

I shook my head.

"I knocked, but you didn't hear me."

"I was vacuuming."

"So I heard. Anything wrong?"

Sometimes I think my children know me too well. "Just mad at your aunt Sister."

"What'd she do now?"

"Said I needed to learn to be more tolerant."

Haley giggled and I began to smile. "I hit her with a cookie."

"You didn't!"

"Right between the eyes."

"I can't believe you did that, Mama."

"I can't, either."

Haley's face sobered. "She okay?"

"What do you mean, is she okay? Of course she's okay. It was a soft chocolate chip cookie. I wouldn't hurt her, for God's sake. Besides, a crowbar wouldn't dent your aunt Sister's hard head."

"But the crumbs could have gotten in her eyes and scratched the cornea, especially if she was wearing her contacts. What color were her eyes today?"

"I don't know. I didn't pay any attention." I was starting to get worried. "That couldn't really happen, could it?" I watched Haley take a long swig from the can of Pepsi and the light dawned. "She called you, didn't she?"

Haley spluttered Pepsi down the front of her shirt and grabbed a napkin from the coffee table. "Oh, Lord, I would have loved to see that!"

"She called you at work to tell you I hit her with a cookie?"

Haley wiped her chin and mopped at her shirt. "I was at home. She called to tell me she had a date for me for the Hannahs' party and that I couldn't say no. She just happened to mention that the two of you had had an altercation."

"Was she very mad?"

"Didn't seem to be. I asked her why, if she had a spare man floating around, she didn't fix Debbie up, but she said Debbie already has a date, as my mother well knew. What's she talking about?"

"Henry Lamont. You're not going to believe it, Haley, but he seems to have moved in with Debbie. Your papa and I had dinner over there with them last night, with Debbie and Henry, and you wouldn't believe it. Your aunt Sister got mad because she wasn't invited."

"He's really moved in? She hasn't known him but a few days."

"Tell me about it."

"You like him, though, don't you?"

"Well, yes."

"But—?"

I told her about Henry's records, about Debbie's

house being the one he had grown up in. She seemed to think it strange but not alarming.

"He has good memories of that house. Maybe that's it. Have you talked to him about it? Or to Debbie?"

I shook my head. "I just found out about it today."

"Well, I'm sure it's just a coincidence. Good karma and all that." Haley wiped the Pepsi-can ring from the table. "It's time Debbie found a nice man. Maybe Henry's it."

"Maybe."

"Well, if I'm going out on a date Thursday night, I need to check and see if there's still anything in the attic I can wear."

What she was talking about was old cocktail and evening dresses she hadn't bothered to take with her when she got married. They've been hanging there for years.

"Maybe you better buy something new," I suggested. "Those are pretty old." I didn't want to discourage her, because this was the first time I had seen her this enthused about something in a long time.

"Dressy stuff doesn't go out of style."

"Let's go see," I said.

Haley pulled down the attic steps and went up while I got out of my heels, suit and pantyhose. Feeling more like myself in jeans and a T-shirt, I climbed the almost vertical steps. As I reached the top I could see how the wind was brushing small limbs of the oak tree against the window. The huge closet in the attic had been lined with cedar. Haley was already in there with the lights on.

"Tornado weather," I said, coming around the corner.

She was sitting on the floor crying. Across her lap was spread a black velvet evening dress embroidered in a random pattern of white crocheted medallions that looked like huge snowflakes.

"I wore this to the leadout the night Tom and I got engaged," she said.

"Oh, honey." I knelt and held her. She cried like a baby, hiccuping and gasping for breath. I held on. Finally the sobs began to slow. We heard the wind and the first drops of rain hit the roof. Haley pushed the dress away slowly and I took it and hung it back up. My knees ached from having knelt so long.

She got up, her breath still coming in short sobs, and looked at the rack of dresses. "It's time to move on, isn't it, Mama?"

"We'll go to Lillie Rubin's tomorrow and buy you the most gorgeous outfit."

She turned out the lights and we stepped into the main room of the attic, dim with its one rain-streaked window.

"Blue," she said. "I think blue. But I can't go until Wednesday."

"Blue it is. And Wednesday you and I have a date."

We started down the steps, Haley first. "By the way," I said, "who is the man your aunt Sister is fixing you up with?"

"His name's Kenneth somebody. That's all I know. He's a musician."

Oh, my God. Mary Alice was madder at me than I had thought. She was fixing my precious daughter up with the leader of the Swamp Creatures! I was glad Haley couldn't see my face. I think it would have scared her.

She wouldn't stay for supper. She held a cold washrag against her face for a few minutes and then put on some makeup. She took a couple of Tylenol and said she would try to beat the worst of the storm home. I told her to be sure and watch the TV newscasts for tornado warnings and go to the basement if she heard the sirens. She promised she would. After living my whole life in

Alabama, I still get nervous as a cat when storm warnings go up.

When she left, I put the vacuum cleaner back in the closet and the dust rag under the sink. Enough. I stretched out on the sofa with the new *Time*, but I couldn't get interested. I was fuming. I could not believe my sister was sending my daughter out with a cinnamon-smoking, greasy, broke Swamp Creature. And that my daughter was looking forward to buying a new dress for this creep. It had never occurred to me that Mary Alice could be so vindictive.

I got up, went into the kitchen and fixed a cup of spiced tea. It smelled like fall, like the first cold front, the Christmas that would soon be here. The rain, surprisingly, had stopped, and the last rays of the setting sun shone through a break in the clouds at the horizon. This is not a good sign during tornado weather, but it was beautiful, a golden band that made the October Glory maple in the backyard neon-bright.

I sipped the tea and did what I knew I had to. I called Mary Alice. She answered.

"Are you calling to apologize?" she asked as soon as I said hi.

"No."

She hung up. I called back and got her answering machine. "I just wanted to tell you I can't believe you'd hurt Haley deliberately. Even when I've been maddest at you, I never thought you would be cruel to my children."

Sister picked the phone up. "What are you talking about?"

"Haley's date you fixed her up with. She's actually excited about it. Buying a new dress. I can't believe you'd do that to her."

"Do what? He's a nice man."

"Tell that to somebody who hasn't seen him."

"When did you see him?"

"What do you mean, when did I see him?"

"When did you see him?"

"We're beginning to sound like Abbott and Costello here. You know when I saw him. At your house this afternoon."

There was a pause. "Kenneth was here? How did I miss him?"

It was my turn to pause. I was beginning to figure out what had happened. "Did you fix Haley up with Kenny the Swamp Creature?"

"Of course not. Why would I fix Haley up with somebody who smokes cinnamon and God knows what else?" She hesitated, realizing she had dug a hole and fallen into it. "Even though he's very nice, you understand."

"Then who's Kenneth?"

"Kenneth Singleton. He plays the cello in the symphony and teaches at the School of Fine Arts. His wife was killed in a plane crash a couple of years ago. I've been trying to get him together with Debbie, but you seem to have taken care of that."

I refused to acknowledge that barb. "I apologize," I said.

This seemed to placate Sister. "Have you hemmed your dress?" she asked.

"I'll do it tonight."

"At least three inches."

"At least."

"And watch the weather on TV and go to the basement if you hear the sirens."

"You, too."

The golden streak was gone from the sky and the

wind was gusting again. I heard the garage door open. Fred was home, thank goodness. Home to canned soup and toasted cheese sandwiches and my arms on a stormy night.

Fourteen

Two separate lines of storms rolled through that night. The first came around nine o'clock, and we dutifully obeyed the TV warnings and the sirens and went to the basement with flashlights and a battery radio. The brunt of the storm was south of us, and though we had some high winds, we didn't lose our electricity. We were in bed by ten-thirty, only to be blasted out around three in the morning. Thunder shook the house and the trees were leaning viciously. As we went down the basement steps, we heard glass shattering, and I remembered the tree limbs that were brushing against the attic window. At times like this, you just pray a broken window is all the damage you'll have.

We lost our electricity this time. We got back to bed around four-thirty and the phone rang at six.

"Mary Alice," Fred said, handing me the phone. I don't think he even woke up.

"A tornado hit the Skoot, Mouse!" Sister said.

"Bad?"

"Of course it's bad."

Fred rolled over and looked at me inquiringly. I put my hand over the phone. "A tornado hit the Skoot 'n' Boot."

"Why am I not surprised?" He got up and went to the bathroom, stretching as if every muscle in his body were sore.

"The sheriff's office called me," Mary Alice said. "I'm going up there to see what's what. I'll pick you up around eight. Okay?"

"I don't want to go. We don't have any lights. We don't have any coffee or *Good Morning, America*, and the attic window is broken. It's probably raining in."

"The sun's shining, and I'll bring coffee." Mary Alice hung up.

"Will you tell me," I asked Fred when he came back from the bathroom, "why yesterday, when I went to tell my sister I wouldn't have anything more to do with the damn Skoot 'n' Boot, I got so mad at her I threw things, and here I am going back up there with her?"

"Because your sister is Mary Alice."

I pushed back the covers and felt for my slippers. "I guess so. Sometimes I swear I think I need some counseling on assertiveness." Fred looked around at me but didn't say anything. I found my slippers and robe. "I'm going to go check on Woofer, bless his heart. I'll bet he was scared to death last night."

"In that igloo under the deck? I'll bet he didn't even wake up." Fred opened a dresser drawer and got out underwear and socks. "Is the Skoot 'n' Boot gone?" He sounded hopeful.

"Sister just said it was bad."

"I think that place is jinxed," Fred said, heading for the shower. He stuck his head back around the door. "Even Nature's in on it."

I padded out to the kitchen. Woofer was busily chasing a chipmunk across the backyard. The chipmunk won easily, diving into one of the many holes they have riddled our yard with and disappearing. Woofer barked happily when I went out to give him a biscuit and pet him. The yard was full of small sticks and leaves that had been blown down by the storm. There were no large limbs, though, and all the trees were still standing.

When I got back inside, I heard Fred pulling down the attic steps to go check on the window. I couldn't make coffee without electricity, but the ice was still frozen in the ice maker. I put some cubes in a cup and poured Coke over them. Caffeine was caffeine.

"I need some plastic," Fred yelled.

I got the Saran Wrap from the cabinet and took it to the attic steps.

"Not that!" He looked down from on high like a figure in a Michelangelo painting. "I need real plastic!"

"This is real plastic."

"Like the drop cloth we used when we painted the den. You know where that is?"

I certainly did, and I was beginning to not appreciate the tone of his voice.

"Bring a broom, too!"

I drank about half the cup of Coke and helped myself to a lemon wafer on the way through the kitchen. The sugar should help the caffeine along.

Plastic and broom were at the back of the utility closet. I took them to Fred. "Nails," he said. "Hammer, dustpan, garden scissors."

It was too early for a scavenger hunt, but what choice

did I have? It was my broken window, too. I helped myself to a couple more lemon wafers on my way through the kitchen.

"I need the mop, too," Fred yelled.

I collected everything and returned to the attic steps, holding the items up while Fred reached down.

"Did you know God's left-handed?" I asked.

"What?"

"In Michelangelo's painting, God's left-handed. See? You're reaching down with your right hand but God's using his left. I read that somewhere. I think. Maybe it's Adam who's left-handed."

"I need a wastebasket, too."

"We really should do some traveling, Fred, you know?"

"We'll travel, Patricia Anne." He disappeared back into the attic.

"Is it a big mess up there?" I called.

"Nope. We're lucky."

The phone rang and I went to answer it. It was Alan calling from Atlanta. Were we okay? The storm had gone through there around daylight and had weakened considerably, but he'd heard on *Good Morning, America* that there was a good deal of damage around Birmingham.

I assured him we were fine, just a broken window and no lights, and he should call Freddie and tell him. I got to speak to my two precious grandsons and told them we would see them soon.

I was sitting at the kitchen table eating cookies and drinking Coke when Fred came in. "All fixed," he said. "I'll put the glass in this weekend."

"That was Alan on the phone. Just checking on us."

"That was nice. They okay?"

"Fine." I held out the cookie box, but Fred shook his

head. "I'll stop by McDonald's and get some breakfast. Some coffee, anyway."

"We've got cereal. I don't know why I'm eating these damn cookies."

"Well, it beats throwing them." Fred laughed like hell; I didn't.

Mary Alice was right on time, but I wasn't ready. I didn't have any hot water thanks to Fred having taken such a long shower, which meant I had to resort to what Mama had always called a "spit bath." Like many things from my childhood, I never questioned the origin of "spit bath." Probably just as well. The family knew it meant a cold, wet washcloth applied quickly to vital body parts. Adequate, I guess, but certainly not refreshing. Then I couldn't figure out what a person wore to a jinxed country-western bar "hurt bad" in a tornado which actually sounded like a perfect title for a country song. Mary Alice started blowing her horn while I was looking through the closet for an old cardigan sweater. The weatherman had been right about the cold front. The brisk north wind was chilly. I finally opened the door and yelled that I was coming. She was quiet for about a minute.

When I stepped into her car, though, after every neighbor had looked out of his door at least once, she handed me a large Styrofoam cup of coffee. "Here," she said, rather ungraciously, but I was in no mood to argue. I needed coffee.

"I assume you don't have lights yet."

I shook my head. "Do you?"

"The generator's on."

"Of course." I tend to forget little expensive luxuries like automatic generators that prevent you, God forbid, from being without electricity for two minutes.

"It's so noisy, though, I don't think I slept a wink after four o'clock."

Tough. I concentrated on the coffee and looked at the damage the violent thunderstorms had done. Trees were down everywhere. Few streetlights were working, which meant traffic was a complete mess. For once, Mary Alice drove sensibly; she had no choice.

"Did they say how bad the Skoot was hit?"

"Part of the roof's gone. That's all I know."

"What about the insurance?"

"Depends."

That didn't sound like a topic of conversation Sister wanted to pursue. In fact, she turned the radio to the Golden Oldies station she loves. Between Tony Bennett's San Francisco and Frank Sinatra's Chicago, the announcer assured us that our Birmingham had suffered only minor damage from last night's storms. I assumed that meant his lights were still on and his trees were standing.

Mrs. Fly's curb market seemed undamaged. The pumpkins were still stacked neatly. We had gone only about a mile farther when we could see where a tornado had touched down. Bent and broken trees on either side of the road showed where it had crossed over on its way to the Skoot. Fortunately, it had cut a narrow swath. A minor tornado, the radio announcer would probably have said.

We could see the damage at the Skoot before we pulled into the parking lot. The window wall where the black curtains had proclaimed SWAMP CREATURES had collapsed, and the roof had come down almost intact, giving the structure the appearance of a one-sided A-frame.

"Good Lord," Mary Alice said. She drove in and

parked. A couple of cars on the road slowed while their occupants stared at the damage.

"Let's get out," she said.

"Are you crazy? What about electrical wires and stuff?"

"Watch where you step, Patricia Anne." Mary Alice got out of the car and headed toward the collapsed part of the building. Debris was scattered across the parking lot—limbs, leaves, papers—and she leaned over to pick some up. Like me, she had worn jeans, and the sight of Mary Alice's rear end as she leaned over in tight jeans did about as much as the coffee had to restore my good humor. I got out of the car and followed her, watching where I stepped. Snakes and downed power lines are two things that demand my instant respect.

Most of the structural damage seemed to be at the end of the building, the part where the dance floor and the stage were. We got down on our hands and knees and looked under the edge of the roof. We could see bricks and shattered tiles.

"I'm going in the front door," Mary Alice said. "I think it's safe over there, don't you?"

"Hell, no, it's not safe! This whole damn place is unsafe. It's the unsafest place I've ever been in my life! In what? A week? There's been a murder, unbelievable vandalism, dope found in the place, and now a tornado hits it. You think the rest of the roof's not going to fall? Don't bet on it. Not to mention getting fried by a few hot wires."

"Oh, for heaven's sake, Mouse." Mary Alice rummaged through her purse. "I hope I have the keys."

"What do you need the keys for? Just go through the hole in the wall. And aren't you forgetting the little matter of the police having the place quarantined, or whatever they call it?"

"That was before the storm. I'm sure they wouldn't mind us going in and just seeing the damage from the inside. Aha!" Mary Alice came up with a key chain shaped like a huge four-leaf clover, which struck me as highly ironic for the Skoot, and started for the front door.

"Aren't you coming?" she asked when she realized I wasn't behind her.

"Is your phone in the car?"

"Yes."

"I'll just wait out here where I can call 911."

"Well, be that way!" She unlocked the door and walked in. I held my breath. "See?" she called. "It's perfectly safe down at this end." I noticed she didn't slam the door, though.

I squatted down and tried to look under the collapsed roof again. Pieces of black curtain material stuck out in several places like a ruffle. But since the wall had fallen in, not out, with the roof just sliding down, you couldn't see anything beyond the bricks and tiles. I got up and walked toward the front door. "You okay?" I called.

"Come on in. It's fine."

I stuck my head in the door. Sunshine was pouring through the hole where the roof had separated.

"See?" Sister said. "It's not so bad." She was standing close to the edge of the dance floor. "The kitchen's fine, and look what I found." She held out the glass boot that had been inlaid in the floor. "It's not even broken. Just popped right out when the roof hit the floor, I guess. I think that's a good sign, don't you?"

"A good sign of what?"

"That the Skoot's going to come back stronger than ever."

The only thing I could figure was that she was in shock. Denial, certainly. That place was the biggest mess I'd ever seen in my life. "Bulldoze it," I said.

She laughed. "Don't be silly. Insurance will pay for every bit of this, and I think while I'm at it I'll enlarge the dance floor. Line dancing takes up a lot of room." She came over and handed me the boot, which weighed a ton. "Here hold this for me. We'll put it right back in the new floor. And look at this, Mouse. See where the bar angles off? If it were straight, it would be much more efficient." She wandered over to the bar.

"Bulldoze it," I said again. "What do you want me to do with this boot?"

"Put it in the car. I don't want it broken."

"I'd feel better if you'd get out of here."

"In a minute."

I lugged that heavy boot to the car. It was a two-foot-tall, high-heeled cowboy boot made out of glass of different colors, and even though it was hollow, it was heavy. I dumped it on the backseat and saw that some debris had gotten into it. I reached in and pulled out wadded, wet paper. I looked around for the dumpster, but the tornado seemed to have deposited it somewhere else. Probably in the next county. Maybe Oz. I stuck the damp paper into my pocket.

"You got a measuring tape?" Sister called.

"No." I shook my head. "Get out of there!"

"In a minute."

I walked around back, watching for downed power lines, to see how the old apple orchard had fared. I was agreeably surprised. The apples were all on the ground, but there were few broken limbs. The apples would need to be picked up soon, though. We should stop and tell Katie McCorkle on our way home.

"You ready?" Mary Alice said, coming around the building. "I've been waiting for you."

Liar, liar, pants on fire.

"I think I'll get a different kind of tables and chairs,"

she said as we turned out of the parking lot. "Those captain's chairs take up so much room and they bruise your thighs."

"Bulldoze it," I said.

The curb market was open when we got back. Fly and Jackson Hannah were sitting on the end of the old pickup we had seen the third time we had gone to the Skoot, the one whose driver I had felt sorry for until Sister set me straight about who he was. Time and too much alcohol had taken their toll on him, but he was still handsome in a dissipated way. You could see that he had once had the charm and charisma his nephew, Richard, had now. Rougher edges, but that could be attractive, too. Today he had on a plaid flannel shirt and khaki pants that were freshly laundered and creased. I suspected it was because this was the first cool day and he had just moved into his seasonal uniform. But maybe that wasn't fair. Fly wore a pair of Nikes, his concession to the season. No socks.

Both men got down off the truck and came over to speak to us. Fly introduced us to Jackson Hannah and said Katie was home with a migraine and he was keeping the store. Jackson was helping him.

"Y'all want a pumpkin?" Jackson Hannah asked. "Bargains."

"No, thank you," we both said.

"We've been out to the Skoot 'n' Boot," Mary Alice added. "What a mess."

"You the new owner?" Jackson ran his hands down the creases in his pants as if he weren't used to them.

"The snakebit owner."

"Seems like it, don't it? I rode by there this morning and thought, Lord, that place is nothing but trouble."

"Did you have much storm damage?" I asked.

"A couple of trees in the pasture. Lost our lights for a while," Jackson said.

"We're okay, too," Fly said. "But storms make Katie so nervous she can't sleep. Walked the floor all night. Like that would help." He scuffed at a small streak of dirt with his Nikes. "Just gave her a headache."

"Sara has a headache this morning, too," Jackson said. "Dick's wife?" We nodded. "She's having that big party out in her backyard Thursday and she says the yard's a mess and it's going to be cold."

"We're invited," Sister said.

"Well, wear boots and a coat."

Sister laughed. "I've met her. She'll pull it off fine."

Jackson grinned. "You're right. Sara can take care of her problems."

"Speaking of which—" Fly pointed toward Richard Hannah's car, which was turning into the parking lot. Dick pulled up beside us and lowered his window.

"Morning, everybody. Mrs. Crane, I heard about the Skoot. I'm sorry."

"I think the insurance will cover it," Mary Alice said.

"That's good." He looked at his uncle. "Uncle Jackson, Sara says can you please come help her? She's got a crew coming from a lawn-care company in Birmingham, but she's got a lot of errands to run. She said she'd feel better if you were there supervising. I'd do it, but I've got about ten meetings today and I'm already late."

"Consider it done."

"Thanks, Uncle Jackson. I've got to run. Ladies. Fly." He was gone so quickly, it was almost like he had never been there.

"Well, guess I better go see what I can do." Jackson Hannah hiked his khaki pants up over his ample stomach and started toward his truck. He turned and grinned. "See? I told you Sara could solve her problems."

We told Fly about the apples and he promised to pass the word along to someone in The Gleaners, Katie's group. It looked like Katie would be out of commission for the day. But the apples would be picked up, and thanks.

"He's such a nice man," Mary Alice said as we headed home.

"Hmmm," I said.

"Let's stop at the chicken place for lunch."

That suited me. The morning's lemon wafers had long ago disappeared.

Fifteen

We stopped again at Kentucky Fried Chicken. The restaurant was extremely busy; a lot of people were still without lights. We finally got our order just as a couple was leaving a corner booth. Mary Alice made a beeline for it. Once there, she was considerably slowed, since booths are not made for people Sister's size. She pushed her way in, though, managing as she was doing it to move the table at least a foot in my direction. I squeezed in and shoved against the table.

"I can't breathe!"

"Of course you can," Sister said. "I'm comfortable and I'm considerably larger than you are, Patricia Anne."

I shoved the table again, succeeding in moving it a few inches.

"Quit that! You're sloshing the coffee."

I was still squeezed in tightly, but I could breathe. And I didn't have to worry about spilling anything in my lap. I reached into the box and pulled out a drumstick. I had consumed enough fat over the past few days, I realized, to plug up arteries the size of a water hose. I really was going to have to start watching it.

Mary Alice poured two packages of Sweet 'n Low into her coffee and stirred it with a little swizzle stick. Steam came up in little puffs. "Umm, smells good," she said.

I took a bite of the wonderful greasy chicken, which was so hot I had to grab for the water. I was still rolling it around on my tongue when I heard, "Afternoon, ladies." I looked up and saw Sheriff Reuse balancing five boxes of chicken dinners.

"You been out to the Skoot?" he asked.

We nodded. I was still trying not to burn my tongue and Mary Alice was simply not being friendly.

"I was sorry to hear about the damage."

Mary Alice scowled. "Tell me something I'll believe. That place has been nothing but a pain in your butt."

The sheriff smiled. "True."

"What's the status on Ed?" Mary Alice asked.

"Very cold." He smiled as if he had said something clever; we just looked at him.

"You heard anything?"

"Not yet, but we will." He nodded. "Y'all enjoy your lunch."

"I think I hate that man," Mary Alice said, watching him walk away in that ramrod way of his.

"He's just doing his job."

"He's so damn serious about it. And he acts like he thinks we know something he doesn't."

"We do. A little bit." It was as good a time as any. I put down my chicken and told her all I knew, starting with my lunch with Bonnie Blue, when she had told me about Ed trying to rape Doris Chapman and Henry coming to the rescue and the trip to the hospital to have Ed's head sewed up. I told her about going to Doris's house and how nice it was and that she was spending the winter in Florida; about Fly keeping her dog and lying about it. I told her about Ed's cut weenie and Henry's dead wife, dead from an overdose, and that Henry had lived in Debbie's house when he was a child and that he had almost been sent to prison but had ended up at a halfway house, which was where he learned to cook.

The whole time I was talking, Mary Alice didn't say a word, just sat there sipping her coffee. Finally, out of breath and out of information, I leaned back. She still didn't say anything.

"Well?" I said.

"Oh, I already knew all that."

"What?" I said it so loudly, people in the next booth turned to look.

"Debbie told me last night. She and Henry have been doing a little investigating, too."

"And you didn't tell me?" I couldn't believe this.

"You didn't tell me, either."

"I was going to yesterday when I went to your house and the Swamp Creatures were there."

Mary Alice rubbed a finger between her eyes. "Ah, yes." She looked out of the window for a minute. "You know, Mouse, there's just one thing I can't figure."

"What?"

"What does it all mean?"

After sixty years, my sister could still surprise me. Not only could she keep secrets, she could actually wax philosophical about them.

"God knows," I said. "Let's eat."

Which we did for a few minutes. Then I said, "I suppose you have Doris Chapman's Florida address and know what she and Ed were arguing about, since it obviously wasn't a rape attempt.'' The sarcasm dripped.

Sister smiled her know-it-all smile. ''Apartment 901, Emerald Waters Beach, Highway 98, Destin, Florida.''

''Know the zip code?'' She couldn't miss the sarcasm this time.

She grinned broadly. ''Better. I know the phone number.''

''Did you tell Sheriff Reuse any of this?''

''Did you?''

I shook my head.

''He probably already knows it, anyway,'' Mary Alice said. ''At least he's leaving Henry alone.''

I shivered in spite of the warmth in the restaurant and the coffee. ''I think it's time we told Sheriff Reuse everything we know, Sister. I was just trying to make sure Henry was all right, and he seems to be. Don't you think we ought to butt out now?'' A picture flashed through my mind of Ed's body being loaded into the ambulance. I put my hands around my Styrofoam coffee cup to warm them.

I couldn't believe she agreed with me. ''You're right. This is the sheriff's job.'' She bit into a biscuit. I felt an enormous sense of relief. We were dealing with violence here, something we were certainly naive about. Best to stay as far away as possible.

''I'll call and talk to him,'' she said. ''But first, I think I'll try and get Doris. I've called a couple of times and haven't gotten an answer. Probably out on the beach.''

''Let the sheriff call her. What are you going to ask her anyway?''

''If she'll come back to work when the Skoot 'n' Boot's finished.''

"Why don't you just ask her if she knows who killed Ed Meadows?"

Mary Alice put the biscuit down. "You think she does?"

I couldn't tell if she was serious or not.

The electricity was back on when I got home. I did some much needed housework. I mopped the kitchen floor, changed the sheets and began gathering a load of wash. And all the time I was thinking about Mary Alice not being surprised about the facts I'd told her, of her casualness. Of course Henry had been surprised when he found out Debbie was living in his old house. Delighted. Small world, wasn't it? And she was beginning to see what I saw in Henry, how much promise the boy had. And, like Debbie said, anybody could make a youthful mistake and usually did. Henry had come through his stronger and wiser.

I hoped she was right.

Now I piled sheets and towels on the bedroom floor. The jeans and shirt I had on could go in the same load. Both had a considerable amount of mud on them. I stepped out of the jeans, automatically felt in the pockets and discovered the paper I had taken out of the glass boot. I started to throw it into the wastebasket but saw it was an envelope that had actually been folded several times. Inside was a thick paper, the kind legal documents are printed on.

I pulled it out, opened it and looked at Ed's marriage certificate. The State of South Carolina duly declared that Edward Raymond Meadows and Wanda Sue Hampton were husband and wife, Charleston, South Carolina, February 17, 1980. It was signed by Edgar Bunyan, Pastor, First Baptist Church, and the witnesses, Helen Bunyan and Marilyn Cox. Folded within the certificate was a picture, obviously taken right after the ceremony. A young Ed and Wanda Sue smiled at each other, standing on what must be the church steps. She had on a street-length white dress and there was a circlet of flowers in her hair. She was plump—probably still baby fat, she looked so young—and her dark hair fell over the shoulder that was turned to the camera. Ed was dressed in a gray suit and red tie. The crease where the picture had been folded came right between them as if foretelling what would happen.

"Whoa," I said. "Whoa." I sat on the edge of the bed and studied the document and the picture. Well, now we knew the name of Ed's wife, and even if they were divorced, she should know the names of relatives. She was the one who had taken care of her in-laws' belongings when they had died and Ed was in the Navy. I picked up the phone to tell the sheriff what I had found, but dialed Mary Alice instead. Here was something new she wouldn't know. As usual I got her answering machine and told her to call me.

The certificate and the picture were still slightly damp from having been down in the glass boot. On the other hand, I realized, this was not debris that had blown into the boot during the storm. I looked at the creases in the paper and in the envelope. I had reached into the boot and pulled out what I thought was trash and hadn't considered at the time that the "trash" was not only farther down than any wind would have blown it but also was far too neatly folded. A picture flashed through my mind, the memory of the dance floor and the lights, red, green, pulsing, and the boot that had a dark spot in it. That was what I had been trying to remember a couple of days before: something wasn't quite right with the boot. While we were dancing to "Rockytop," I had skimmed over the boot and thought something was wrong with one of the lights, or that there was a flaw in the colored glass. It had seemed so unimportant at the time, a nothing.

I picked up the marriage certificate and looked at it again. This was the reason the light hadn't shone through one small spot on the boot. Edward Raymond Meadows had folded the certificate four times over the picture and hidden them in the boot before the boot was inlaid in the floor.

"Shit!" I said to my reflection in the mirror. "Shit, shit, shit!" I knew I had discovered something important, something I should turn over to the sheriff immediately. I reached for the phone and nearly jumped out of my skin as it rang.

"Mama?" Haley said. "You okay? You sound funny."

"I'm fine. I was just going to call Sheriff Reuse. I found out the name of Ed Meadows's wife."

"Who told you?"

"I found the marriage certificate in the glass boot from the Skoot 'n' Boot. A picture, too."

"Oh." A pause. "Well, you still want to go shopping tomorrow?"

Haley may look like Fred, but sometimes she acts like Mary Alice. You would think from her reaction that a marriage certificate hidden in a glass boot was an everyday occurrence. "Call me when you get off from work," I said.

I laid the certificate and the picture on my dresser, took a quick shower, then put the clothes in the washing machine. Afterward I called Sheriff Reuse, who was in and who picked up the call immediately.

"Enjoy your lunch, Mrs. Hollowell?" he asked.

"Yes. Did you enjoy all of yours?"

"They were great." I remembered he didn't have

anyone to fix him meals at home and my conscience hurt me. Just a little.

"Anything I can do for you?" he asked.

"I know the name of Ed Meadows's wife."

"Wanda Sue Hampton?"

I was totally deflated. "You already knew."

"Mrs. Hollowell, all we had to do was feed Ed Meadows' name into the computer of South Carolina's public records, and there it was."

"I thought you were looking for her."

"We are. Mrs. Hampton-Meadows seems to have disappeared. Probably remarried and not using her maiden name. We lose ladies all the time like that. We're working on it, though."

I assumed he meant he was working on finding Wanda Sue Meadows, not on changing the archaic system of names that females have always been burdened with. Sheriff Reuse did not strike me as a feminist.

"Well, I just thought you ought to know," I said.

"And we thank you for your help. You find out anything more, call us."

I said good-bye and hung up. I could just see him sitting there at that perfectly clean desk, smiling that superior smile of his because I had actually thought I had some news for him. I kicked the washing machine, which was making an ungodly noise and succeeded in doing nothing but hurting my toe. And then I remembered I hadn't told the sheriff how I had found out Wanda Sue Hampton's name. Well, damned if I'd call him back! If he'd been any good at his job, he'd have asked.

"When you remarry, Haley," I said, getting into the car, "I want you to keep your maiden name."

" 'Haley Hollowell' is too alliterative," she said.

I bristled. "I happen to like it."

"I know you do, Mama. You gave it to me."

"Haley Marie Hollowell is all the name you need. I should still be Patricia Anne Tate."

Haley looked over at me. "What's your problem, Mama?"

"Sheriff Reuse says they lose women all the time because they change their names."

"Bet Aunt Sister's been lost a lot, then."

"It's not funny," I said.

"I'm assuming you called and told him Ed's wife's name."

"He already knew it. He just can't find her."

Haley nodded. "The name-change thing."

"Yes."

"Am I detecting a certain annoyance at one Sheriff Reuse?"

"He was patronizing. Like why was I telling him something he already knew. Didn't even give me a chance to tell him the marriage certificate was hidden in the boot."

"Seems to me that's pretty important information."

"Well, there's nothing on that certificate he doesn't know. Where it had been couldn't be too important."

"But why would Ed hide it? Go to so much trouble?"

"Who knows?"

Haley pulled into the shopping-center parking garage. "Maybe you ought to call the sheriff back."

"Why?"

Haley parked expertly in a small space between two vans. "Because," she said, cutting the switch, "I don't have a good feeling about this. Never have. You and Aunt Sister shouldn't be involved in something so obviously dangerous. Don't you realize that the person who slit Ed Meadows's throat and vandalized the Skoot is someone you've probably met up there?" She took the key out of the ignition and reached for her purse. "Stay away, Mama. Please."

"I'll call the sheriff back," I promised.

In the quiet elegance of Lillie Rubin's, the Skoot 'n' Boot seemed far away. Haley tried on several blue dresses, finally choosing a clingy shift with a sequined jacket. It was wonderfully flattering on her and she knew it. She preened before the mirror in a way that did my heart good. Thank God for Monday's tears. They seemed to have been the release she needed. There was even color in her cheeks.

The saleslady who saw me admiring a red dress on a mannequin assured me they had it in my size.

"Try it on, Mama," Haley insisted.

I did. The bodice was fitted; there was a wide embroidered belt, and a full chiffon skirt that ended just above my knees. I thought it looked terrific.

"It's too young for me," I said, twirling in front of the mirror.

Haley and the saleslady both said, "Nonsense," which was all I wanted to hear. My daughter and I left with new dresses.

"Now shoes," Haley said.

"Whoops," I said.

"What?"

"It's a garden party and they're working hard to get everything fixed from the storm, but I don't know how much they can get done in such a short time."

"Then I'll just stay on the porch," Haley said, breezing into the most expensive shoe store in the mall. "They do have a porch, don't they?"

"Probably," I said. "They have everything else."

"How did we get invited, anyway?"

"It's a fund-raiser thing. People were 'invited' to contribute so much to attend."

Haley looked surprised. "You contributed to Richard Hannah's campaign?"

"As a matter of fact, I did, but not enough to get all of us invited to his home. This is your aunt Sister's clout we're partying on."

"I didn't think the Hannahs needed any fund-raisers."

"I'm sure they don't. They just have to act like they do."

Haley nodded. "Makes sense."

Well, maybe it did, I thought.

We both ended up buying shoes. With heels. Then, on the way home, we stopped at the drugstore and bought a hair streaking kit for Haley, the kind that has a plastic cap with little holes that you have to pull the hair through with a crochet hook. It looks like torture the Spanish Inquisition guys would have bragged about, but it makes Haley's red-blond hair come alive. This would be the first time she streaked her hair since Tom died. Another good sign. We also got a rinse for my hair called "Spun Sand." If it turned out to be the color of Mary Alice's, I could shampoo it out. I hoped.

Just after we parked in my driveway, Debbie's car pulled in beside us.

"Hey, y'all," she said, getting out and eyeing the packages we were removing. "And have we made the Visa people happy today?"

"Come see," Haley said.

"Okay. I brought you something, Aunt Pat." She moved around the car to open the passenger door and lifted a foil-wrapped casserole off the floor. "Henry sent it. It's shrimp and chicken and pasta, and broccoli and God knows what else." She loosened a corner of the foil and sniffed appreciatively. "Boy, that smells good."

I groaned. "In a white sauce, I'll bet."

"Some kind of cheese," Debbie said.

Your cholesterol, my conscience reminded me. *Fred's cholesterol.*

Shut up, I told it, accepting the casserole and agreeing with Debbie that it did, indeed, smell wonderful. "Come on in," I told her. "You've got to see our dresses."

They carried the packages into my bedroom while I put the casserole on the stove and turned the water on for tea. It was chilly in the house, so I went into the hall to raise the thermostat. Fred had checked the furnace several days before and it came right on, blowing the smell of first heat of the season through the ducts. I could hear the girls talking in the bedroom. I went back in and saw Debbie holding up the glass boot.

"In here?" she was asking Haley.

"Where I found the wedding certificate?" I answered her. "Yes, here they are." I took the documents from my dresser drawer. "And the picture."

Debbie picked them up and held them so Haley could see, too.

"All folded and down in the toe of the boot?"

"Yes. They were definitely hidden there."

"How did you find them?"

I went through the story of the roof caving in on the dance floor and how we rescued the boot so we could put it back in later. The kettle began to whistle on the stove, and Debbie and Haley followed me into the kitchen while I finished the story. They sat at the table, still studying the document and the picture as I fixed tea and set out cookies.

"I didn't think you were interested," I told Haley, handing her a cup of tea. "When I first told you, you acted like a wedding certificate hidden in a boot in a dance floor was something that happened every day."

"I was just halfway listening," she admitted.

"Well, I think it's important." Debbie held the paper up to the light as if she were searching for some secret message. "I think what we've got here just might be the reason Ed Meadows was killed."

I nearly spilled my tea. "*Why?*"

"I don't know. But why would he have gone to so much trouble to hide it? I mean, he had to have *planned* this. It must have been put in when the floor was laid. And I'll bet this is what the vandals were looking for, too. They really tore the place up, didn't they?"

"And hid dope in the bathroom," Haley added.

Debbie got up, opened the junk drawer by the sink and got out an old envelope and a pencil. "Okay," she said, sitting back down. "Let's see what we've got."

"What are you doing?" Haley asked.

"Just making a list. Henry and I've already been working on one. But, Aunt Pat, maybe you can add to it. I guess it's more of a diagram than a list."

"Where is Henry?" I asked.

"School."

"And the babies?"

"With Richardena." Debbie drew a circle at the top of the envelope. "Okay, Aunt Pat, give me the name of someone at the Skoot."

"Henry," I said.

Debbie wrote his name into the circle.

"Bonnie Blue Butler."

Debbie drew another circle and put the name in.

"Doris Chapman, the Swamp Creatures, Fly Mc-Corkle, the students who help in the kitchen—whatever their names are—Sheriff Reuse, Mary Alice, the man Ed bought the place from."

"Don't forget Wanda Sue Hampton," Haley said, looking at the picture.

"And Ed Meadows."

"I've got him in the middle," Debbie said, holding up the envelope for us to see. "Okay, let's see if we can get any connections. Just free-associate and see if anything jumps out at us. We're assuming now that the marriage certificate is at the core."

"He got married in Charleston," I said. Debbie drew a line between Ed and Wanda Sue Hampton and wrote "Charleston" on it. "He was in the Navy," I added.

"Stationed in Charleston?"

I shook my head. "It was his home. His parents lived there."

"And he showed up here when?"

"I think when he bought the Skoot. About two years ago, maybe three. Probably when he got out of the Navy."

"Could he have served twenty years? Be eligible for retirement?"

Haley spoke up. "The paper gave his age as forty-one. If he went in at eighteen, it would work out. Why?"

Debbie drew an anchor beside Ed's name. "I don't know. We're just thinking here." She tapped the envelope with the pencil. "Any other connection to Charleston?"

"Maybe Doris Chapman is Wanda Sue Hampton," Haley said, "and Ed was messing up her new life and that's what they were arguing about."

"He had PMS," I said. "Bonnie Blue said she and Doris talked about it."

"You mean like every fourth week?" Haley smiled.

"Henry said he had mood swings, but he didn't say they were regular," Debbie said.

"Men don't notice things like that. Bonnie Blue said they were like clockwork," I said. "She said they knew when to stay away from him, he'd be so mean."

"Hmm." Debbie wrote "PMS" by the circle with Ed's name in it.

"You want a regular sheet of paper?" I asked.

Debbie shook her head.

Haley pointed to the certificate. "He was black-mailing Doris and she was giving him a hard time every month about the payments."

"She lives way beyond the means of a waitress at the Skoot," I said. "She's got a new town house and she's planning on spending the winter in Florida."

"Maybe she inherited some money," Haley said. "And she could be working in Florida."

"Fly McCorkle has her dog and lied about it."

"Good, Aunt Pat." Debbie drew a line between Fly and Doris and wrote "dog" on it. "Could he be a boy-friend who's giving her money?"

"He doesn't have a pot to pee in. And I got the idea he's pretty well tied to his wife's apron strings. She runs a curb market right off the interstate. Seems like a real nice person. She'll probably be at the party Thursday night. She's some kin to the Hannahs."

"A curb market would be a perfect place to sell drugs," Haley said. "You could hide them in all sorts of vegetables."

"Speaking of which," I told Debbie, "when I got to your mother's yesterday, one of the Swamp Creatures was out on the porch smoking dope. Your mama said it was cinnamon, but it wasn't."

Debbie wrote "dope" by the Swamp Creatures' cir-cle.

"Where are we now?" Haley asked, looking at Deb-bie's envelope.

"We've got to find Doris Chapman," Debbie said.

"Your mother has her phone number," I said. "I thought she got it from you."

Debbie looked startled. "Not from me."

"She's been trying to call her. We've already figured out she's involved some way."

"I'll bet she's Wanda Sue," Haley said.

"We'll let Sheriff Reuse find out, okay? It's his job, remember. That's what both of you have been telling Mary Alice and me, not to get involved in anything dangerous."

"You're right, Aunt Pat." Debbie picked up the certificate and studied it again. "Did Mama give you the phone number by any chance?"

Sixteen

When Debbie left, I followed her to the porch. I was still not happy about the speed with which Henry Lamont had moved in on her, but I couldn't think of a way to broach the subject. I knew she was a mature, capable woman, but I also knew she was vulnerable. Standing on the steps, looking up at me in the late-afternoon sun, she seemed especially young.

"Do you know this Kenneth your mother has fixed Haley up with?" I asked, skirting the issue.

"Mama says he's terrific." Debbie laughed. "She's had her eye on him for me, but I guess she gave up."

"Your mama told me she's decided she likes Henry."

"You're so subtle, Aunt Pat. Why don't you just come out and ask me what's going on with Henry and me? You've been dying to since the other night."

"Okay. What's going on with Henry and you?"

"We're friends. I think he's the nicest man I've met in a long, long time, and something may come of it, I just don't know. But I think there's a chance. He nearly flipped when I gave him my card and he saw I was living in his old house." She smiled. "I think he thinks I'm his fate or something. He says there's no such thing as coincidence."

"I hope he's wrong. About the coincidence."

Debbie examined her palm as if she could read her future there. "He hasn't moved in, and I haven't slept with him, Aunt Pat."

I was old-fashioned enough to be both startled and relieved at this announcement. "Fine, darling. You just take your time. There's nothing like getting to know each other well."

"He could be the twins' father, though."

"What?" I wasn't sure I had heard her right.

"He was a donor at the sperm bank at UAB when he was a student. They keep that stuff frozen, you know."

"Good God Almighty!" I spluttered.

Debbie burst out laughing, and in a moment so did I. We laughed so hard we both were crying. We were just calming down when Haley came to the door, asking what had happened. That started us all over again.

Debbie left, still giggling, dabbing at mascara that had streaked under her eyes and leaving me to explain to Haley why we were laughing so.

"Aunt Sister's going to find out who the father is, " Haley said.

"Oh, I don't think so," I said. Knowing Mary Alice as I did, Fay and May were Henry's, no doubt about it, from now on.

Sleep came in waves that night. I would sleep deeply for an hour or so and then come wide awake. Finally, to keep from disturbing Fred, I went into the den, lit the gas logs and settled on the sofa. The full October moon, the "corn moon," shone through the skylights and streaked across the floor. It was hard to believe that a few nights before, tornadoes had been tearing up lives. I pulled the afghan around me and watched the flames dance around the logs. Red, green. I awoke with a start. Damn. I hadn't slept the night before. This was not good. I needed some rest.

I went into the kitchen and got some milk and aspirin. The moon was so bright through the bay window, I didn't have to turn on the light. Outside, the trees moved slightly; down the street a light came on. Another insomniac. Other than this, everyone was asleep on this first cold night. In his igloo, Woofer slept, too old and too warm to bay at the moon. I went back to the sofa, curled up in the afghan and didn't know anything else until the sun woke me shining in my eyes.

My first thought was that it was going to be awfully cold tonight for a garden party, for any kind of outdoor party, including a bonfire, and that I had spent all that money on a dress nobody would see because I was getting out my winter coat. So I would smell like mothballs instead of L'Air du Temps. Damned if I was going to catch pneumonia for the sake of vanity.

The phone rang and I reached for it.

"They have a big heated tent," Mary Alice said.

"Okay, thanks." I hung up and went to get my robe. The bed was empty; Fred had tiptoed out again. Hadn't even had coffee. Damn it! That man drove me crazy by being so sweet that I could never stay mad at him. I went into the kitchen to put the kettle on and stepped outside to give Woofer his treat. God, it was cold!

Woofer had his mouth open and the dog biscuit was halfway there when I thought about what had just happened. Had I dreamed Sister had called about a heated tent? I gave Woofer the biscuit I had in my hand, threw a couple of others into the yard and went in to call her.

"What?" she said.

"You just called me, didn't you?"

"Of course I did. What's the matter with you?"

"I thought I was dreaming. I was just waking up and thinking about the cold and the party and you called about a heated tent and it just blended together."

"Have you had your coffee?"

"No."

"I thought not. Call me back after you do."

Which I did, but all she wanted to know was if I wanted to borrow one of her evening "wraps," since Debbie said I had actually bought a new dress. And I said I would wrap myself in my coat, thank you very much. The conversation was a short one.

Once a week, I tutor at a junior high school. I thought when I volunteered that I would be tutoring English grammar, but as it turned out, the work involved a little bit of everything. The math teacher would probably have been startled to hear me explain how to divide fractions by standing them on their heads, but the kids seemed to understand, and I enjoyed working with them. The one-on-one teacher-student relationship is what every over-worked teacher dreams of.

I took a shower and dressed. Before I left for school, though, I called Sheriff Reuse. He had to be notified about the marriage certificate having been hidden in the boot. Fred had made no bones about it. "My God, Patricia Anne," he had said, picking up the heavy boot to slide it back under our bed, "Debbie's right about this thing being important. What's the matter with you?"

"The sheriff was patronizing," I had said.

"I don't give a good goddamn if he's rude as hell. Go call him."

"Now? It's after eleven o'clock!"

We had finally agreed to wait until morning. The sheriff wasn't in, though. The man who answered the phone said he would take a message. I left my number but told him I wouldn't be in until after three o'clock.

"He's gone to Atlanta," the man said. "Won't be back till late."

"I'll be here until six," I said. Fred wasn't going to like this, but I had tried.

As the day went along, my mood improved. One of my students, who was having a hard time understanding percentage, had a real breakthrough. It was another of my "stand it on its head" solutions, and it worked. I should have been teaching math all these years, I decided. Lord knows the papers were easier to grade. And several people told me they liked my hair, which had turned out a light ash blond. By the time I got home, I was looking forward to the evening. The temperature had rebounded into the high seventies, as it does this time of year in the South, and it looked like the Hannahs were going to have a nice, though chilly, night for a party.

The sheriff hadn't called, but Bonnie Blue had, and so had Haley. Bonnie Blue said she would call later, and Haley wanted to borrow my black evening bag if I wasn't using it. She would come by after work.

I took Woofer for a quick walk and still had a couple of hours to pamper myself. I soaked in a bubble bath with a mask slathered on my face, pumiced my heels, painted my toenails. When Haley came in, I had just dampened my hair and sprayed curling mousse on it. "At my age," I admitted, "it takes a lot of upkeep."

"At your age, I should be so lucky."

My sweet Haley. I hoped her date would be everything Sister had promised. Maybe even be *the* one. Well, the thought wasn't so far-fetched.

At five I called Sheriff Reuse's office again. He still wasn't back from Atlanta, the man said, and yes, my message for him to call me was there. Could *he* help me? I thought not. I hung up, hoping Fred wouldn't be too upset. The boot wasn't going to go anywhere. It was just a piece of hollow, colored glass, anyway. As for the marriage certificate, the name Wanda Sue Hampton seemed to be fairly common knowledge.

"It's the fact that the certificate was *hidden* in the boot, Patricia Anne. *Inlaid* in the floor!" I knew exactly what Fred would say.

Which he did. I soothed him by saying the sheriff would call at any minute and that I had done all I could to reach him.

At least I thought I had soothed him. "Give me the phone," he said. "What the sheriff's number?" I sat on the sofa and watched Fred's face while I listened to his side of the conversation.

"Sheriff Reuse, please.

"When will he be back?

"I need to talk to someone who's working on the Ed Meadows murder. The one at the Skoot 'n' Boot.

"My name is Fred Hollowell.

"Yes, my wife called earlier."

Fred tapped on the table. "Nobody?

"Atlanta?

"Of course it's important.

"No. I need to talk to the sheriff.

"Thank you. You have my number." Fred hung up and turned to me. "There, Patricia Anne. He'll call soon as he gets in from Atlanta."

I've been married to this man for forty years. I know when to keep my mouth shut.

He went in to take a shower and I closed my eyes and said my mantra. It was just beginning to work when the phone rang. I grabbed it, thinking it might be the sheriff.

"Hey, Patricia Anne," Bonnie Blue said. "Guess who called me this morning? Doris. Doris Chapman."

"She did? Is she home?"

"Probably by now. She called from Destin, though. She's going to the Hannahs' party tonight, and Mary Alice said all of y'all were going. Anyway, Doris wanted me to go to Goldstein's and get her mink coat out of storage."

The two things registered simultaneously. Doris was going to be at the party and she had a fur coat. A mink.

"She had to call the folks at Goldstein's and give them her storage number and give the number to me, and even then they weren't too happy about it. I finally told the woman, I said, 'Hey, look at the size of this coat and look at me. I steal a mink, I'm getting one big enough.'" Bonnie Blue laughed. "Anyway, I thought you'd want to know she's going to be there tonight."

"I sure do, Bonnie Blue. Thanks. Are you going to be there?"

"Absolutely. I was invited to tend bar. Damn glad to get the job, too. Come by and get some orange juice."

"Will you point Doris out to me?"

"You can't miss her. She'll be the one the animal rights' activists are picketing. And with good reason." Bonnie Blue laughed at the scene she had conjured up. "Hey, I better go. I'll see you tonight, okay?"

"Okay. And thanks, Bonnie Blue."

I hung up and went in to tell Fred that Doris had a mink coat and was going to be at the party. "She's Wanda Sue, I'll bet you. And she was blackmailing Ed."

Fred had just stepped out of the shower, and I took the towel to dry his back.

"But what about?" he asked, reaching around and cupping my butt.

That I couldn't answer. Nor did I have time to.

Seventeen

Fred is neither a partygoer nor a party-giver. I get him to Sister's parties on New Year's Eve and the Fourth of July, and the whole family comes to our house for Thanksgiving. Sometimes we ask old friends in for supper. But lately we've been doing less of that. I don't know why. I used to complain that we didn't socialize enough, but I think I'm becoming more like Fred as we get older. It's just so comfortable to eat supper while we watch *Wheel of Fortune*.

"All those people," he complains when we come home from Sister's parties. "I can't remember their names."

I know the feeling.

He was in a good humor, though, as we turned into the Hannahs' driveway, in spite of the fact that the sheriff still hadn't called and that this was most certainly a big party. "I really like that dress," he said.

"Thank you."

"Sure you aren't cold? I've got a couple of jackets in the trunk."

"I'm fine. But thanks." When push came to shove, I'd gone with L'Air du Temps and the threat of pneumonia instead of health and the smell of mothballs. As for the jackets, I'd have to be in the last stages of hypothermia to put on one of Fred's old nylon windbreakers over my new red dress. I thought about the grease stains on them. Maybe I'd just have to die.

We pulled up behind a Mercedes whose female passenger was alighting in a flurry of sequins, high heels and furs. Her escort wore a tux.

"Hey," Fred said, pointing at the man. "Hey."

We've been married so long, body language accounts for the majority of our communication.

"Formal wear was optional, Fred. You opted not to."

I don't know what his answer would have been. A rap on the window made both of us jump. A smiling young man was standing there.

"Good evening," he said when Fred let the window down. "I'm Douglas and I'll park your car for you. Just pull up to the steps."

The Mercedes was already being whisked away by a Douglas look-alike. We pulled up as instructed.

"Your name, sir?" Douglas asked. He wrote the name on a numbered card and handed Fred a duplicate.

"Where are you parking them?" Fred wanted to know.

"In the field by the stable, sir."

"Don't you have a lot of mud out there?"

I saw Douglas cast a quick glance at Fred's 1989 Honda, which was already the worse for wear. "The field's dry, sir. Y'all have a good time, now.'' He got in the car and drove off.

"It's got to be a loblolly out there," Fred grumbled. "Mud up to the bumpers."

"It won't hurt the car," I assured him.

"Bet that Mercedes gets stuck." Fred brightened at the thought.

Dick and Sara Hannah were standing at the door greeting their guests. I thought then, and I still think now, that they were shining that night, that the aura surrounding them wasn't a trick of the lighting. Blond and petite, Sara wore a dark green velveteen sheath that ended well above her knees and brought out the green of her eyes. I thought the dress was demure with its high neck and long sleeves. Later, when I saw the back, or rather what little there was of the back, I realized "demure" was hardly the right adjective. Dick, like Fred, had opted for a dark suit.

"Mrs. Hollowell," Dick said. "We're so happy you came." I was impressed that he remembered my name. Granted, he was a politician, but he had met me only a couple of times.

I introduced Fred, and Dick introduced Sara. I knew she had been working for days to clean up the storm damage and getting everything ready for the party. But there was no sign of tiredness, not even a slight shadow under her eyes. Sara Hannah glowed this night.

"Mrs. Crane is already here," she said. "And I believe your daughter—Haley?"

How did these people do this? I couldn't remember the names of the people in my Great Books group. I wondered if there was some trick they knew. Some association thing. Like thinking about a crane at a hollow well.

"They're out at the tent, I believe. Right out the side

door. There's a bar out there as well as in the library.
Be sure and make yourself at home.''

We thanked her and moved into the hall as some more
people came to the front door.

"Mr. Hill, welcome," we heard Dick say.

"How do they do that?" Fred asked. "I'd go to parties more, Patricia Anne, if I could do that."

"God knows," I said. "And no, you wouldn't.
You're just an old recluse."

He patted me on the butt. "Not so old."

A blue-and-white tent was set up in the side yard and
was huge. Barnum and Bailey would have been able to
get along fine with this tent. A wooden walkway with a
railing led to it from the steps. Inside there was a
wooden floor and dozens of white tables and chairs,
many already occupied. Each table was topped with a
navy-and-white-striped cloth and a bouquet of daisies.
On a small stage to one side of the tent, Jimmy Gerald's
band, which had been playing for Birmingham functions
since V-J Day in 1945, was gamely charging through
"In the Mood." Several couples were already dancing.

"Oh, my," I said. "This is so Gatsby-ish."

"So what?"

"Like *The Great Gatsby*. You know. I'll bet if we
looked out, we'd see the light on the pier."

"They got a pond this close to the house?"

"I'll rent the movie," I said. "Let's find Sister and
Haley."

"There's Mary Alice." Fred nodded toward the dance
floor. "Dear God. Look at that, Patricia Anne. She looks
like a butterfly that got too close to Chernobyl."

She did. She had on a caftan that seemed to be made
out of several layers of soft, flowing silk, each a different
color. Lavender blended into rose, into blue, into green
as the orchestra finished the song, more or less together,

and Bill, yes, dipped her. I should have known.

"He's stronger than I thought," Fred said.

"Shut up." I speared him with my elbow. Mary Alice had spotted us and was motioning toward a table on the other side of the tent. The silky material of the caftan was caught at her wrists with rhinestone cuffs, which gave her wings. A fortune, I thought. She had spent a fortune on that outfit. "You tell Mary Alice she looks good."

"She does. She just reminds me of the butterfly house at Callaway Gardens."

"Tell Haley she looks pretty, too."

"That won't be a problem."

We wound our way toward the table Mary Alice and Bill had headed for. I saw, to my relief, that Kenneth Singleton was a very nice-looking man. He and Haley had their heads close together and were laughing at something. He hopped up immediately as we approached. Mary Alice made the introductions and Fred and Kenneth shook hands.

"You look beautiful tonight, Baby," Fred told Haley. Then he turned to Sister. "And I like that outfit, Mary Alice."

She laughed. "You're such a nice liar, Fred."

We sat down and Kenneth offered to go get us drinks.

"Where's the bar?" I asked.

"On your left as you came in."

"We were looking at the dance floor," Fred explained.

I stood and looked over the tables to see if I could spot Bonnie Blue. Kenneth jumped up politely.

"Sit down," Sister said. I don't know which one of us she meant, but Kenneth sat down immediately. I said I would be right back and headed across the tent to the bar. Behind me, Sister was explaining to Kenneth that it might look like I couldn't wait for a drink but it wasn't that at all.

"Maybe she's got a bladder infection," I heard Bill say. "My wife—"

I knew I was going to have to get Haley and Kenneth away from that table.

The bar was doing a booming business. No wonder we hadn't seen it when we came in; the crowd was three-deep around it. I could hear Bonnie Blue, though. "Black Jack and water, white wine, vodka tonic!" She sang the orders out.

"Orange juice!" I yelled.

She located me and grinned. "Orange juice coming up. Hey," she said to the people standing between us, "let this lady up. Can't you see she's diabetic and about to have an insulin reaction?" The crowd parted quickly for me. "Here, honey," she said, handing me the juice. "You'll feel better in a minute. Just try not to spit it out like Julia Roberts did in *Steel Magnolias*."

The crowd moved away from us immediately. "You seen Doris?" I asked.

"No. I had to get to the party. But I don't think she's here yet. Least she's not out here in the tent. Most of the good food's inside, though. She could be there. But you know, Patricia Anne, I don't think she knows a thing. She said Ed just jumped her and she thought he was trying to rape her."

"You asked her?"

"Well, when I talked to her on the phone. Sort of."

"Point her out to me when you get a chance," I said.

I got Fred a beer and headed back to the table. Mary Alice and Bill were on the dance floor again, dancing this time to "Moonlight Cocktail." Doing a pretty good job, too. At the table, Kenneth and Fred were deep in a discussion of whether or not utility stocks were a good investment. Haley's eyes looked slightly glazed.

"Let's dance," I told Fred.

He looked at the dance floor. "There's no room."

"All the more fun."

He got up reluctantly, promising Kenneth that he would return in short order to finish their discussion.

"Nice, sensible man," he said as we headed to the dance floor. "I think Haley likes him."

"Good," I said. "Let's go get some supper."

"Thought you wanted to dance."

"There's no room on the dance floor."

He looked a little puzzled, but he followed me out of the tent.

Supper was set up not only in the dining room but also in the den. Desserts were arranged on an adjacent glassed-in porch. We got plates and were trying to decide where to start when Katie McCorkle came out of the kitchen with another casserole. She was dressed in a simple black dress and pearls. Her hair was pulled back into a becoming French braid.

"Good," I said. "You're feeling better."

She put the casserole down and shook hands with Fred after I had introduced them. "Yes, thank God. That's the only thing that gets you through a migraine, knowing that every moment you're getting closer to the end of it."

I pointed to the loaded tables. "Surely you didn't do this."

"Some of it. And Sara did some, too. Most of it came from a caterer in Birmingham, though."

"Tell us where to start."

"With the shrimp. And try the remoulade sauce."

We started down one table.

"Just come on around me," said a beautiful red-headed woman who was also filling her plate. "It all looks so good, I can't decide."

"Looks to me like you're doing a pretty good job," said Katie, who had emerged from the kitchen again.

The woman looked at the abundance of food she already had on her plate and giggled. "Guess you're right, Katie."

"Doris," Katie said, "these nice folks are Patricia Anne and Fred Hollowell. And this is Doris Chapman." Katie turned back to Doris. "Mrs. Hollowell's sister bought the Skoot."

Doris's eyes, which were round, seemed to get rounder. "Oh, my. There's been a lot of trouble up there, hasn't there?"

"Lots," I said. I was trying to relate this drop-dead-gorgeous woman with the Doris whom Henry and Bonnie Blue had described, the nondescript, plain waitress.

Doris reached over and took a hefty helping of the casserole Katie had brought out. She obviously wasn't into calorie-counting. Nor did she need to be. She was wearing a lavender knit column dress that ended just above her ankles. A generous slit to mid-thigh facilitated walking. Not that one would do a lot of walking in that dress. The dress bumped, rolled and wiggled just the right amount in all the right places. I kicked at Fred as she leaned way over to spear a pickle. Like I said, most of our communication is nonverbal.

"Not guilty," he whispered. But I knew he was. I've got that man's thoughts pegged.

"Ed and then the tornado." Doris paused. "Does the potato salad have mustard in it, Katie?"

"This one does; that one doesn't." Katie picked up a bowl of fruit that was about half empty and disappeared into the kitchen. Doris pushed the casserole over on her plate and put a spoonful of nonmustard potato salad by it. I studied her. Was it possible there were two Doris Chapmans here tonight? The red hair could have come from a squeeze bottle like mine. But the rest of her? Unless it had been darker in the Skoot 'n' Boot than Henry and Bonnie Blue had realized.

I tested the waters. "You seen Bonnie Blue?"

"No. She's out in the tent." Doris selected a piece of ham. "I'm starving. I'm going to go surprise her soon as I eat. She had to come to the party early, so she left my coat with the McCorkles." Doris laughed. "They didn't know who I was. I'll bet she won't, either."

So something *was* different. "Why not?"

Doris held her loaded plate away from her and turned slowly, pointing. "Hair red, nose job, chin, forehead heightened, face-lift, boobs, hips, tummy tuck, liposuction on my thighs and the fat put into my butt." She turned so we could see a nicely rounded derriere that was made out of fat thighs.

"Good God," Fred said. "It looks great."

Doris smiled. "Doesn't it?" She seemed as delighted as a child, which was fine. I've never been tempted to go the cosmetic-surgery route myself; I've earned every wrinkle and sag.

"Y'all come eat with me. The steps in the foyer would be a good place, okay?"

"We're right behind you," Fred said. And he meant it. He didn't give a damn if God or a plastic surgeon was responsible for the way Doris looked in the lavender knit dress. It was the result that he liked. Men!

The steps turned out to be a good place to eat. We had an unobstructed view of the front door and saw when Richard Hannah, Sr., and Jackson arrived. Richard, Senior, was in a wheelchair, the result of a small-plane crash during his second campaign for governor. The accident had killed his wife. A large man who looked like he might be a professional wrestler helped Richard, Junior, get the chair over the threshold, and then he left. Jackson, who entered behind his brother, stood for a moment, looking around. He saw us on the steps, gave a wide grin and started toward us.

"Daddy Dick!" Sara had left her duties at the door for a moment, but now she entered the hall. "Daddy Dick!" She ran to the man in the wheelchair and leaned down to hug him. That was when I first saw that her dress had no back to it. Jackson had turned away from us when Sara appeared and now was watching her and his brother.

"Daddy Dick," Doris murmured. "That has interesting connotations, doesn't it?" She crossed her leg so the slit in her dress fell open against the step, much to Fred's admiration.

"Do you know a Wanda Sue Hampton?" I surprised myself, blurting it out like that.

"No. Why?"

"I thought you might."

"I know a Wanda Sue Eddington."

"Could she have been Wanda Sue Hampton before she married?"

"That *was* before she was married. Let's see. Her name now is Ellis, I think, or maybe Ellington. Something like that."

I took a bite out of an angel biscuit and wondered why somebody didn't come up with a solution for women's names.

"What did you say her name is?" Doris asked.

"Wanda Sue Hampton."

The tableau in the doorway had changed slightly. Sara was now leaning over Daddy Dick, her cheek against his balding head. Daddy was beaming and son was smiling, too, standing over them, one hand on his wife's head and the other on his father's head like a blessing.

"I see Paris, I see France." Jackson was standing by the stairs, gazing at the way Doris's skirt fell to the side.

"I don't have on underpants." She giggled.

He twirled an imaginary mustache. "Let's rush to the gazebo, my dear."

"After a while. Let me finish my supper."

Jackson patted her leg and walked toward the tent. Fred and I must have had startled looks on our faces.

"My boyfriend," Doris explained. "Jackson Hannah."

Well, that explained the mink coat, the town house and the plastic surgery.

"Is Wanda Sue a friend of yours?" she asked.

I told her the truth, about the boot and the marriage certificate being hidden, about Henry ("He's an angel," she interrupted) being under suspicion. I didn't have anything to lose, and after all, she had worked at the Skoot. Maybe she could add something.

While I was talking, she was devouring her food with her perfectly capped teeth.

"Druggies," she said when I had finished.

"I think so, too." It was the first time Fred had opened his mouth in ten minutes. Doris and I both jumped.

"Personally," Doris said, "I think that macho Swamp Creature, that Kenny somebody, might have something to do with Ed's murder. He's stoned half the time. Dealing, too."

"You sure?"

"Saw him. The sheriff knows it. I told him." Doris stood up and brushed the crumbs from her dress with a napkin. "Thanks, y'all. I enjoyed supper."

At the front door, Sara had left Daddy Dick's side and was greeting more guests with her husband. Richard,

Senior, had disappeared, probably into the dining room.

Doris stepped over us. "Would you mind taking my plate back?"

"Sure," Fred agreed readily.

"I'm off to the gazebo."

We watched her slide through the line of guests at the buffet tables.

"She's not at all what I expected," I said.

When we got back to the tent, Debbie and Henry had arrived. When Henry found out we had been in to supper, he immediately wanted to hear about the food.

"Some kind of rice," Fred said, "and a real good casserole."

"And ham and angel biscuits," I added. "Fruit."

Debbie laughed. "I think we better go check it out for ourselves, Henry." She turned to Haley and Kenneth. "Want to go?" They did.

Jimmy Gerald and the boys in the band were huffing through "I'll Be With You in Apple Blossom Time," and Mary Alice and Bill were still dancing. "Want to dance?" I suggested.

Fred groaned. "Good God, no. You shouldn't have let me eat that last roll, Patricia Anne."

I reached into my purse and handed him a Tums. "Please forgive me."

The music ended and Sister and Bill came back to the table. They were red-faced, out of breath and happy.

"Where are the kids?" she asked.

"Supper."

"Haley likes Kenneth." The wooden fold-up chair groaned as Mary Alice sat down.

"Good. We met Doris Chapman."

"She's here?"

"She's Jackson Hannah's girlfriend."

"You're kidding."

"Good-looking girl," Fred chimed in.

"Doris?" Mary Alice looked surprised. "Do you remember Doris Chapman being good-looking, Bill?"

"I don't remember Doris Chapman," Bill said.

"You would now," Fred said.

I gave him the schoolteacher look. "She's had everything done that plastic surgeons know how to do."

"She's gorgeous," Fred said.

This time I pinched his leg. The secret is in the twist.

"What?" he asked. "What?"

"Well, good for her," Sister said.

"And she's definitely not Wanda Sue Hampton."

"Who?" Sister asked, and I remembered I hadn't told
her about the marriage certificate and the picture.

"It's a long story," I said. "I'll tell you later. Right
now I want to know more about Haley and Kenneth."

Mary Alice was happy to oblige. She sipped her white
wine and gave me a total background check including a
glowing financial report on Kenneth Singleton. She finished with "I had him picked out for Debbie, you
know" and a shrug.

"Henry's a doll," I said.

"Henry's a cook."

"A chef," I corrected her. "An artist. He'll do well."

"Birmingham does need an elegant new restaurant,"
she said. I saw where this was going and wondered how
it would sit with Henry. "Snow peas like little flowers . . ." I tuned her out.

The bar's business had slowed down. Many people
had brought their supper back to the tent, and Bonnie
Blue and her helpers seemed to be pouring more coffee
than anything else. The band had taken a break and it
was relatively quiet in the tent. The lack of sleep from
the past two nights was beginning to catch up with me.

"Wouldn't it, Patricia Anne?"

I jumped. Mary Alice looked at me and frowned. "Well, wouldn't it?"

"Absolutely," I said, wondering what the hell I had just agreed with.

"And lamb. I always said if somebody in Birmingham knew how to cook lamb, they'd make a fortune."

"I love lamb gravy," Bill said.

"Patricia Anne bought some mint jelly in Gatlinburg one time that was the best I ever put in my mouth."

This was scintillating party talk. I looked around at the other tables. What were those people talking about? From the looks of the plates, food probably. I sighed.

"Want to sneak out to the gazebo?" I asked Fred.

"What's out there?" Bill asked.

"Doris Chapman and Jackson Hannah."

"Really?" Mary Alice seemed intrigued.

"Well, they were. Cold as it is, they'd be gone by now," I said.

"Maybe." Fred grinned.

Bill got up. "Want us to bring you anything?"

"We didn't even look at the desserts, Patricia Anne," Fred said.

"I'm sorry, Fred. I can't let you eat dessert."

He stuck his white-coated tongue out at me. "Let's go look."

The Hannahs had moved away from the front door and were circulating among their guests. Dick introduced the four of us to his father, who was holding unofficial court in the front parlor. I remembered him as a vigorous young governor and it was painful to see him so disabled. He was still a handsome man, though. It was easy to see where his son had got his looks.

"Are you by any chance the Hollowell who owns that steel-fabricating place right off Arkadelphia?" he asked Fred.

Fred said he was, pleased that Richard, Senior, was familiar with his business.

"I've been meaning to get in touch with you. We're looking for some competitive bids on roof bolts for the mines. You handle that kind of thing?"

Fred had died and gone to heaven. We left them ten minutes later, chatting about A-36 carbon steel and rods and shafts.

"Thy rods and thy shafts, they comfort me," Mary Alice said.

"Well, they give us this day our daily bread."

"That's not funny, girls," Bill said. Mary Alice rolled her eyes at me.

Bill and Sister went into the dining room and I headed for the porch, not that I was planning on getting dessert, but to see what was there. The spread was unbelievable, ranging from pecan pie to chocolate mousse to fruit tarts. I hoped Henry had brought something to take notes on.

I couldn't resist a small helping of blueberry trifle, telling myself I would just pick the blueberries out of the whipped cream. I took the bowl and wandered over to the window. The backyard was dark, probably because the Hannahs didn't want their guests tromping around on their storm-soaked grass. By the light of the full moon, though, and the lights that streamed from windows, I could make out the swimming pool, the children's swing set and, in the background, what must be the gazebo.

"Mrs. Hollowell?"

I turned to see a beautiful young woman in a short, strapless black sheath. Her dark hair was pulled back into a French braid and caught with a black bow. Her eyes were such a pale blue, they were startling against her tanned, olive skin. Someone I had taught, I thought, and smiled at her.

"Yes," I said.

"I'm Fussy." She saw I didn't have a clue to what she was talking about. "Fussy Moran. We met at your sister's? The Swamp Creatures?"

"You're Fussy?" I almost said, "The bag lady?" but I caught myself in time.

"Yes, ma'am."

"How did the anniversary party go?"

"It was fine." Fussy held up a plate with a piece of cake on it. "This is for Granddaddy. He loves lemon pound cake."

"Your grandfather's here?"

"He's Richard Hannah."

"Good Lord," I said.

Fussy giggled. "I know. My mama says I'm climbing fool's hill with the Swamp Creatures, but I really enjoy it. She's Dick's older sister, by the way. Maryann. She and my daddy are both around somewhere. Let me take this to Granddaddy and I'll find them and introduce you. You aren't here by yourself, are you?"

I shook my head. "My husband and your grandfather are discussing bolts and rods."

"Oh, Lord. I might as well eat the cake myself, then." Fussy broke off a piece of crisp crust and popped it into her mouth. "Great!"

It was all I could do to keep from staring at her. I still found it hard to believe that this was the same girl I had met at Mary Alice's.

"Sara and Dick know how to do parties," she said. "They've got a great pool. I wish they could have used it tonight. Some designer did it so it fits into the landscape. It even has a little creek that runs into it." Fussy took another bite of cake and put her plate down. "Come on, I'll show it to you."

"You sure it's all right?"

"They won't care. I want you to see the stones in the waterfall. I've never figured out if they're fake or not."

"I don't want to mess up my shoes." Fussy might be a Hannah who didn't have to worry about things like that, but I was a Hollowell and had spent seventy bucks on these red heels.

"We'll go through the pool room. There are all kinds of slippers and flip-flops out there. I don't want to get mud on these, either."

I looked down and saw what looked like glass slippers on Fussy's feet. I just hoped when she pulled them off she didn't turn back into a Swamp Creature.

It felt good outside, a crisp October night. Fussy turned on the lights in the pool and we walked across the lawn to the spot where the water dropped over a shelf of rocks and into the pool about three feet below. Fussy was right. It was a beautiful pool that Mother Nature would have been proud of.

"Feel those rocks and see if you can tell if they are real."

I pushed up the sleeve of my dress and leaned over.

"Oh, my God," Fussy said. "Oh, my God!" She turned so quickly that she bumped against me and both of us nearly ended up in the waterfall. By the time I had recovered my balance, she was running to the other end of the pool. I could see what she was running toward, though—a large, dark, floating form.

I got there just as she dived into the water. She surfaced, grabbed the man (I could tell now it was a man) and started swimming toward me.

"Help me!"

I jumped in and swam toward her.

"Shallow end," she gasped.

I grabbed the man's arm, and together Fussy and I kicked and pushed until our feet touched the bottom of the pool. We pulled him to the steps and up onto the apron, where we turned him over and Fussy started CPR.

"Help!" I screamed, running up the kitchen steps. "Somebody come help us!"

Several people came to the windows to look out and someone opened the kitchen door. "Get some help!" I screamed to the person standing there and then ran back to Fussy. I knew CPR. We had been required to learn it as teacher in-training.

"Move over!" I said. But Fussy was no longer working on the man.

"He's dead," she said.

"Maybe not! You can't tell!" I pushed her aside and saw that yes, indeed, you could tell. Blood was still running from the great gash that had opened his chest, but he was dead.

"It's Uncle Jackson," Fussy whimpered. But I already knew that.

Eighteen

It was after midnight before we were allowed to go home. Much of the time was a blur. I remember the sounds of people shouting and running down steps. I remember lights flaring and hearing Haley scream, "Mama!" And then Fred was there, wrapping me in his coat, trying to help me up while Fussy and I held hands across Jackson's body, still thinking, maybe, that we could cheat death.

And then there were the shakes, shivering so hard that hot water in a tub couldn't stop it, and a doctor, one of the guests, who asked had I been drinking? No. This will make you feel better. A pink pill. Valium? Probably. And it did. Enough for me to answer the sheriff's questions. Enough to see the you-again? look on Sheriff Reuse's face when he came in and saw me wrapped in one of Sara Hannah's robes, chenille, just like everybody wears, nothing fancy. Better enough to ask about my new red dress, which I knew didn't count for much in the scheme of things but which was the only Lillie Rubin, new red dress I had ever had, and to be assured by Mary Alice that her cleaners would fix it as good as new.

I told the sheriff all I knew, which was nothing, and Fussy told him all she knew, which was nothing, and the guests were finally allowed to go home, but not, according to Mary Alice, until they had trampled every blade of grass around the pool and destroyed any evidence the sheriff might have been able to use, such as a footprint.

Richard Hannah, Sr., who had had heart surgery the year before, had been put to bed with a sedative. Richard, Junior, dealt with the newspeople, who had arrived before the sheriff. Finally he gave up and turned his job over to the wrestler guy who had accompanied the elder Richard. He handled them, I understand, by standing on the front steps and growling, "Go away." Sara and a red-eyed Katie McCorkle said good night to the guests, who were escorted through the tent and away from the media.

Sheriff Reuse was kind; he looked tired, and I remembered he had been in Atlanta all day. "Take some vitamin C," he told me when I sneezed. And finally: "Go home and get some rest. I'll talk to you tomorrow."

We had to leave by way of the tent since the media seemed to have set up residence on the Hannahs' front steps. I was glad they didn't get any pictures of me. I was still wearing Sara's chenille robe and had topped it with Fred's coat. One of the deputies took us to the pasture where our car was parked. It was the last car there and it looked tiny and welcoming in that field. All

I wanted to do was get in it, go home and sleep for a couple of days.

The deputy stayed to make sure the car started all right, and then he turned left toward the house while we turned right toward the main road.

"What do you think?" Fred asked.

I was almost asleep. "About Jackson?"

"If the two murders are connected."

"I don't even want to think about it," I said. "I'm just going to go home, lock the door and not go out again. In sixty years I've never seen any violence except on TV, and here I've seen two murders in a week. Murders." I felt the shivers beginning again. I closed my eyes and said my mantra. It didn't work.

"I wonder if this will hurt Dick Hannah's election bid." Fred swung up the interstate entrance.

"Maybe help it," I said. "Who knows?"

There was a sudden rustling in the back and a dark figure rose from the floor. This is it, I thought. This is the murderer and we're dead.

"I'm sorry, Fred," Doris Chapman said, "but you have got to stop the car. I've got to pee so bad my eyeballs are floating."

"No problem," Fred said. "I suddenly need to go myself."

"Thank you," Doris said, getting out of the car.

"You're welcome," Fred said. A few moments later, he got out for his turn.

Doris was in the backseat again, and my heart was still beating about a hundred and fifty even with the Valium. "What the hell is this about, Doris?" I asked. "You could have given us a heart attack."

"Oh, Patricia Anne, I've never been so scared in my life!" She started sobbing. Sobbing interspersed with wailing.

"Good Lord!" Fred said, getting back in the car. "What's the matter?"

"Jackson's dead. We're all going to be murdered."

"Not me," I said. "I'm going to go home and lock all my doors. Not come out again."

Fred reached over and took my hand. "What are you talking about, Doris?"

She leaned over the seat between us. "Either of you have a Kleenex? I just used the only one I had."

I fished one out of my purse. "Talk," I said, handing it to her.

"I saw Jackson murdered. Right there in front of me. And I loved him. I really did." She sobbed into the Kleenex. "I'm so scared. I know I'm next."

"Who killed him, Doris?" Fred asked.

"Katie McCorkle."

"Katie? She couldn't kill a fly," I said.

"She could with a butcher knife, Patricia Anne. You weren't there."

"No, she wasn't, Doris. Tell us about it." Fred sounded like a TV psychiatrist.

"Are you going to believe me, Patricia Anne?"

"I'm sorry," I said.

"Well, I met Jackson in the gazebo and he was glad to see me, but surprised because he didn't know I was coming, and I told him I'd had a message from him on my phone in Destin that he wanted me to be sure to come to this party. Anyway, he said he was going to get some champagne to celebrate and he went into the kitchen. None of the lights were on in the back, but I saw him coming back down the steps and then I saw Katie coming down after him. She called his name and he stopped by the pool and they talked for a minute and then Katie stabbed him." Doris shuddered. "And he fell into the pool and she washed the knife off. Just leaned over and rinsed the blood off right where Jackson was. That's when I took off. Climbed the railing and hid behind that thing that pumps the waterfall. Good thing, too. She went over to the gazebo and looked around. I saw her." Doris shuddered again. "I'm next."

"Of course you're not," Fred said.

"But why would Katie McCorkle kill Jackson Hannah and want to kill you?" I wanted to know.

"Beats me," Doris said. This time we both knew she was lying. "I knew I had to get out of there, though. I went around where they had the car tickets, and while they were out parking cars, I found out what kind of car you had and where they had put it. They were more organized out there than they looked. Then I hightailed it out to the field and found it. I thought you never would come, though."

"I'm the one found Jackson's body," I said.

"Oh. I'm sorry."

"And why us, Doris?"

"Well, you were so nice at supper, and I had to hide *somewhere*."

"We'll take you to the police station," Fred said.

"Oh, no! Please don't."

"You have to tell them what you saw, particularly if you think you're in any danger."

"Think? Hell, I know it."

"All the more reason," Fred said.

"I can't. I just can't tonight. Can't I just go home with you while we figure out what to do?"

"What is this 'we' business?" Fred asked. "How can 'we' figure out what to do if 'we' don't know what's going on?"

"I told you, Katie killed Jackson."

"And you need to tell the police. I'll take the Gardendale exit."

"No! Wait!" Doris put her head down on the back of the front seat. "There's some stuff I haven't told you."

"Then maybe we better go home," Fred said. Why do I ever underestimate this man?

"Thank you," Doris said again. She sat back and was quiet except for an occasional hiccup or sniff. I thought about what she had told us. Katie McCorkle? Tiny Katie whose church group gleaned for the poor? The wound in Jackson's chest had been a gaping hole. How in the world could that small woman have opened him up like that? Even with a sharp butcher knife. And why? *If* she had really done it. Maybe it had been someone who looked like her; Doris could have been mistaken. After all, the only light was from the windows. But Doris had watched them standing there talking. She had seen Katie rinse the knife off in the pool. What had Katie done then? Gone back inside and cut some more ham for the buffet? My stomach did a flip.

"Talk about something," I told Fred. "Anything."

"Katie McCorkle's pearls were gone," Fred said. "When we were in the living room talking to the sheriff."

"Talk about something else," I said. "She probably put them in her purse. Talk about the Grand Canyon."

"The Grand Canyon?"

"Sure."

"It's real big, and you can take helicopter rides into it and camp down in the bottom of it."

"That's better. Are we going to go there when you retire?"

"Absolutely."

"Those were beautiful pearls." Doris spoke up from the backseat. "I noticed them when we were getting our supper. Opera-length. Didn't look like Katie."

"I must have noticed them, too," Fred said, "to remember she didn't have them on later."

"Oh, for God's sake." I lifted Fred's coat over my head and covered my ears with my hands. When Fred woke me up as we pulled into our driveway, I was dreaming Mary Alice and I were in a red convertible. She was driving, and we were hell-bent for the rim of the Grand Canyon.

Fred fixed coffee while Doris took a hot shower and put on one of my nightgowns and Sara Hannah's robe. I had switched to my own pink chenille one. The short nap had refreshed me. Maybe I was getting used to sleep deprivation. I had even combed my hair, brushed my teeth and put on lipstick, which I was happy I had done when Doris came out. Even with her eyes swollen from crying, she was still gorgeous. I began to have serious doubts concerning my adamant stand against cosmetic surgery.

Fred had just poured each of us a cup and was getting the milk out of the refrigerator when there was a loud knock at the kitchen door.

"Oh, shit!" Doris disappeared under the table. I couldn't think that fast, maybe because of the Valium. By the time I was ready to hit the floor, Fred was saying, "It's Mary Alice," and letting her in.

She swept in, still in her butterfly caftan but with a fur coat on. "Who's that under the table?" she asked.

"It's Doris Chapman," Fred said.

Mary Alice sat down at the table and leaned over. "Hi, Doris," she said. "I've been wanting to talk to you about coming back to work at the Skoot 'n' Boot."

"Thank you," Doris said, "but I don't think so."

"Well, you've got a while to think about it." Sister turned to me. "I just came to check on you, Mouse. I was proud of you diving into the pool that way to rescue Jackson Hannah.''

A wail came from under the table. Mary Alice leaned down again. ''What's the matter, Doris?''

''He was her boyfriend,'' I explained.

''Oh, I'm sorry. I wondered what she was doing under the table.''

Fred caught my eye and held his hands together in a V. He says Mary Alice's thought processes are like a train that occasionally veers from the main line. ''Let me pour you some coffee,'' he said.

''You poor thing.'' Mary Alice helped Doris get up. ''I don't know what the world's coming to. People didn't get murdered when Patricia Anne and I were young.''

Fred snorted, but it seemed to me that Sister was right.

''Doris saw it happen,'' I said.

''The murder?''

Doris was back in her chair by now with her head on the table. ''Katie McCorkle,'' she mumbled.

''What did you say, dear?'' Sister asked.

''She said Katie McCorkle killed Jackson Hannah.'' I was beginning to feel like an interpreter.

''Oh, surely not!''

''She saw her stab him with a butcher knife,'' Fred said, sitting down and stirring his coffee.

''Oh, my God!'' Mary Alice reached over and patted Doris's arm. ''How awful. And I'll bet Sheriff Reuse just upset you more. That man's a martinet. Remember I told you that, Patricia Anne?''

''He doesn't know about it,'' I said.

''Doesn't know about it? Why not?''

''Let Doris tell you,'' Fred said.

Doris lifted her head. ''It's a long story.''

''I've got time.'' Mary Alice slipped out of her coat

and leaned forward, her butterfly wings cascading around the end of the table.

Doris told the same sequence of events she had related in the car, and Mary Alice asked the same questions we had: Why didn't she go to the police and why should Katie want to kill her?

"This is between you and me, and you've got to help me. Okay?" Doris took a paper napkin out of the holder in the middle of the table and held it to her eyes.

"Okay," Mary Alice agreed.

Doris sighed. "Old man Hannah and Katie have had a thing going for a long time."

"I thought they were cousins," I said.

Fred frowned at me. "Let her tell her story."

Doris continued. "Anyway, this went back a long time."

"What about Fly?" Sister asked.

"Shut up, Mary Alice," Fred said.

"I think he knew about it," Doris said. "Anyway, it had been going on for a long time. Even when Jackson ran for governor. You remember that?"

All three of us nodded. Jackson's antics on TV would be long remembered.

"Richard, Senior, talked him into that. Jackson didn't really want to be governor. Probably couldn't have handled it, anyway."

We all nodded again.

"Not that he wasn't smart. Jackson was plenty smart." Doris wiped her eyes with the napkin. "He just wasn't a politician. You know?"

We nodded.

"But if Daddy Dick told him to jump, there Jackson would be, asking how high. I think part of it was guilt. Jackson was piloting the plane that killed Millie Hannah and crippled Richard, Sr. Did you know that?"

Our heads moved sideways.

"Well, he was. It caused a whole lot of his problems, I think. His drinking got worse and his wife quit him. He'd been going to AA for a couple of years when I met him, though. He'd come in the Skoot to see Ed and he'd drink a Coke. Or a root beer. Diet. First time he asked me out, he ordered a real expensive bottle of wine and didn't touch a drop. I got to take it home." Doris cried a little. "First time I ever ate she-crab soup."

Mary Alice opened her mouth to say something but didn't. Fred might have kicked her.

Doris straightened. "The thing about it is this. Ed Meadows had the Hannahs by the short hairs about something. They were paying him off to the tune of five thousand a month. Jackson asked me if I would deliver an envelope to Ed, and I looked in it and saw six big ones. I asked him, 'What the hell is this?' and he said, 'A gambling debt. One of them's yours.' So I took it. I think that first one paid for my eyes. But when Jackson found out, he said, 'That money's a present.' And he paid for everything else I had done."

"They were paying Ed sixty thousand dollars a year?" Fred sounded amazed.

"Something like that. I don't know what for, though. I swear to God I don't."

"I think I do." I got up, went into the bedroom, then came back with the marriage certificate and the picture. "These were hidden in the boot in the dance floor. There's got to be some connection."

"Wanda Sue Hampton," Doris exclaimed, looking at the name on the certificate. "That's who you were asking me about."

"I thought you might be her. She."

Mary Alice studied the picture. "Down in the glass boot?"

"You remember I brought it home so it wouldn't get broken? I thought there was trash in it."

"I don't recognize her." Mary Alice handed the picture to Doris, who looked at it carefully.

"I don't know who she is, but I'll bet you're right. This is what he was holding over them." Doris passed the picture on to Fred. "I didn't finish my story, though. "Ed was using. You know, drugs?"

We all three nodded.

"Most of the time he was okay. Unless he mixed it with alcohol. But I know that Swamp Creature guy was dealing and Ed was letting him use the Skoot. Probably for his supply. I saw some deals going down in the parking lot, not much, but God, I hate drugs. My first husband died tripping. You remember LSD?"

We did.

"I called that TV Crime Stoppers program and reported it. I don't know if they did anything about it, though. I left pretty soon after that. Ed jumped me in the cooler and nearly scared me to death. He'd have hurt me, too, if it hadn't been for Henry. Anyway, Jackson said it was time for me to leave, so I went to Florida. Had my face done down there."

"Wait a minute," Fred exclaimed. "I know who this is." He handed me the picture. "Imagine her blond, Patricia Anne, and about twenty pounds lighter. She's had her nose done, and probably her eyes and chin. But look carefully, honey. You can still see her."

I looked at the picture, imagining the young woman blond, skinny, with a different nose, larger eyes and a more prominent chin. As if from a negative, an image began to emerge. "Oh, my," I said. "It's Sara Hannah."

Mary Alice grabbed the picture and studied it. "I don't see it," she said.

Doris was looking over her shoulder. "I do. That's who it is."

Fred got up, poured us more coffee and opened a package of Lorna Doones to celebrate.

"That's what he was blackmailing them with, all right," I said, taking the picture back. "Sara Hannah is Wanda Sue Hampton."

"But wait a minute," Sister said. "It's no disgrace to have been married before. Not even for a politician's wife. That information wouldn't be worth a thing."

"Oh, but it would," I said. "Sheriff Reuse found the marriage records, but he didn't find a record of a divorce. He's still looking for Wanda Sue Meadows."

"Sara Hannah's a bigamist?" Doris's eyes were perfect round circles.

"Well, Sister's right. They wouldn't be paying him much to keep him quiet about being her first husband," I said.

"Not good for politics," Fred said, biting into a cookie.

"But, and I know this is all speculation, why would she have married Dick Hannah without getting a divorce?"

"Probably thought she had one," Doris said. "My second husband was in the Marines and I signed the divorce papers he sent me and then he didn't file them. I thought I was rid of that man a whole year before I was. See, they can get a divorce done real cheap in the service."

"Would it be worth killing Ed for?" Mary Alice asked.

"For Richard, Senior, it would. He wants that boy of his in the Senate so bad he can taste it," Doris said.

"And that's what jumped the ante." Fred brushed crumbs from the table into his hand. "Our friend Ed went way up on the amount. Probably wanted a 'final' big payoff, and I'll bet he thought you were going to bring it, Doris. That's why he got so mad that day in the cooler. Hadn't you just given him some money?''

Doris nodded. We all looked at each other, pleased. Then Doris tuned up. ''But why did Katie kill Jackson? And why is she after me?''

''We're going to have to sleep on that one,'' Fred said. ''I can't think anymore.''

''I'm staying here.'' Sister groaned and got up. ''You got a nightgown I can wear, Patricia Anne?''

Fred saved the day. ''Try some of my pajamas, Mary Alice.''

Nineteen

The sky was beginning to lighten when I finally fell into a deep sleep. When I awoke, it was almost eleven and I could hear the shower running. My throat felt scratchy, as if I were catching a cold; not surprising after the frigid swim of the night before.

Fred and Doris were sitting at the kitchen table eating waffles with syrup.

"You want some?" Fred asked, holding up his plate.

I shook my head and got orange juice out of the refrigerator and a vitamin C tablet from the cabinet. "I'm catching a cold."

"It's the only thing you can do," Fred said.

"What?" I asked, sitting at the table. "Catch a cold?"

"I was talking to Doris," he said.

"Good morning, Doris." She nodded my way without

taking her eyes off Fred. She was still wearing Sara Hannah's robe, but she had on eye makeup, blush and lipstick and looked smashing.

"I know it," she agreed.

"They'll give you protection."

"She'll get out on bail, though." Doris shivered. "And they'll probably charge me with something for delivering the money to Ed." She pushed her plate away. "I just want to go back to Florida."

"And let Jackson's murderer get away with it? Knowing she's coming after you?"

Tears brimmed in Doris's eyes. "I know you're right. I'm just scared shitless."

Mary Alice came in, dressed in Fred's cranberry-colored silk pajamas. Her hair was wet and, like me, she wore no makeup.

"I am dying," she announced and headed for the coffeepot. "Where are the aspirin, Mouse?"

"You sick?"

"Headache."

I sneezed. "I'm getting a cold."

"This has been a week of bad karma." She opened the cabinet that I had pointed to and poured several aspirin tablets into her hand. Then she sat down at the table, lined the tablets up in front of her and proceeded to chew them up one at a time, occasionally taking a sip of black coffee. "You look like you just walked out of Merle Norman's," she told Doris. "How on God's earth do you do it?"

"It's tattooed," Doris said.

Mary Alice nodded and chewed on another aspirin. "Very nice," she said. "Was it painful?"

"Hurt like hell."

"I have a low-pain threshold," Sister said. "Should I consider it?"

"No. The stupid thing was they did one side at a time. I wouldn't have gone back the second time if I could have made the other side match."

Fred pushed his chair back. "Do we ask the sheriff to come here or do we go out there?"

"Out there," Mary Alice said. "I've got to go home and get dressed."

"Me, too," said Doris.

"And I need to go by the shop for a few minutes." Fred looked at me, but I just shrugged and sneezed. "I'll go call him."

"Don't you just love men sometimes?" Mary Alice said.

"Sometimes," I agreed.

Doris looked out of the window and shook.

Fred came to the door. "He'll meet us at one o'clock and please don't be late, because he has to be somewhere at two."

"That martinet," Sister mumbled.

We agreed to meet at the sheriff's office. I would take Doris by her place to get dressed. Fred and Sister left, and I threw on a pair of jeans and a sweatshirt that proclaimed June 9, 1992, had been Doo Dah Day at the Birmingham Humane Society. Which reminded me. I ran out with some dog biscuits for Woofer and a promise of a long walk later. He's so good.

I asked Doris if she wanted to borrow any of my clothes, but she said she would just wear Sara's robe and pray we didn't have a wreck. I wondered if Mary Alice had been talking to her.

It was after twelve when we got to Doris's town house. She hadn't questioned the fact that I had gone right to it without directions.

"I'll hurry," she said, unlocking the door to a beautifully decorated living room that I immediately fell in love with. The dominant colors were peach and green, blended together so artfully I didn't know how she could bear to leave the place to go to Florida.

She noticed the look on my face. "It's nice, isn't it?"

"It's beautiful."

"I'll give you the name of my decorator." Bless her heart, I think she was serious. "There's a TV over in that cabinet, and Cokes in the refrigerator. I won't be long."

I sank down into the luxury of the sofa. It was a forest green with small peach flowers on it. The chair beside it had the same colors in a stripe, another in a flame design. If I tried to mix all these patterns, I would end up with a mess, not this soothing blend. I could feel myself relaxing. Maybe I *should* get the name of Doris's decorator.

The doorbell rang and I came straight up.

"Don't open it!" Doris hissed. She was standing in the bedroom doorway with a towel wrapped around her. "Let me look." She crossed the room and pulled the drapery back an imperceptible amount. "Mrs. Stannard," she said in obvious relief. "My neighbor. She's got some flowers. Will you get them, Patricia Anne?"

"Sure."

Doris disappeared back into the bedroom as I opened the door to the same lady who had told me about Fly McCorkle having Doris's dog. She was carrying a large basket of cut flowers: mums, daisies, rubric lilies. Like the living room they were going to grace, they were perfect.

"Oh, my," I said.

"They're something, aren't they?" She looked around. "Didn't I see Doris?"

"She's getting dressed. Won't you come in?"

Mrs. Stannard shook her head. "Just give her these.

Tell her somebody left them on my porch this morning, but they're for her." She handed me the basket. "I should be so lucky."

"You and me both," I said. I thanked her, closed the door and put the flowers on the coffee table.

"Aren't those beautiful!" Doris cried. In the mirror's reflection, I could see her wriggling into a pair of jeans. "See who they're from, Patricia Anne."

There was a knock on the door. Mrs. Stannard had forgotten something. I opened it to Katie McCorkle, who held a small dog under one arm and a small pistol in the other hand that was pointed right at me.

"I brought the dog back," she said, letting him drop to the floor.

I backed away from her.

"Buffy!" I heard Doris squeal as the dog ran into the bedroom. And then: "Oh, God."

"It's me, Doris," Katie called. "How are you today?"

Doris appeared in the doorway. "What do you want, Katie?"

"Finish getting dressed, honey. We're going over to the Skoot."

"She's got a gun, Doris," I said.

"Just a little one." Katie looked at the gun and smiled. "Remember when Nancy Reagan said she carried a gun, but just a little one? I loved that."

"Why are you doing this, Katie?"

"You were in the gazebo last night. I'm sorry Patricia Anne had to get involved, though."

Patricia Anne was sorry, too. My mind was racing. The small cellular phone Fred had given me for Christmas was in my purse on the sofa. If I could get to it . . .

"Mind if I sit down?" I asked.

"Fine." Katie reached over and got my purse. "I'll

just take this. And, Doris, don't you try anything. Put
on some sneakers and let's go.''

I sat down on the sofa. ''Why are you taking us to
the Skoot?''

''That place is in terrible shape since the storm. Part
of the roof's just hanging in the air. Defying gravity. If
it fell in and somebody happened to be under it, I'd hate
to think what would happen to them.''

''But why are you doing this, Katie? And why did
you kill Jackson?'' I asked.

''Too long a story to tell now. Got your shoes, Doris?
Okay,'' Katie reached into her purse and brought out a
roll of electrical tape. ''Put this around Doris's wrists,
Patricia Anne. Wind it real tight. One of you has to
drive, and I don't want any smart moves out of the other
one.''

Doris held out her arms obediently and I started wrapping the tape around her wrists.

''That ought to do it,'' Katie said. She took a small
pair of scissors from her pocket and cut the tape. If I
were clever enough, I could grab those scissors. Katie
smiled at me. No, I couldn't.

What was happening was so far from anything I had
ever experienced, I didn't know how to react. Katie
McCorkle looked like the same old hippie who sold soup
mix at a curb market. Her bell-bottom jeans were the
same, her gray-brown hair was pulled back into a ponytail and she had the same sweet, friendly smile. But she
was holding a pistol on us. We were going to have an
''accident'' at the Skoot 'n' Boot. She had struck Jackson Hannah so hard, she had split his chest open.

''Let's go,'' she said. She reached over to the bouquet
of flowers and pulled a few out. ''Here, Doris, hold these
just in case that lady next door is watching. She's a real
nice lady, but I think she's a snoop.''

Buffy danced around our legs, wanting to go with us. "I'll come back and get you," Katie said, pushing him back and closing the door. "Don't worry about him, Doris."

We marched to the car in what must have looked something like a wedding procession to Mrs. Stannard if she was looking out. A shotgun wedding, though she wouldn't have been able to see the small gun in the palm of Katie's hand. I got in the driver's seat and Katie opened the passenger door for Doris. Then she got in the back and handed me the keys she had taken from my purse.

"Okay," she said.

"You want me to go up the interstate?"

"Why not? Get there faster."

I started the car and drove out of the complex. A small wall of mailboxes stood at the entrance and I considered aiming for them, but I decided it wouldn't work. To start with, there was no one around to come running to see what had happened. And Doris would be hurt. She would slam into the dashboard and hit her head on the windshield. Plus, we would both be shot in the head immediately. That was the biggest deterrent.

Doris was not in good shape. The flowers in her hands were shaking as if a windstorm were battering them, and she kept sniffing and wiping her eyes and nose on the sleeve of her shirt. I wasn't much better, but at least I had the driving to think about.

"Hey," Katie said, leaning forward. Doris and I both jumped. "What kind of eye makeup you got on, Doris?"

"It's tattooed."

"I wondered why it wasn't running."

"She said it hurt," I added. "When they did it."

"Looks good."

"Thank you." Doris wiped her eyes again on her sleeve.

We were passing a row of cardboard signs that had been stuck in the ground, advertising the upcoming election. Richard Hannah, Jr., gazed at us with a slight smile. What in the world were we doing? he seemed to ask.

"I'll bet you both were going to vote for Dickie, weren't you?" Katie said.

We nodded.

"He's beautiful, isn't he?"

We agreed.

"And brilliant, too. Levelheaded. Never let his daddy's money spoil him." Katie sighed. "I wish you could vote for him."

Both of us did, too.

"He'll win, anyway," she said. "He'll be President someday."

A piece of the puzzle had slid into place when I saw Richard smiling in the posters. Or at least I thought it had.

"You're a distant cousin, aren't you, Katie? There's a definite family resemblance."

"You think so?" She sounded pleased. "He's my son. Nobody knows but you and me and Richard, Senior. And Fly, of course. Jackson did, but he told me I better not hurt Doris or he just might have a few things to tell the press." She giggled. "Loose lips sink ships."

Loose lips sink ships? This woman must be older than I thought.

"Oh, God," Doris wailed.

"He's a fine son," I said. "I know you're proud of him."

"The light of my life."

"Nutty as a fruitcake," Doris whispered.

"I heard that," Katie said, "and I probably am. About

my son, anyway. You don't have any children, Doris.
What do you know?''

"You're right, Katie.'' Actually, I agreed with Doris,
but there was no use antagonizing this woman. I needed
time to think. ''I've got three and they're the lights of
my life, too.''

"But they're not running for the Senate. Mine is.''

"And going to get it, too.'' I thought for a minute.
''You know, Katie, I was in labor with Freddie for almost twenty-four hours.''

It did the trick. ''I was in labor with Dickie for forty-
eight. Probably should have had a cesarean, but Millie
was scared to take me to the hospital.''

"Where was he born?''

"The Hannahs have a retreat near Knoxville. A big
house up in the mountains. All the family would visit in
the summer. That's when I got pregnant. You know I
almost got an abortion? I was only sixteen. But Richard
wouldn't hear of it. Hey''—she touched my shoulder—
''turn on the interstate.''

I turned and went up the ramp, past posters of a smiling Richard Hannah, Jr.

"But what about Millie?'' I asked. ''She couldn't
have been too happy about her husband and a sixteen-
year-old.''

"Ha! Millie was tickled to death. She had him coming
and going on this one. Richard was about to divorce her
because she couldn't have any more children, couldn't
give him that son to carry on the sacred Hannah name.
And now he'd been screwing around with a sixteen-
year-old whose baby just might be a boy. Anyway, she
did a great job of planning it, told everybody she was
pregnant, and when I began to get a little plump, she
and I went to Tennessee to see the fall leaves, and oh,
my, she almost had a miscarriage. No traveling. Bed rest.

Quiet, which meant no company. I was stuck up there with that woman for months. Richard came up to visit, but we couldn't go anywhere. No TV and it snowed. The plan worked, though. Everybody was amazed at how quick Millie got her figure back. And Richard had his son.''

"What did you do? Go back to school?''

"Went to Europe. Bummed around. Met Fly. Didn't come back here until Dickie was a teenager. Not that I didn't want to, God knows. But it was best. By that time Richard was governor and Millie was Mrs. Society. They didn't care how much I saw Dickie, long as he thought I was just his cousin.''

"And you and Richard got together again.''

"What do you mean, got together again? There's always been Richard and me. And Dickie.''

Coming from this family, I thought, Richard Hannah, Jr., was born to be a politician. His mother wasn't who he thought she was, his real mother was a murderer and a nut case, and he wasn't even married to his wife. To say nothing of his father, who was guilty of statutory rape and paying blackmail money, and who had probably hired a couple of thugs to do Ed Meadows in. And his uncle Jackson, who had done God knows what.

"Where did you meet Fly?'' I asked.

"In Stockholm, on this youth-hostel boat. I bought him a coat 'cause he was freezing. The Alabama weather suits him better. The curb market was his idea, you know? A good one, too. Long as we never had to make a living with it.'' Katie paused. "And we didn't, of course.''

"That's nice,'' Doris said.

I looked at her.

"Next exit's the Skoot,'' Katie said.

"Oh, God." Doris buried her face in the flowers again.

I looked at the clock. It was only 12:45. Fred and the sheriff wouldn't worry about us being late for a half hour or more. Anyone going by the Skoot 'n' Boot wouldn't think anything was unusual if he saw a car there. I needed to attract attention out here on the interstate, but I couldn't think of a way. Flashing the lights wouldn't help. Anyone who saw them would think I was signalling that the highway patrol had its radar gun aimed down the road. Besides, Katie would see the lights flashing inside. All I could do was exit and head for the Skoot.

The sky was a brilliant blue. The storm had washed all the haze from the air and left everything shining. "It's a beautiful day," I said.

"Yes," Katie agreed. "Hurry up. I'll bet Fly's tired of waiting for us."

"Fly's there?"

"He didn't know you were coming, Patricia Anne. He's going to be upset. He likes you."

A twinge of hope fluttered in my chest for a moment. But only for a moment. Fly would do whatever Katie wanted him to. And that included killing me along with Doris.

The old truck with the butterfly painted on it was parked on the side of the building, just as it had been the first time I saw it. Fly got out and shuffled toward us, grinning, the most genial aging hippie one could ever hope to meet.

"What are you doing here, Patricia Anne?" he asked.

Katie answered for me. "She brought Doris home."

"Oh, that's too bad." Fly looked very sad.

"You don't have to do this, you know," I said. "Doris and I won't say a word about anything. We'll sign an oath in blood. I swear. Here." I held out my finger.

"Don't grovel, Patricia Anne," Katie said.

"I wasn't groveling," I said. "I just happen not to want to die today."

"You were groveling," Fly said. "Be like Doris."

Doris's body might be there, but her mind was in never-never land. She clutched the flowers stiffly in hands held away from her body, and her eyes were blank.

"She's in shock," I said. "That's dangerous."

Katie and Fly both laughed appreciatively.

"Okay," he said. "What we're going to do is play a little game of hide-and-seek. Now, what you and Doris are seeking, Patricia Anne, is hidden right under here." He pointed toward the collapsed part of the Skoot. "Go ahead, crawl under there. I'll come behind you part of the way."

I looked around at the fall trees, at the sky and the sun. I took a deep breath of the clean, crisp air. Katie and Fly were right. I'd been groveling. I got down on my hands and knees and started crawling.

"Go right behind her, Doris," Fly said.

There were bands of sun shining through the broken slats of the roof.

"Wait a minute." Fly said. He came around me and crawled toward a support beam that was still intact and holding up a contiguous part of the roof. "Right here," he said. He backed away and I crawled over to the beam. I saw immediately what he was going to do. A rope was tied around the beam; the other end was probably tied to his pickup.

"Don't be thinking you'll have time to get out of the way," he said. "The whole roof's coming in. But just in case you do—" He picked up a board which I hadn't

noticed before and hit Doris a hard blow on the side of
the head. She fell across me without a sound.

"Wait," I said. But the swish of the board was the
last thing I heard.

Twenty

The light was there at the end of the tunnel, just like I had known it would be. "It's okay," I heard a familiar, loving voice say. "It's okay, Patricia Anne. You're safe, darling."

Fred's voice. Fred had beaten me into heaven? How had he done that?

"Oh, Mouse, I love you so much. Don't be dead. It's all my fault."

Mary Alice was in heaven, too? And taking the blame for something? How about that! Heaven was going to be okay.

The light began to swing back and forth.

"Hold it still," I said.

"Open your eyes again, Mrs. Hollowell," a woman's voice said.

"Not unless you hold that light still."

"I promise."

I opened my eyes. Two Freds leaned over me. Two Mary Alices, two doctors with two lights. "I'm not dead, am I?"

Fred was squeezing my hand. "No, darling."

"We're putting in an IV, Mrs. Hollowell," the doctor said.

"Am I in the hospital?"

"Not yet, Mouse. You're still at the Skoot." Mary Alice's voice was shaky.

I thought for a moment. There was something I needed to know. Finally it came to me. "Is Doris dead?"

"No, darling. We got here just before they collapsed the roof. You're both going to be okay." Fred squeezed my hand.

"I hurt everywhere," I said.

"This will help." The doctor stuck a needle into my arm, and I didn't know anything else for a long time.

When I awoke, Mary Alice was sitting beside me working a crossword puzzle.

"Hi," I said.

"Hi." She put the puzzle down. "You want anything?

"Some water?"

"Sure." She picked up a glass and held the straw to my lips. The water tasted wonderful.

"Fred's gone home to get some sleep," she said. "He was here all night."

"Is it the next day?"

"Yep, and I'm supposed to ask you how many fingers I'm holding up." Mary Alice shot me a bird. I was too groggy for anything but a smile.

"Is Doris okay?"

"You both are. Thank God."

"But how did you know we were there?"

"I was behind you on the interstate. I saw you coming down the ramp and wondered who the third person was in your car, and I got close enough to see it was Katie. Then I called the sheriff. Told him I was following you, that you were in trouble."

"You were following me all the time? I didn't see you."

"You're not a good defensive driver."

"Did they get Katie and Fly?"

"Red-handed."

I shuddered. The answer was a little too apropos.

"They're in jail and charged with all sorts of stuff," Sister said.

"Who killed Ed?"

"The sheriff thinks Fly and a couple of the elder Richard's thugs. Pretty much like we figured. Ed had been blackmailing Sara for some time. She couldn't handle it anymore and told Daddy Dick the truth. I think he figured Ed would never let go, especially if Richard, Junior, got elected to the Senate. So he put a stop to it."

"It was Fly called us, wasn't it?" I asked sleepily.

"Yesterday?"

"No. From Debbie's. A long time ago, I think. And played the tape saying I was going to kill you."

"He was trying to scare us, let us know we were vulnerable. He was in my house and yours, too, at least once, trying to find out about us, if we knew anything."

"In my house?"

Sister nodded. "So much for my alarm system."

I shivered. "Bulldoze the Skoot, Sister. Flatten it."

"I'm thinking about it."

Richard Hannah, Junior, didn't win the election, though I voted for him and so did the rest of my family.

What happened wasn't his fault, and I think he would have made a good senator. But by then he had had too much descend on him. He and Sara had a quiet wedding at City Hall and left with the children for Europe. Sheriff Reuse says they are living in France, in Provence. Maybe, someday, they'll be healed enough to come home.

Richard, Senior, was not charged with anything. According to his testimony, he knew nothing. Jackson had been responsible for planning Ed's murder and for carrying it out. There was no evidence to the contrary, and Fly McCorkle refused to talk. The McCorkles' trials are set for next spring.

As for Fred and me, well, Mary Alice gave us a fortieth anniversary party, not at the Skoot, of course (though she still hasn't bulldozed it), but at her house, which is almost as large. It was a mild November, the kind we have in the South sometimes that confuses dogwood trees so much, they bloom. French doors were opened to the terrace and we could see the lights of the city below us, planes landing and taking off. The furniture was pushed against the walls, and the Swamp Creatures (without Kenny) made the hills come alive.

Henry and Debbie showed up, one carrying Fay, the other May. But the surprise of the evening was Haley arriving with Sheriff Reuse, who actually laughed several times.

We learned the Tush Push and the Achy Breaky, and the skirt of my red dress swirled like I knew it would.

"Hey," Fred said. "Hey." And we held each other tight and danced right on out the door, right into the warm, starry night.

"My Fred," I murmured.

"My Ginger."

I'll take forty more years with this man.

Discover Murder and Mayhem with

∽ Southern Sisters Mysteries ∽
by
ANNE GEORGE

MURDER ON A GIRLS' NIGHT OUT
978-0-380-78086-0/$6.99 US/$9.99 Can
Agatha Award winner for Best First Mystery Novel

MURDER ON A BAD HAIR DAY
978-0-380-78087-7/$6.99 US/$9.99 Can

MURDER RUNS IN THE FAMILY
978-0-380-78449-3/$6.99 US/$9.99 Can

MURDER MAKES WAVES
978-0-380-78450-9/$6.99 US/$9.99 Can

MURDER GETS A LIFE
978-0-380-79366-2/$6.99 US/$9.99 Can

MURDER SHOOTS THE BULL
978-0-380-80149-7/$6.99 US/$9.99 Can

MURDER CARRIES A TORCH
978-0-380-80938-7/$6.99 US/$9.99 Can

MURDER BOOGIES WITH ELVIS
978-0-06-103102-1/$6.99 US/$9.99 Can

Photo by E.A. (Buster) George

ANNE GEORGE was the Agatha Award-winning author of eight Southern Sisters mysteries: *Murder on a Girls' Night Out, Murder on a Bad Hair Day, Murder Runs in the Family, Murder Makes Waves, Murder Gets a Life, Murder Shoots the Bull, Murder Carries a Torch,* and her final book, *Murder Boogies With Elvis.* Her popular and hilariously funny novels reflected much of her own experiences. Like Patricia Anne, Anne George was a happily married former schoolteacher living in Birmingham, Alabama, and she grew up with a delightful cutup cousin who provided plenty of inspiration for the outrageous Mary Alice. A former Alabama State Poet, cofounder of Druid Press, and a regular contributor to literary and poetry publications, Ms. George was also the author of a literary novel, *This One and Magic Life,* which *Publishers Weekly* described as "silky and lyrical." She had been nominated for several awards, including the Pulitzer for a book of verse entitled *Some of It Is True.* Anne George passed away in March 2001.

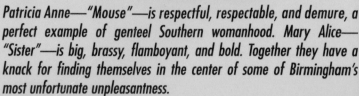

A Different Kind of Sister Act

Patricia Anne—"Mouse"—is respectful, respectable, and demure, a perfect example of genteel Southern womanhood. Mary Alice—"Sister"—is big, brassy, flamboyant, and bold. Together they have a knack for finding themselves in the center of some of Birmingham's most unfortunate unpleasantness.

Country Western is red hot these days, so overimpulsive Mary Alice thinks it makes perfect sense to buy the Skoot 'n' Boot bar—since that's where the many-times-divorced "Sister" and her boyfriend du jour like to hang out anyway. Sensible retired schoolteacher Patricia Anne is inclined to disagree—especially when th~~e foir~~ and stabbed dead body dangling in th~~e~~ ~~h~~as some questions for Mouse and he~~r~~ ~~.~~..re ine last people, besides the murderer, of course, to see the ill-fated victim alive. And they had better come up with some answers soon—because a killer with unfinished business has begun sending them some mighty threatening messages...

www.avonbooks.com

Mystery

ISBN 978-0-380-78086-0